CW00683597

V.P. NIGHTSHADE

The First Time In Forever

Vampiris Bloodline — A Paranormal Vampire Romance Series Book 3

First published by Sohmer Publishing 2022

Copyright © 2022 by V.P. Nightshade

All rights reserved. No part of this publication may be reproduced, stored, or transmitted in any form or by any means, electronic, mechanical, photocopying, recording, scanning, or otherwise without written permission from the author. It is illegal to copy this book, post it to a website, or distribute it by any other means without the express written permission of the author, except for the use of brief quotations in a book review.

This is a work of fiction. The characters involved are wholly imaginary. Names, characters, businesses, places, events, and incidents in this book are either the product of the author's imagination or used in a fictitious manner. Any resemblance to actual persons, living or dead, vampire or human, or actual events is purely coincidental. Any trademarks, service marks, product names, or named features are the property of their respective owners and used only for reference. Opinions of the characters are not necessarily those of the author.

Cover Design Images used under license from Canva.com

EPUB ISBN: 978-1-7374885-8-3

Paperback ISBN: 978-1-7374885-9-0

Hardback ISBN: 979-8-9863081-0-4

First edition

This book was professionally typeset on Reedsy.
Find out more at reedsy.com

For My Facebook Reader Fans – This is the book that you voted for.
I hope that you love it!

For my sons.
No matter what you do in life, remember to always do what makes you happiest.
Do not ever stop dreaming or working for what will make you genuinely happy.
I love you!

For Romana Disrud,
My partner in crime, my biggest fan, thank you for being there throughout the journey!
I definitely wouldn't have taken it without you!

As always, to that grumpy man who pays my bills!
I love you, baby!

Contents

Preface

After the release of Now, Always, Forever (Book 2), I thought it would be fun to set up a poll on The Choice Fans private Facebook Group to ask my 'super fans' what book in the Vampiris Series that they wanted to read (and consequently me to write) next. I gave them three choices (hey, it is all about The Choices!): The prequel (Nichola's life leading up to Leila or Book 0), Book 0.5 (Rom and Esmeralda's love story), or Book 3: The First Time In Forever.

They chose to continue the story with The First Time In Forever, and though surprised, I am glad that they did! Because I had a blast writing this novel!

It was really fun for me to get some meat and bones on the various family relationships that exist within this series. And to give more insight into the vampire world and some of the dangers that they face (with some of the blood and gore that comes along with it).

The only drawback to this fan-based decision was that I did not have a name for my heroine. I knew her character, but she never told me her name!

I hope you love Anisa as much as I now love her. She might be sweet, but never forget, she is one strong-willed, purposeful young lady, who knows exactly what she wants! It was kind of neat to see how this new character started and how she developed over the course of the book. It was also good to see how Devin developed and grew in this novel, too! Love truly does change us in the best possible ways.

So, to you, my readers, who I appreciate so much, thanks for reading The First Time In Forever, Book 3 of the Vampiris Series! I hope that you have as good a time reading it as I had writing it! This book continues the Tsoukalous Vampire Family's storyline that you all love.

As always, I hope it makes you laugh, cry, get mad ~ and at the end fills your heart with love!

V. P. Nightshade – Friday, May 13th, 2022

P.S. I just realized that I completed this novel on Friday the 13th – SPOOKY! Let's hope that Friday the 13th turns out to be a lucky day!

Author Notes

The First Time In Forever: Notes from the Author

1: This work contains coarse language, explicit violence, and mature sexual content.

2: Trigger Warnings: This is a Paranormal Vampire Novel, and features incidents of:

Attempted Rape, MA 18+ Content and Language, Violence, Blood, Gore, Angst –

if any of these bothers you, do not read this book!

3: Vampires do not exist (that is our story, and we are sticking to it)!

This Novel is part of the Vampiris Bloodline Series!

Series Books in Order:

The Choice (Book 1)

Now, Always, Forever (Book 2)

The First Time in Forever (Book 3)

This is the third book in a series! It does not contain any cliffhangers, but does have overlapping characters with their own stories and agendas. In order to fully enjoy this book you should have read Book 1, The Choice, and Book 2, Now, Always, Forever or you will not understand the character motivations or enjoy this book to the fullest. Please read The Choice and

Now, Always, Forever first!

Epigraph

"I don't believe in perfect relationships, and I believe even less in perfect people.
But I believe that there are people in this world who would swim oceans for you.
Those who would fight to their last for you.
Those who would fight their last for you.
And not make you feel like you are too fast, or too slow
or that anything you could want is out of their way.
Because wherever you are is the only place they really long to be.
I believe that you must wait for that.
And that sometimes you have to fight for it.
Fairy tale romance only ceases to exist if you choose not to believe in it.
I do not believe in perfect relationships, and I believe even less in perfect people.
Hell, I do not believe in a lot of things.
But I still believe in perfect love."
~ Carson Patrick Bowie

Prologue: January 2022, Kerrville, Texas

My life definitely hasn't turned out how I thought it would! I used to have plans, hopes, dreams, GOALS! I had planned on a lucrative and unexciting career writing contracts for large corporations, maybe doing some traveling, living in a big house, and being respected for my skill as an attorney. Instead, of all my plans and arduous work coming to fruition, over the last few months my life has kind of been adrift.

Why? Well, I am not what I seem. Hell, I am not even human, I am a vampire. Well, I am not really a full vampire either. That's the being adrift part. I am in two separate phases and though I need something, want something, I couldn't tell you what it is, and I don't see an end in sight.

Where do I find myself? On a dusty ranch in Kerrville, Texas building small homes for a bunch of wolf shifters I seemed to have inherited from my friend. One of the few people who I had thought would be around long enough to help me through this crazy vampire transition. That was another fucking curve ball that life threw at me. God, I missed that old cowboy!

So, a high-powered attorney I am not, a full vampire I am not; but it seems that now, I am an adrift, over-educated construction worker. The shit that life throws at you! It's so out of my control, it's almost like somebody is writing my life for me!

* * * * *

I steadied the sheet of drywall as Ric, Mitch's Beta, secured it with an electric screwdriver to the studs in the wall of the single-story home that we were building for one of the ranch's wolf-shifter families. My mother gave my brother Zachary and I the idea of building the small homes when she found out that the whole pack shared the enormous packhouse at the ranch and all slept together in a partitioned barracks. Mitch and Ric, as Alpha and Beta, and Lenyx the pack Gamma, were the only ones with separate quarters in the packhouse.

Though the pack was small, it appalled my mother that the families weren't housed separately and that the children didn't have their own space. She complained that it was one thing that the single adult wolves who worked the ranch slept in barracks, but the few pack families should have separate spaces to live.

Zachary and I agreed and were working on completing the single-family home projects. With my mother's mate, Nick's help, we created a small housing layout around the main packhouse over the last four months; creating streets, digging wells, installing septic tanks, and laying foundations to get it done, ever since we had taken over the more than 8000-acre ranch that we had inherited from Billy Burke. It was a big project, but it was highly satisfying to see how excited the wolf-shifter pack was over the new improvements to their living conditions.

Though we all pitched in to build as much of the homes as possible, Nick had been truly invaluable helping us hire the various experts such as the architect, foundation company, plumbers, and electricians. Experienced in the many areas of construction and planning due to building his own resorts he was the one that we called when we had questions and Nick had never failed to come through.

It almost made me feel bad for giving him so much trouble over the past couple of months while I was in Peru. Almost. Smiling, I remembered his many lectures on decorum and behavior to Fred and me as we attempted to run our moving gambling hell under his nose in the resort. Rolling my eyes I shook my head remembering his beleaguered tones as he complained about my drinking and 'womanizing' (as he called it) in the staff village. He always wanted to take the fun out of living.

Drinking aside, it wasn't my fault that the women who worked at the resort pursued me! My allure to the opposite sex and my sexual stamina since I had started transitioning into a vampire was off the charts and I could not help it if they talked about it with each other. They wanted it and I wasn't opposed to it. So, who was I to tell them 'no'? It wasn't like I was biting or feeding on them!

I could feel the frustration of my situation flow up my spine causing my skin to prickle in goosebumps. Admittedly, I was a little all over the place with my transitioning into a full vampire. I figured after several months that I would be done transitioning by now! Sure, I was stronger, faster, my eyesight and hearing were excellent, and my body had developed some great muscle definition. But I was still a little hormonal, and somewhat quick to anger. Yeah, I was better now than when this all started, however it wasn't over! No fangs had appeared in my mouth as yet. To be honest, as far as I was concerned, I was okay with that, as I didn't seem to be lusting to open a vein in anyone around me for the time being.

Though I wished it were over. Until it was, everyone felt they needed to keep an eye on me. Nick made sure that I rarely went anywhere on my own, 'just in case'. It irritated me to have a babysitter all of the time, even if I understood the logic behind it.

Uncle Man had told me, when I asked, that each vampire transitioned at their own pace and not to worry about it; my body was developing to be an apex predator: lean and attractive to my main source of prey. Which just happened to be humans. Though I was with my mother on that thought. No way, no how; and just gross!

Still, Uncle Man was not a vampire, only a companion; so though he had a lot of experience helping vampires' transition, he didn't have any firsthand knowledge about what it actually felt like to go through it himself.

I probably could talk to Nick about it. But, though he and I were getting a long better, he was still my mother's mate, not my father, and I just wasn't quite comfortable discussing my transitioning issues with him.

I sure wished that Billy was still alive.

"Hey, Dev! Would you give me a hand unloading this truck?" Zachary called to me.

"Where's Dene?" I yelled back.

"One of the kids fell off their bike and he is checking him out." Zachary's loud voice came back through the open front door, and I could hear him opening the truck doors and tailgate.

"Yeah, give me just a sec, brother!" I called in return still holding the sheet of drywall in place as Ric continued to place the screws.

"Boss! Boss!" Fred yelled in a panicked voice, and I heard him running toward the house that we were working in.

I scowled in irritation as a pang erupted in my chest. I had told him not to call me 'Boss'. One, I didn't feel like his boss and two, it reminded me of Billy. Still, he insisted on it. It was the one thing that Fred didn't listen to me about.

"Over here!" I hollered as Ric nodded to me that it was safe to let go of the drywall. The dark haired, green-eyed wolf shifter smiled at me, sensing my frustration with Fred. Both he and Mitch had respected my wishes to not be called 'Boss', but instead referred to me as Mr. Sutton. I wasn't sure that I was comfortable with that formality any better.

If it hadn't been for Zachary resigning his detective's position with the San Antonio Police Department, I wouldn't have anyone here at the ranch who referred to me just by my name. Zachary had told me that he still had some issues over how it had went down with that vampire serial killer, and how much of it had to be covered up. I knew how much he had loved that job and how good he had been at it. But he told me that he couldn't stick around, knowing that he had lied to his partners and the public.

My chest ached with both anger and sorrow, as I thought about how this sucky vampire legacy of ours had interfered with both of our hopes and dreams, and even though I was sorry that his life had been impacted too, selfishly, it was nice being able to share this huge responsibility of making this ranch function and taking care of the people who depended on it, with my brother.

I put my hat and sunglasses on and walked out of the house to the truck where Zachary was unloading tape, spackle, and paint. I was thankful every day for the sunblock product that Dr. Lambert had developed! At least I was able to function and get work done around the ranch during the day because of it.

"Boss, we got us a visitor!" Fred panted as he ran over to the truck under the harsh Texas sunshine, his dirty-blond colored, straw like hair floating around his head as he skidded slightly in his cowboy boots to abruptly stop in front of me.

"Who is it?" I asked sharply. I wasn't expecting my mother and Nick for another two days.

"It's that little gal!" Fred told me staring at me with his hazel eyes in excitement, and I could feel dread overtake me as I returned that look. "You know, that pretty little gal. Rom's daughter."

"Son of a bitch!" I ground out.

* * * * *

Walking around the living room of the ranch house, I curiously gazed at the dead animal heads on display, the comfortable looking oxblood-burgundy leather furniture, white and brown patterned cowskin throw rug on the polished oak floor and the wood-paneled walls.

I was fascinated by the huge set of cow horns mounted on one of the walls. They were wider than I was tall. I wonder how large a cow would have to be to have horns that size?

Landing in San Antonio International Airport a few hours ago, had been just like landing in any other large city in the world. But, driving the rental car that I had gotten out here to this huge expanse of land? The further northwest I had gotten from San Antonio the stranger it had gotten; the more rugged, hilly, and deserted the land had become, and when I had pulled off of the interstate and through the entrance of the ranch gates, I had to drive what seemed forever down a dusty dirt road to finally get to the ranch house. It was so isolated!

Looking out the window, I could see the construction taking place about a thousand yards from the main house; it was like a small town was being built. That must be where the shifters were going to live.

10

Everything about this place; everything about this house; and especially everything about this living room screamed 'Cowboys live here'. To me it was like a foreign land; but a land I was willing to invade because the thing that had pulled me here was the most important thing in the world to me. I knew this deep inside my soul.

I suddenly felt a tugging inside of me; like someone had reached inside and given my soul a squeeze. I heard the backdoor open and slam shut, then hurried stomping footsteps on the tiled floor in the kitchen. My heart thundered in my chest as I spun toward the sound.

* * * * *

Devin rounded the corner and stopped to stare at her in shock, unable to keep his eyes from roaming over her small curvy form dressed in tight jeans, boots, and a clingy pink blouse. He let his eyes travel over her long wavy golden-brown hair, finally settling on her large, innocent, cerulean blue eyes.

His eyes softened for half a heartbeat as they met hers, then turned hard. "What are you doing here, Anisa?" His question a gravelly demand laced with anger.

"You know why I am here." Her words were direct but achingly soft as she walked to him to affectionately gaze up into his clove-colored eyes. She had always marveled how his eye color changed with his moods sometimes they were a warm, gentle pecan-color with gold specks; but today they were a dark, spicy clove, probably because he wasn't happy to see her. Or at least that was what he was telling himself.

Devin stared down at her in dissatisfaction and something more. Shaking his head, he ran his hand through his silky dark hair. He replied in an exasperated tone. "Listen, you are a nice kid, but I am not *the* guy, and I am not going to take advantage of you…"

"You know you want me." Anisa's beautiful blue eyes suddenly held him entranced, and he found himself frozen in place as she wrapped her arms around his waist, running her hands over his back to embrace him.

He swiftly tried to back away from her only to end up pinned against the wall of the living room with her lush breasts pressed against his body.

11

Awareness flowed over his skin as the hair on his body stood on end, his heart pounded, and he grew immediately hard! Lightheadedness overtook him for a moment then he grabbed her shoulders tightly, holding her back from him; trying to give himself some breathing space before he ended up acting on his body's desires.

"You got to stop this, Nessie!" Devin growled harshly. "No good is going to come of it and you are only going to get hurt! I am not a fucking saint you know!"

"I know that you feel it too, Devin. The connection, the need to be with each other…"

The musical sounds of her voice made his body ache with longing and his cock to throb. "Damn it, Nessie! Knock it off!" He turned to anger to keep himself from making a huge mistake. "The only thing you are feeling is horny! You just don't have enough experience to understand what you are feeling is natural; but that doesn't mean its transcendental! It doesn't mean that we are soulmates." As he panted out the words his heart pounded hard in his chest.

"If you would just…" Anisa wrapped her arms around his neck, and he clutched her arms desperately to stop her.

"No way!" He exclaimed pulling away from her. "I don't fuck virgins and then dump them, and I guarantee you that's exactly what would happen. I am not that big of a bastard, and besides your Dad would kill me. Literally end me!" He finally disengaged her arms and leapt about six feet away from her; his vampire speed making him much faster than she was. "Nessie, if I was doing this to you it would be considered assault! Or stalking at the very least!" Despite his words, his voice sounded panicked.

Anisa heard that panic and knew that he was weakening. Her eyes roved over his tall, lean, hard-muscled body noticing his erection, and she smiled beguilingly at him as she once again fixed him with her eyes and started to approach him. "I know that you feel it too." She said to him calmly as he shook his head negatively at her. "Just grasp my hand and I will pull you through. You will feel what I feel, Devin." She held her hand out to him.

Meeting her blue eyes with his own, the look that he gave her was one of terror and confusion because he found himself wanting to reach for her hand. Wanting to reach for it desperately.

Suddenly Devin's cell phone rang, startling him out of the spell she had woven around him, and he quickly reached into his back pocket to retrieve it. "Mom!" He answered in immense relief. "Yes, she's here! Okay." He extended his arm tentatively to hand Anisa the phone, like he was afraid that she would grab him by the arm. "It's for you."

She took the phone from him curiously, answering, "Hello?" in her bright and cheerful voice.

"Anisa! What are you doing?"

Devin's sharp vampiric hearing heard the male voice coming through the speaker.

"Oh! Hi Daddy!" Anisa answered vibrantly, in an excited childlike voice.

Devin took the opportunity to high-tail it out of the house and run back to the construction site. He didn't care that he was leaving his cell phone behind with her and if he had to sleep in the packhouse tonight to stay away from her that's what he would do.

He could only handle so much temptation before he broke; he was just a vampire after all.

Katerini, Greece

I *don't know why we have to have everyone here while we are supposed to
be spending time alone on our vacation!* Nichola's grumpy voice came
across to Leila through their mind-link as they were getting in one of
the two mid-sized limos that met them at the Thessaloniki airport, to head
to his oceanside resort. *Thank goodness the new jet seats seventeen!*

Nichola, Leila returned, holding Princess's small, padded carrier out for
Devin to take it and place it on the floor of the limo. *We had to bring Devin,
he's still transitioning, and you had already said that you wanted Zachary to come
to meet your nephew to discuss a job working with the small council. Also, Mitch
and Ric needed a way to get to the shifter tribunal and you know that Zachary
and Devin want to go with them. Neither Mitch nor Ric have mates, and this is
an opportunity for them to meet with other shifters.*

You understand that there are concerns for conflict in the region, correct?
Nichola started.

Yes, Nichola. Leila's thoughts were getting exasperated. He had been
irritated since they had left Texas when he realized that everyone was
planning to go with them to Greece. His snarky thoughts had been popping
in and out of her head the whole time, and he had been silent to the point
of rude toward the rest of their traveling party. *That is why they moved the
tribunal location to Skopje in Macedonia. They had thought about Bucharest but
decided that it was too populated. Skopje is really a perfect location, they don't*

even have to fly to get there from here.

But it doesn't happen until next month! So we are stuck with them until then! Frankly, I do not care about whether or not the wolf shifters find mates, or volunteers to increase their numbers at the ranch. All I wanted was for us to spend time together; alone! Frustration shown in his beautiful amber eyes and Leila pierced him with an exasperated look of her own at his complaining. He changed tactics quickly when faced with her annoyance. *That being said, I don't see why Aleksei, Iris, Rom, Es, and that daughter of theirs has to be here too!* He glanced back at the second limo to see the others, the two aforementioned wolf-shifters, and Fred, getting into the limo.

Nichola, Leila looked at him and she tried to keep her thoughts patient. *You know that Aleksei and Iris want to visit with the boys for a few weeks since Zachary is now traveling with us, and Anisa would have just found a way to get here on her own if we hadn't brought the others. That would have really upset Rom and Es again! You know Anisa is convinced that she and Devin are soulmates.*

The boy says 'no'. He should feel it before she does; she's not even close to transitioning yet! Nichola's thoughts were infuriated. This whole Anisa-Devin thing had caused strife between he and Rom, and he was less than happy with the whole situation. As far as Nichola was concerned, Rom needed to stop spoiling his daughter and put his foot down about her behavior.

Well, Devin is under a lot of pressure with his own transition you know. Leila responded. *Maybe he feels something, but just doesn't know what it is yet. Besides, I was still human when I could feel you, and I was just a child. Anisa is an adult; she feels something.*

The boy should just take her to bed and fuck it out of her system! Then he could just walk the fuck away! Nichola thought angrily at her.

Nichola! Leila's thoughts were shocked. *I did not raise him to be that sort of man and Anisa is an innocent! Besides, what if he were to bite her? Rom would have a fit. Not so much Es; but Rom is very protective of Anisa.*

Too protective by far. Nichola agreed. *If she were my daughter, I would lock her up for chasing after a man who didn't want her. No means no!*

Really? Leila looked at him skeptically and her teal eyes twinkled as she gave him a slight smirk.

Gazing at her expression Nichola realized how he must have sounded to her, especially after their own experiences. He returned her smirk with a small sheepish smile of his own. *Well, most of the time.*

* * * * *

Devin and Zachary watched their mother and Nichola. It was totally obvious to them that they were having some sort of mental conversation by the expressions flowing across their faces. The boys looked at each other and then simultaneously rolled their eyes.

They still weren't used to their mother's relationship with her soulmate or how it all worked between them. The only thing that they were positive about was that they were absolutely crazy about each other, and they had never seen their mother happier. That made their relationship good enough for them.

"You sure that you and that Anisa chick aren't soulmates?" Zachary asked Devin looking out the back window toward the other limo.

"Hell, no! I couldn't even imagine her being able to be inside my head; she's driving me crazy enough as it is." Devin told Zachary only to become the focus of Leila and Nichola.

"It doesn't quite work like that." Leila started.

"Are you sure that you feel nothing at all towards her?" Nichola asked and Devin looked at him in surprise. This was the first time that he had directly asked him any questions about the situation.

"No. I don't feel anything." Devin looked him straight in the eye.

"Well, if that's the case then you won't mind me tapping that." Zachary said to him out of the blue.

"Zachary!" Leila exclaimed appalled.

"Don't even think about it!" Devin growled out in a dangerous tone.

"So, you sure you don't feel anything, bro?" Zachary smirked at Devin's attitude.

Nichola looked at Devin expectantly. "It's a reasonable question."

"Well sure, I guess!" Devin hedged. "I mean she is really pretty and nice. But she is so damned young and naïve. If she was older and you know, knew what the score was…"

"Knew what the score was?" Leila asked incredulously, stunned at this conversation going on between her two grown sons and Nichola.

Devin ignored his mother's question and continued to focus on Nichola. "If she gets wrapped up with somebody like me, she's bound to get hurt. Besides," and here Devin fixed Zachary's blue eyes with his own clove-colored ones, "if she is too young for me, then Bro, she's definitely too young for you! Not to mention the fact that Rom would kill either one of us."

"She is an adult." Nichola said simply.

"Yes, she's twenty-two." Leila agreed.

"Not where it counts." Devin pointed to his head and then his heart. "She's horribly immature and spoiled. Look what she's done already, chasing me all over the world! Luckily for her, I am not as bad a guy as Nick thinks I am, or I would have had her in Peru where she gave me plenty of opportunity and just broken her heart. Besides, she kind of acts like I am some toy that she just has to have."

"Well, if you don't want to be her toy, Dev, I can be her toy." Zachary said suggestively, teasing him with a smirk, his blue eyes sparkling.

"Zachary!" Leila said shocked.

"Well you raised them!" Nichola blurted out and Leila's eyes flashed at him in anger, causing him to immediately try to recover. "What I mean is, that I offered to raise them."

"That's any better?" Leila demanded.

Devin punched Zachary in the arm and Zachary punched him back.

"I have never claimed that you were a 'bad guy', Devin." Nichola loudly interrupted their mock fighting. "I only ask that you behave in a more responsible manner. I always attributed that irresponsibility on your own youth." He glared at both of them.

"That's only because you are old as dirt, and you have forgotten how to have fun." Devin teased him with a grin.

"Oh, I don't know about that." Nichola looked over at Leila giving her a sexy, impish smile, which she returned reaching over to hold his hand.

Devin and Zachary both scoffed and rolled their eyes in mock disgust.

* * * * *

"Ani, are you sure about this?" Esmeralda asked her daughter in the second limo, fixing her with her beautiful sea blue eyes, as she ran her fingers through her long blonde hair that she had pulled over her shoulder. She could tell that Nikolaos was upset, and couldn't deny that it was like they were being foisted on him because of this situation. Plus, she was tired and tense from the long, and stressfully silent plane ride to Katerini.

"I am positive, Mother! I know what I am feeling." Anisa said flashing her cerulean blue eyes at her in irritation.

Leave her alone. Es heard Rom's voice in her mind. *The girl says she knows!*

Well, Devin doesn't. Es returned in exasperation. *Men don't like women who pursue them! She's just making this worse. He has to come to his own conclusions. Because she is so strongly pursuing him, right now he is just avoiding her. It is not helping.*

Well, you pursued me! Rom leered at her.

And if I remember correctly, you ran as fast as you could!

Rom smiled at her, his teeth bright white against his swarthy skin. *And you caught me! If they are mated, it will work itself out.*

It would be different if she were a vampire or at least transitioning. With her still being wholly human and with him saying no, I honestly don't know what to think. Esmeralda fretted, nervously combing her fingers through her silky hair, worried about her headstrong daughter's future happiness.

I trust our daughter to know what she is feeling. Devin is young and not fully transitioned, you know that can be a time of confusion; I am sure that is factoring into it. They just need some time. Don't worry. Rom reached over and held her hand tightly to comfort her.

* * * * *

They had been driving for an hour, and night had fallen along the Greek shoreline, exhibiting a beautiful display of twinkling stars in the midnight blue sky which flashed over the waters of the Aegean Sea. They pulled up to the guarded gates and then into the long drive of a large, bright-white marble, villa with a dusky-pink tiled roof, which was aglow in external lighting. Pulling up to a columned portico, several employees rushed out to greet the limos opening the doors as they stopped.

Nichola stepped from the limo reaching back to assist Leila. They were greeted by a smiling, good-looking, olive-skinned vampire with chestnut brown hair and striking large brown eyes.

He extended his hand to Nichola, and they clasped each other's forearms warmly. "Uncle, it is pleasant to see you!" He said in accented English.

"Aris!" Nichola smiled proudly. "Your English is coming along well!"

"Thank you, Sir!" He bowed his head slightly, shyly at the praise.

"Leila, this is Aristides Tsoukalous. The majordomo of the Víla Xenia and one of my nephews. Aris, this is my lady." Nichola's voice rang happily with pride as he looked at her. "And these are my two sons, Devin and Zachary." He indicated them as they got out of the limo, surprising Leila, and the boys.

"My lady and young masters, welcome to Víla Xenia! We are so happy to be hosting you." He took Leila's offered hand and gave it a swift kiss.

"You are one of Nichola's nephews?" Leila asked surprised.

"Well a half dozen times removed my lady. But essentially, yes." The vampire said with a smile, and it was so infectious that she returned one of her own.

"Aris!" Mansuetus clasped the vampire on the shoulder jovially. "It is good to see you! Is that boy here yet?" Mansuetus inquired looking around.

"Mansuetus! How are you, my friend! Yes, he arrived about an hour ago." Aris returned smiling.

Nichola pulled Leila inside the villa as the employees scrambled to unload the luggage from the limos. Devin looked down to see Anisa standing next to him, staring up at him adoringly with her piercing blue eyes. He sighed deeply in irritation, intentionally ignoring her, and started to follow Nick and his mother before he heard behind him, "Hey, there! I'm Zachary. May I escort you inside?"

He whirled around to see his brother hold out his arm to Anisa with a soft smile, clasping her hand to his arm as she took it, and then lead her past a shocked Devin into the villa. Zachary threw a wicked, white-toothed, teasing grin over his shoulder at him, and Devin gave him a glare that should have set him on fire.

"Devin, would you escort your Auntie Iris inside?" He heard a soft sultry voice next to him causing him to take his focus off of his brother and Anisa. "Aleksei is directing the luggage and I must admit I am tired of all of this traveling."

"Sure, Aunt Iris." He smiled down at her dark-haired beauty, holding his arm out to her. "I myself am a little tired too."

＊ ＊ ＊ ＊ ＊

Anisa looked around the busy lobby of the villa in wonder, keeping a firm grasp on Zachary's arm. The walls of the interior were brightly white-washed plaster, and the floors were a smoothly polished, gray-veined marble. There were no sharp lines at all, with curved corners, and archways into public rooms off of the lobby. The ceilings were lined with stained teak planks. The furniture was also made of teak and had white cushions and brightly-colored pillows of sea-blue and the occasional scarlet. The chandeliers were made of thousands of small sparkling pieces of crystal, like galaxies against the dark teak ceilings and there were assorted sizes of bronze standing lanterns throughout the lobby. The villa was a light, airy, beautiful, seaside palace.

"Oh!" Anisa exclaimed looking at everything around her with interest, her beautiful, innocent eyes were wide.

"It is pretty, isn't it?" Her mother stepped up beside her. "This is one of my favorite resorts that Nichola owns. It is too small for large council gatherings, but I have been here with your father a few times during small council meetings. This is such a pleasant place to stay, and the area is absolutely lovely."

"Why don't we go into the bar and get something to drink while they are getting us settled in our rooms?" Zachary said holding his arm out to Esmeralda as he saw Fred holding Princess's carrier, directing the bellhops with Zachary and Devin's luggage. "Fred," he called out to him. "Come meet us in the bar when you are done getting Princess settled."

"Sure 'nuff, Boss." Fred replied, his voice full of Texas twang.

"Leila, we are going to the bar." Es called out.

"You go Lady Tsoukalous." Cassie, Leila's companion, told Leila. "It's going to take me a few minutes to get you and Lord Tsoukalous unpacked."

"I am going to find that boy!" Mansuetus told Nichola impatiently heading down a hallway.

"I need to meet with my nephew about a few things, i psychí mou, go and take Devin and Iris with you." Nichola gave her a quick kiss, looking at and nodding to Devin next to her.

Leila reached out and took Devin's other arm and they all started heading for the bar. As they did, they passed Dene, who turned his face away and headed in Nichola's direction. Iris turned her head away also, looking down with a pensive expression.

* * * * *

As Zachary helped Anisa and Es into seats at a large table, Anisa watched Devin's tall muscular form leisurely walk into the bar escorting his mother and aunt with her heart in her eyes. She had never felt a connection like this in her entire life to anyone. It was more than some schoolgirl crush. It was a desire born of an erupting volcano, burning all previous feelings that she had ever had for anyone else to ash.

She felt his emotions throughout her body like they were her own. She knew he wanted her and knew that he battled that desire with everything that he was. She didn't understand why. If he would just give in once; she knew that he would come to realize that they had been created for each other.

Anisa tried to comprehend his confusion, after all she hadn't immediately realized the bond between them herself.

She remembered to when they had first met in November. After she had been around him for just a brief time, she had felt he was a truly kind, quiet, attractive young man who seemed a little sad. Then she had learned from his mother, that his friend had been killed when they had been hunting down a dangerous murderer: a vampire serial rapist and killer of young girls. Devin had been there to witness his death, and it had affected him deeply.

His friend had left Devin and his brother his ranch and various other holdings. Now, Devin was under some stress trying not only to improve the lives of the people that depended on him; but also, trying to cope with the various aspects of transitioning.

Unused to having someone at a vampire resort so close to her in actual age, let alone another American, Anisa had sought him out to get to know him better. Often times their families had spent the evenings together dining and dancing. Though he never once asked her to dance, he did spend time speaking with her about their time in college, how he and his brother, who was at their ranch in Texas, were learning their way and trying to improve the lives of the wolf shifters who lived and worked on the ranch, and how his life and career goals had changed since starting his transition. Anisa had found him to be quick-witted, humorous, and adventurous.

Once she found out that he, his companion Fred, and Mansuetus were searching for Incan treasure, she had begged Mansuetus, who doted on her, to go. Not thrilled to see her on that first trip, Devin tried to dissuade her from coming, explaining that he feared for her safety. It wouldn't be the first time that someone got hurt in the caverns. She swore to him that she would stay with them every step of the way and would be careful.

Excitement flowed over her like water rushing over a waterfall to crash into the rocks below, as she remembered entering the antechamber that they had broken through to find gold and silver relics and works of art. Devin's eyes sparkled in triumph, but after walking the chamber and not finding any written documents, which had been an important discovery to his friend, they shown dully in defeat.

She'd only meant to give him a comforting hug after seeing his grief, but as soon as she felt his warmth against her and heard the thumping of his strong heart, she knew that there was something special about him. As he returned her hug gently, the scent of sweet coffee, pastries, and a hint of mint flowed over her senses, the blood rushed through her veins like a fast-bubbling spring; and the effervescent feeling flowed to her heart, seizing it with a gasp, then to her head causing her to sway in dizziness, and finally to her womb, wetting her panties in desire.

She gazed up into his eyes in wonder, taking in the beautiful pecan color and noticing for the first time the small gold flecks which seemed to swirl around his irises. She remembered licking her lips in anticipation of kissing him.

He stared down into her eyes in surprise, roving over her face and concentrating on her lips before stopping himself halfway to fulfilling that kiss. Suddenly he pulled away, putting distance between them. He left her to approach Fred and Mansuetus who were exclaiming over an artifact, throwing a bewildered look back over his shoulder to her.

* * * * *

He avoided her like the plague after that, barely even speaking with her over the next several weeks as she and her mother helped him and his mother with the large council Companion Act packages that they put together before the discussion and vote. Because she was just a human, she had not been allowed into the large council meetings. Curious about the process and how everything worked she had sought him out.

He answered her questions, but without any pleasure, and did not invite her curiosity about the process. Finally, frustrated, she blurted out, "Devin, have I done something to offend you?"

"No." He told her coolly.

"Then why are you acting like you don't like me?" She blinked up at him with hurt in her eyes, and a frown on her lips.

"I like you just fine, Nessie." He told her with a smile at her pouting face.

"Nessie! I don't like that. That's like the Loch Ness Monster." She exclaimed irritably.

"It's definitely a monster's name." He had chuckled teasingly and walked away.

She had frequently sought him out after that, going with he, Mansuetus, and Fred to the cave, to collect and catalogue the find. Sometimes he would ignore her, other times he would tease her mercilessly, before retreating.

The more time that she was around him, the more she could sense his emotions. She could tell when he was happy, sad, angry, frustrated, and on occasion, when she wasn't totally paying attention to him, she would catch him watching her speculatively.

The evening after the Large Council session ended, all of the vampires in attendance were dining and dancing. At their shared table, she could tell

23

that both Devin and his mother were upset about how the Companion Act had been modified.

She and her mother had been terribly angry with her father over his part in 'watering down' the act as her mother had accused him. Sometimes her father was entrenched in keeping the status quo of the vampire community and could be extremely intractable; at other times he seemed highly progressive. His unreasonable thoughts of 'companions running wild' had infuriated her mother so much that she had sat next to him in bitter silence; at least until Charles Peake, her mother's longtime friend and a member of the Small Council, had come to claim her for a dance. Esmeralda had accepted readily throwing Anisa's father a harsh look.

As Esmeralda left for the dance floor, Anisa looked over at Devin and asked him quietly, "Would you like to dance?"

"Sure." He told her distractedly, glaring in her father's direction.

Once on the dance floor, Devin absently enfolded her in his arms for a waltz, still glaring at her father's back. Once he pulled her close, he gazed down into her eyes with a look of shock.

She had met his glowing eyes with her own, feeling his sudden burst of need. His body stiffened as he moved her throughout the dance, and she was almost overwhelmed with his warring emotions: lust, need, confusion, fear.

As the final notes of the music rang over them, he immediately stepped away from her and hurriedly left the dance floor almost running for the exit.

Anisa had followed him sedately; sensing his location as she finally made her way outside. She found him leaning against the wall of the front of the hotel, hiding in the shadows, his arms tightly holding his torso like he was afraid that his body would break into a million pieces. He looked like he was in pain, and she approached him with her hand outstretched.

"Devin…" she started hesitantly.

"Nessie! What are you doing out here?" He moved out of her reach. "Go back inside. Now." His voice was harsh.

"Are you okay?" She asked him softly.

"I am fine. Go in. Now." He schooled his features into an emotionless mask.

"You don't look fine, Devin." She came closer to him, and ⅂ moved away from her, but he was halted by the wall of the buⅰ

"Leave now. Please." His voice was shaking and low as he lⅽ from her searching eyes.

She reached out to touch him on the chest and faster than she could see he snatched her to him, whirling her around to push her roughly against the wall of the resort holding her in place with his body pressed tightly against hers.

"Is this what you want, Nessie?" He whispered severely in her ear, sending bursts of pleasure pebbling over her skin. "I have tried to stay away from you, but you have been relentlessly tempting me for over a month." He ran his lips from her ear down the side of her neck, the soft texture of his mouth leaving a fiery trail, to bury his nose against her throat. "God, you smell delicious." He groaned breathing deeply of her. "You smell like chocolate, popcorn, and wild figs. I could just eat you." He nipped her with his teeth emphasizing his words, causing her breath to catch in her throat.

She felt his hands slide up her dress bunching it around her waist, to clutch at her ass as he positioned his body in between her legs and ground his erection against her core. She moaned helplessly in response, overcome with the intensity of the sensations spiking through her body.

"That's what you want, isn't it, Nessie? Do you want my cock? You want me to fuck you, don't you?" He whispered once more against her ear as he slid his hand between them and into her panties. He stroked her clit and she gasp out in shock at the overwhelming lust that burned through her. "You like that don't you, Nessie. Would you like me to make you come?" Her gasps turned to pants as his finger steadily stroked her over and over and she clutched his shoulders for support, straining against the feeling of pressure in the pit of her stomach. He moved his hand lower and thrust a finger into her channel.

"Ah! Ow!" She exclaimed unprepared for his action.

He pulled back and looked at her in bewilderment. "Ow?" He met her surprised eyes, glazed over with lust, in the dim light of the front windows of the hotel. "No." He removed his hand from her panties suddenly, shaking his head. "No, no, no. Are you a virgin, Nessie?" His voice was strained and disappointed.

She mutely nodded at him.

He started to pull away from her and she pulled him back. "You know we are soulmates." She stated decisively and she felt him withdraw mentally from her as if a door slammed in her face.

"No we are not." His voice was firm, as he shook his head negatively, pulling away from her and separating their bodies. "No, Nessie. We are not."

"But…" She started to say reaching out for him.

"No, Nessie! We aren't!" He interrupted harshly and moved so quickly it was like he had disappeared in thin air.

Two days later she found out that he had left for his ranch in Texas, and it took her more than a week to find a way to follow him.

* * * * *

Upset by his continued rejection of her, Anisa watched with a hurt look shining in her eyes as Devin avoided her gaze and pulled chairs away from the table for his mother and his Aunt Iris. Barely glancing in her direction, he walked to the bar to join his brother who was ordering drinks.

Esmeralda reached over to pat her hand, and Anisa looked at his mother and aunt who both gave her small sympathetic smiles.

"Don't worry, sometimes men are not very smart in matters of the heart; either their own or anyone else's." Iris's words to her were soft. "If you are truly soul-mated, it will work itself out. Just give him some time to wrap his head around it."

Castor Blood

⌇⌇

"**S**ince when do you not greet us upon our arrival, boy?" Mansuetus demanded in an outraged tone as he walked into the suite. "Did I raise you to be rude?" He said speaking to the back of a tall, slender, young man, garbed in a black fitted gentleman's overcoat and tight black pants and boots, who seemed to be gazing out the window contemplating the choppy Aegean Sea.

"Leave him alone, Mansuetus." I murmured as I leisurely followed him through the door. "I am sure that Castor is upset with me and preferred to not make our conflict known to the rest of the traveling party." I intentionally made my voice low and nonthreatening as I could feel the fury coming from the young vampire. If he knew how pissed I was at his slight toward my mate he would not be presenting his back to me at this moment, no matter how furious he was with me.

"I am not 'upset' with you, Uncle Nikolaos. Though your summons for me and my team to immediately relocate from Kiev and for me to come here did prevent us from ending a cell there." The young vampire turned from the window to face me with his piercing light green eyes. His voice was intentionally soft and emotionless; and both he and I knew that he was lying about his feelings.

"It was imperative that you leave Ukraine. I have it on good authority that a conflict will commence there over the next several weeks." I said to him keeping my voice also deliberately mild, ignoring his lie, and removed my jacket to hand it to Mansuetus. I proceeded to sit down in a wing backed chair, crossing my legs leisurely, to face him as Castor stood before me.

"Rumors, surely, Uncle!" Castor spat; now he shows me his anger. "We could have destroyed that murdering cell if we only had been allowed to stay. Who is there left now to protect our people?" He gestured with his slender hands in frustration. Frustration with me and my authority.

"Do you doubt me, Castor?" I kept my voice soft but pushed my power at the younger vampire, surprising him. I rarely showed my power to my young protégé, but I was irritated by the antics of the many young vampires, humans, and wolf shifters that I had recently found myself surrounded by and was not in the mood to brook insolence. Especially, since this one owed me so much.

He gazed at me surprised for a brief time before answering, "No, Uncle."

"Good. Our people are relocating from the country as we speak. There is no one there for you to protect. The cell will be destroyed in due course when the war starts. Let the humans deal with each other." I steepled my fingers looking over them speculatively to pierce him with my gaze. "Besides, I have another, more challenging, mission I would like you to undertake. Something that will relieve you of your constant ennui and provide you with more of a contest, than slaughtering human hunters."

I almost smiled when he gave a slight roll of his eyes, reminding me sharply of my mate's sons, Zachary, and Devin. Almost. Obviously, most young vampires were alike in their attitudes; despite their levels of existence: untransitioned, transitioning, or fully transitioned.

Of course, it could be that both their mother and I have overly-indulged the three of them, which could account for their insolence.

"Castor!" Mansuetus exclaimed appalled at his behavior.

I held up my hand cutting him off. "Are you afraid of a new challenge, Castor? Are you too young or immature to handle a mission of vital importance to our community that will take the skills of nuance instead of slaughter?" I inquired sharply.

"Of course not, Uncle!" Castor replied, outraged at the suggestion.

"Good. Let us go and discuss the mission with the others then." I stood and walked to exit the suite.

"The others?" I could feel the intense curiosity which I always admired in him, radiate from him as he caught up with me to match my pace.

"Yes. The other members of the team." I continued to walk down the hallway of my villa then looked at him out of the corner of my eye. "Also, I would hope that you will know how to comport yourself around my mate. Especially, since you have lost the opportunity to present yourself as manners dictate." I allowed a small amount of my anger to peek through in that statement. No matter his youth and irritation with my edicts, Castor was educated in our customs, and I shouldn't have to remind him of them.

"I apologize, Uncle." His voice was soft in contrition.

"Not to me, Castor. Not to me." I replied just as quietly as we walked into the bar.

* * * * *

"Oh, my! It is Castor Blood." Iris whispered breathlessly to the table in general as Nichola, Mansuetus and an extremely dangerous-looking, but beautiful young male vampire walked into the bar.

"I wonder what he could be doing here?" Esmeralda sighed in return.

They approached the table and Nichola introduced Leila. "Castor, this is my lady, Leila. Leila, may I introduce my nephew, Castor? Castor is in charge of the Special Investigations Group for the small council." Nichola's voice was affectionate and proud when he referred to the gorgeous young vampire.

Leila held her hand out with a welcoming smile and the youthful vampire took it and bowed low over it, the bangs of his silky, dark, tawny-brown hair falling over his forehead in an attractive cascade. "Lady Tsoukalous, please forgive me for not greeting you earlier." Castor expressed sincerely, his voice pleasing and musical, as he raised his light green eyes to charmingly gaze up at her from her hand.

"Nonsense. I am sure no slight was intended." Leila smiled at him warmly.

"Lady Esmeralda, Lady Iris." Castor bowed in greeting.

"And these are my sons, Zachary and Devin." Nichola said motioning to

29

the boys who stood politely to greet Castor.

Castor raised an eyebrow in surprise before quickly schooling his features and offering Zachary his arm. Instead of clasping his arm as Nichola or Mansuetus would have done, Zachary shook his hand firmly and Devin followed suit.

"You are human." Castor stated in surprise to Zachary. "And American." Castor's voice was full of envy as he faced the boys. "I have always wanted to visit the United Colonies."

Zachary smiled widely nodding to Castor as he realized that the vampire in front of him may physically look like he was the same age as he and Devin but was much older.

What Zachary had come to understand since he was now more exposed to vampires was that they sometimes became very isolated from humanity as a whole. It was like they lived in a totally different and separate world than everyone else on earth. They became fixed in some of their thoughts and habits due to isolating themselves and often times did not accept change readily.

Nick was very progressive in his thoughts and actions, more so than other vampires Zachary had met, but even he still unashamedly called Myanmar by the name of Burma because of some long-ago memory.

"Castor," Esmeralda addressed the tall, slender vampire, breaking up the curiosity of the young men as they took each other in. "May I present my daughter, Anisa?"

Castor walked around the table to take Anisa's hand in his, bending to briefly kiss her fingertips and to gaze flirtatiously up into her blue eyes with a small smile. "A pleasure, Miss Anisa. I have heard so much about you from Lord Romulus."

Anisa blushed in response and Devin gave Castor a sharp look that did not go unnoticed by either his mother or Iris.

Fred, Mitch, and Ric walked into the bar causing Castor's nose to flare slightly. "Wolves." His voice was a low intense growl as he came to stand defensively next to Nichola.

"Castor!" Nichola's faint voice held a note of warning. "These are the others that I was telling you about." He continued smoothly, gesturing to them. "This is Fred, Devin's companion and this is Mitch Matheson, Alpha of the Diamond Wolf Ranch and Maverick McAllister, his Beta. My nephew Castor."

Mitch held out his hand to the handsome vampire and only Nichola's tone and his expectation of courtesy caused Castor to shake it briefly in response.

"Call me Ric." The Beta said with a grin, showing his gleaming white teeth, noticing the vampire's irritation as he held out his hand also.

Castor nodded coldly to the wolf shifter as he shook his hand but with obvious distaste.

"Gentlemen, I have asked Aris to prepare the conference room for us to have our discussion. Let's leave the ladies to their drinks." Nichola leaned down to kiss Leila briefly on the forehead. At her inquiring glance he gave her hand a small squeeze and flashed her an impish grin.

* * * * *

"What do you think that they are up to?" Iris inquired to Leila as she watched the men leave the bar.

"Auntie, you know better than to ask me. It could be any one of a number of things. Nichola schemes, you know." Leila said with a shrug, in acceptance of her mate's idiosyncrasies. "I will try to find out later."

"I am sure that Aleksei and Rom are also involved in whatever it is, as they have not arrived as yet, and I have been expecting them. It's probably Small Council business." Esmeralda spoke with irritation as she sipped her wine. "There always seems to be more business than leisure time in holding those positions."

"You are most likely correct." Iris murmured in response.

"Who was that vampire, Mother? I have never seen him before." Anisa asked her voice full of curiosity.

"That is Castor Blood, darling. He rarely socializes. According to your father he is usually traveling throughout the world investigating. He runs the Special Investigations Group. The group examines vampire deaths thought to be caused by hunters." Es told Anisa.

"Hunters?" Anisa asked bewildered.

31

"Vampire hunters. Specifically, the group investigates the existence of hunter organizations." Iris answered.

"And what do they do when they find these organizations?" Leila asked skeptically.

"What do you think they do, Leila? They destroy them." Es answered surprised by her question.

"You mean he kills people?" Leila asked outraged.

"Are you offended when the military kills terrorists, Leila?" Iris looked at her. "It's the same thing. Vampire hunters are terrorists. In fact, many acts conducted by hunters are attributed to terrorism by human authorities. Hunters do not care whether the vampire is committing crimes against humanity; they only care whether or not someone is a vampire, and they are rarely concerned with collateral damage in their attacks. There have been several cases over the years that hunters have not only killed vampires but have killed humans that were in close proximity to the vampire's location. Most of them believe that the end justifies the means."

"Rom told me that it isn't only vampires that the organizations target. They also target shifters, witches, and their associates like friendly humans, familiars, and even our companions. They don't differentiate between adults and children either." Es told Leila animatedly. "These organizations conduct terror campaigns and some really gruesome murders. They are the reason Nichola is so conscious of the security of his establishments." Es nodded in the direction of a dark suited human who sat alone at a corner table in the bar with his back towards the wall so that he could see all entrances and exits to the large room.

Leila remembered the guards at the gates of the villa, the resort in Peru, and the ones at the resort in Ponce Inlet, Florida. She met Iris's eyes and asked. "Are all these guards truly necessary?"

"Oh, yes. It is especially dangerous here in Europe where the organizations are smaller but abundant, because they are decentralized and autonomous. Superstition and belief in the existence of the supernatural is prevalent amongst European countries substantially more than in America; so it seems that they have more individuals who are willing to join these organizations to help rid the world of its 'monsters'." Iris emphasized the word trying to explain.

"Because Europe is a modern society, these organizations are dangerous because they have access to other dark organizations to obtain modern weapons. These people do not just use wooden stakes and silver knives. Some of them have been in existence for a long time and understand our strengths and weaknesses. They know how to kill us, and it is imperative that we protect ourselves." Iris seemed fearful as she explained. "Even Aleksei's property on the Riviera has a full security detail because of the number of organizations under surveillance."

"Well, why is his name Castor Blood if he is a nephew of Mr. Tsoukalous? Why doesn't he go by the name of Tsoukalous?" Anisa asked.

"Because he is cognizant of the fact that he is only a Tsoukalous bastard.His mother was a gypsy who was the mistress of Jonas Tsoukalous; Aristides human brother." Iris, ever the gossip, answered her.

"How old is he?" Anisa asked wide-eyed.

"He was born in the early 1700s. Why the interest, child?" Iris asked studying her with a wicked smile.

"He just seemed nice." Anisa blushed deeply under the other woman's scrutiny.

"Your father would not like you to develop a deep association with him, Ani." Es instructed.

"Whyever not, Mother?" Anisa asked surprised.

"Because his profession is hazardous, and he is a dangerous individual who associates himself with the dark underbelly of both the supernatural and human societies of the world."

"I thought you said that his job was necessary? You made it sound like what he does helps our community and saves lives." Anisa argued, bristling at her mother's dictatorial tone.

"It does! What he does is necessary to our security. In many ways he is a hero. Still, his lifestyle is extremely dangerous, and it would not do for you to strongly associate yourself with such activity. But what does it matter? You have a soulmate, do you not?" Es asked irritated at Anisa's rebellious tone.

"Of course I do! But I am an adult and allowed to have my own friends! Father cannot continue to dictate who my friends are!" Anisa exclaimed angrily, causing Iris and Leila to glance at each other in concern, as they sipped their porcine blood-laced wine. Obviously, this was an old argument.

"Your father can do many things, Anisa. He cares for your security, more so than he does your so-called happiness, or your need to be your own person." Es told her bluntly.

"His extremely old-fashioned rules are smothering! I am an adult, and he needs to trust me and give me my own space!" Anisa exclaimed with passion.

"The more you claim to be an adult instead of proving it through your actions – the less I believe it!" Es said getting loud as her daughter continued to argue.

As far as Esmeralda was concerned, Anisa needed to be having this beat-to-death discussion with her father instead of complaining about it to herself or airing her displeasure in front of Leila and Iris.

"Ladies!" Iris intervened and Leila fought to hold back laughter, very much reminded of past similar conversations with her own sons. "Why don't we have some more wine?" Iris motioned to the bartender for another round of drinks.

* * * * *

Devin followed Nichola and the others into the conference room looking around in interest only to find both Romulus and Aleksei awaiting them. The room looked elegant but comfortable with its white-washed plaster walls, long teak table, and sea blue upholstered chairs. Everything in the villa spoke of the sea.

Everyone sat around the table and Nichola sat at the head.

"I wanted to speak to all of you to let you know that I have contacted the wolf-shifter pack leaders in the region." Mitch and Ric looked at him in surprise. "You already are aware that due to some political instability in your original meeting location, your conclave was moved to Skopje next month; what you are unaware of is that I have asked the pack leaders to consider a formal alliance with the vampire community during this meeting."

"But Uncle!" Castor exclaimed interrupting.

"Yes, Castor?" Nichola inquired looking at him with patient amber eyes.

"Uncle, what about the war?" Castor asked in confusion. "We don't trust each other! It just won't work." Castor stated heatedly glaring at Mitch and Ric.

"Well, with an attitude like that of course it won't!" Zachary burst out.

"What would you know about it? You're just a human!" Castor's voice was biting.

"Obviously, more than you do since we work with wolf shifters every day." Devin defended his brother.

Nichola raised his hand for silence.

"You are too young to know of the war, Castor." Aleksei corrected calmly. "In fact there are very few vampires still alive who even remember what the war was like; or took part in fighting in it." Aleksei glanced at Nichola. "But two of us are here at this table."

"This is true." Nichola nodded to the elder vampire. "The war is long over. But it would have continued for far longer than it did if the vampires and the warm-blooded shifters hadn't banded together to destroy the Naga. You see, Castor, we have precedent for successfully working together."

Castor looked at the wolf-shifters across the table briefly in doubt.

Nichola continued. "I understand that you have your own reasons for attending the conclave." Here he nodded to Mitch, Ric, Devin, and Zachary. "But I would ask you to negotiate an alliance with the wolf shifter community as a whole." They looked at him in surprise. "You four are representative of what good cooperation between the vampire and shifter communities looks like. Your work together benefits our children and the way we live. We can provide safety for each other. Friendships amongst us benefit our communities. You four prove that theory."

Castor had folded his arms across his chest and leaned against the back of his chair. "Then why am I here, Uncle?" His voice was laced in skepticism.

"Because you have a detailed knowledge of hunter organizations. How they think, how they operate. You're aware of what drives them, and you've been successful in using your knowledge to block their murderous efforts and on many occasions, you've destroyed them." Nichola regarded Castor's obvious reluctance calmly. "The largest threat to both of our communities are the hunters."

Nichola looked at Mitch. "When William took your pack in over a hundred years ago, he did so for the protection of both himself and your pack. Did he not?" He smiled at the alpha shifter warmly.

"Yessir. I wasn't alive then. My grandfather was the alpha at the time though and I heard the stories." Mitch answered calmly, his multicolored hazel eyes brightly flashing from gold to green as he thought back to his former boss with affection. "The area hunters were picking off our pack individually, we hadn't been a large pack at the time, but they had killed so many of us; we were almost decimated.

They even killed our children and as you know our children don't even shift until they are sixteen. But the hunters of that time tortured and killed the families, including women and children, of the wolves they killed. As you know if we die in wolf form we revert back to our human form, so it was easy enough to track down the families of the wolves. Some of the women that had been married to our wolves at the time were human, and no one knew if their children would have ever shifted. It still didn't matter to the hunters though." Mitch paused deep in thought.

"The hunters had no idea about the Boss and what he was. Still he saved Gramps' life. Gramps had been wounded and had been trying to escape the hunters by traveling through the Boss's ranch. The Boss and Fred found him, patched him up, and protected him until he had pulled through the worst of it. They saved him." Mitch nodded at Fred who gave him a small smile. "Then the Boss proceeded to hunt down and kill the whole group of hunters.

He gave my Gramps and the rest of the pack a place to live safely in exchange for working the ranch. He fed us, clothed us, and protected us." Mitch smiled. "The pack has come back, still our numbers are less than what they were before the hunters started killing us. That's why going to the conclave is so important. We are hoping to increase our pack."

Nichola nodded in understanding. "Both of our communities are declining in number every century that passes." Everyone except Rom and Aleksei were visibly shaken by the possible ramifications of that announcement. "That's why it is important that we combine our forces and ally with each other to our mutual benefit. An attack on one community should be considered an attack on all."

* * * * *

From her seat on the covered patio of the suite that Aris had shown her to, Leila sat watching the moonlight gilding the peaks of the waves of the Aegean Sea, as Cassie played fetch with Princess in the fine white sand of the beach. She heard the door to the suite open and walked in to see the villa employees wheeling in covered trays of food.

Nichola walked in after them and smiled at her. "I thought you might want to dine in privacy tonight, agápi mou."

Princess came bounding in to leap up on him with her tiny feet and he swiftly picked her up to receive her small kisses. "Hello, skýlos!" He murmured smiling.

Cassie came in after her nodding her head once, "Lord Tsoukalous. Would you like me to take her?"

"No, Cassie. We will keep her. Besides, I believe that you have a dinner date. We won't need you any further tonight." He told her holding the small dog close petting her soft fur as he nodded to the open doorway.

Leila looked up to see Dene patiently waiting for Cassie with a smile. Cassie returned his smile and said over her shoulder, "Have a good evening, Sir, Lady Leila."

Dene smiled at Leila over his shoulder as he closed the door softly behind them.

Nichola put Princess down and came to enfold Leila in his arms looking down into her teal eyes with devotion as he ran the long fingers of one of his hands through her silver-streaked auburn hair.

She wrapped her arms around his waist and looked up into his amber eyes with adoration. "Who would have thought those two would have made a couple?"

"After all of these years, I still find myself amazed at some things." He told her gently running a hand over her flat belly and bending to gently kiss her.

"Are you sure they won't think that we are rude for not joining them for dinner?" She asked softly against his lips.

"Mansuetus will see to them. Besides, you and I are on vacation." He chuckled quietly as he pulled her close.

A Relationship Is Not For Me

achary, Devin, Mitch, and Ric were standing to one side of the dining room with drinks in their hands watching as Aleksei helped Iris to a seat at a table.

"I can't believe that Mr. Tsoukalous has invited the alpha of the local pack to stay here at the resort." Ric said to them softly in amazement.

"It's one thing that I am realizing about Nick. He makes his mind up about something then goes balls to the wall for it." Zachary stated. "It's almost like he is human. He sure doesn't let time fly, by debating an issue."

"Well, though I am grateful for his confidence, I hope he realizes that alphas are kings to their people. When we make decisions, our people carry them out without question. Just because I am an alpha to my people doesn't mean that I can force another alpha to do something. Not without challenging him for his position over his pack. At least we have a couple of days to prepare for his arrival." Mitch ran a hand through his short chocolate and caramel-colored, streaked hair. He glanced around at the assembled vampires and companions milling about the dining room.

"I am sure that he knows more than he lets on about shifters, buddy. Besides, he should trust us! Because he's right; if anybody has a chance to pull off a treaty between the vampire and wolf shifter communities, it's definitely us." Devin said with confidence. "I am more concerned about that Castor guy blowing shit up. Obviously, he has issues with you guys. Not to mention that he is kind of a jackhole."

"He definitely has some prejudices. But we should try to give the guy some slack. We don't know how he got those prejudices, and people aren't prejudiced by nature." Zachary began in a reasonable voice.

"Bro, he called you a human like it was a dirty thing..." Devin interrupted and anger laced his low tone.

"Dude," Zachary returned with a smile, taking a small sip of his whiskey. "I am a human and in case you don't know it's probably not too far off that most vampires would look at me like a piece of meat; or something less than themselves. Don't worry about me. We need to figure out a way to bring 'Cousin' Castor onboard with getting a treaty completed. If Nick's right, and these hunters are that dangerous to both communities, an alliance is necessary for the survival of all."

"They are so dangerous that we never shift outside the ranch for fear of being discovered." Ric responded, sipping his whiskey, his emerald-green eyes becoming wolfy in his irritation.

"Well, I will see if I can get Uncle Man to spill on him a little later. Figure out what his issue is." Zachary told them looking around as Fred came walking into the dining room. "Let's get us a table and get something to eat."

* * * * *

"That little gal is looking at you again, Boss." Fred leaned close to murmur to Devin as he was cutting his ultra-rare steak.

"Don't make eye contact, Fred." Devin responded under his breath concentrating on his plate.

"But she's a cute gal, Boss." Fred smiled devilishly.

"She wants something more than I can give her and a relationship is not for me. Would you like to be stuck taking care of both myself and her too?" Devin asked in soft exasperation.

"I don't know. I like having women folk around." Fred said looking at the table that Cassie and Dene sat at. His eyes roamed over Cassie fondly.

"How's that going, Fred?" Zachary whispered following Fred's gaze.

"She likes us both." Fred said quietly. "I ain't opposed to sharin', but the Doc needs some convincin'."

"I don't even want to know how that would work out." Mitch murmured.

"That's because you can't see yourself sharing." Ric ribbed.

"Wolves don't share." Mitch's voice came out in a wolfy growl.

"Wolves share. Alphas don't." Ric smiled toothily sipping his whiskey.

"Same thing, as far as I am concerned." Mitch muttered taking a bite of his steak.

"I thought that wolves mated for life? Your wolf is basically the one that tells you who your mate is. That's why we are going to the conclave to begin with, to see if your wolf recognizes their mate, right?" Zachary asked.

"Yes, that's one reason why and we are definitely looking for mates." Ric replied.

"But, more importantly, we also would like to expand the pack. I'd love to get a doctor or a nurse to join the pack. It's nice having the Doc at the ranch sometimes, but we could do with our own permanent doctor. Someone who understands our biology because it is their own." Mitch replied. "But our mating process is remarkably similar to vampires. They know when they are in the presence of their mates.

Still, after speaking with Mr. Tsoukalous the other day about my hopes for this conclave, it doesn't seem to be as instantaneous as ours. We *know* because our wolf knows." Here Mitch glanced at Ric who nodded at him in agreement. "According to Mr. Tsoukalous, vampires, not being two-natured, run into a bunch of other emotions. They may not know instantly when they are in the presence of their mate. The feelings could easily be misconstrued with extreme sexual desire or even an intense desire to feed.

Like wolves, vampires have the ability to love without the mate bond." Here he nodded to Aleksei and Iris who were chatting amiably together at another table. "This could cause the vampire to be confused about their mate or what they are feeling. Especially if they meet their mate after they are already in love with someone else. With wolves, the mate bond represents desire, but it also tells us who our perfect match for breeding is. It's for the procreation of children. Children born of a mate bond have stronger abilities than normal shifter children."

"But Mitch, don't you have any control over it? What happens if you are in love, married, and have kids? Would you leave your family because you finally run into your mate?" Devin asked curiously.

"I am not sure what I would do personally, Mr. Sutton, as I don't know firsthand what it feels like. But I have heard from other packs about wolves rejecting their mates because they have created a life that they aren't willing to give up for them. That rejection is supposed to be agonizingly painful for both. It is one of the reasons why I have never married. I would rather find my mate. Still, I have responsibilities to my pack, and it is coming to a point where it is time for me to marry and have kids. If I don't find her at the conclave, I will probably select one of my she-wolves to be my mate. My pack deserves a Luna." Mitch ate another bite of steak.

"Doesn't sound very romantic." Fred muttered.

Mitch gave Fred a small sardonic smile, "Being Alpha rarely is."

Devin looked up from his plate to find Zachary, a wide, toothy smile on his face, waving his fingers flirtatiously to Anisa across the dining room where she sat with Rom, Esmeralda, Castor, and Mansuetus. She returned his wave cheerfully with a bright smile.

"What are you doing?" Devin demanded.

"Going to ask your girl to dance." Zachary said with a mischievous smile as he quickly stood and headed toward Anisa.

"Dammit!" Devin lowly cussed out in a snarl sitting back to glare at Zachary's retreating figure.

* * * * *

"I don't know why he has to be such a pain in the ass sometimes!" I ground out as Zachary flashed me a roguish smile over Nessie's head as he waltzed her around the dance floor. I swear I am going to have to pound him!

"I thought you didn't like her." Ric grinned at my irritation.

"It's not that I don't like her. She's got it in her head that we are soulmates! We aren't. Like she would know in any case; she's just a human." I explained.

"I thought she has the vampire gene? Isn't there a chance that she could go through a transformation? Like yourself?" Mitch asked waving his fork in the air at him as he continued to eat.

"Well, sure. She could I suppose. That doesn't mean that we are soulmates!

I don't feel it. Sure, she is pretty, and I like her, but I am too young to hook up with someone who believes in forever. You guys have an extended life span, but it isn't too much longer than a human. If nothing bad happens to me, I could live for hundreds if not thousands of years. Nessie is thinking in terms of 'forever'. If that is what she wants, then she deserves it.

But forever doesn't interest me no matter how much I like her. That makes her off-limits to me!" I drank down my whiskey motioning to a waiter. "Just bring us a bottle." I told him trying to keep my voice neutral. "Besides, I have a lot of other things to worry about besides being in a relationship with some crazy girl. We have the local alpha arriving in a couple of days, and the conclave coming up next month, not even mentioning all of the construction that Lenyx is overseeing at the ranch right now."

"If you like each other, I don't see why you don't just simply hook up? We wolves understand that sex outside of mating is only temporary; and that gal ain't no little girl." Ric ogled Anisa appreciatively in Zachary's arms.

I gave him a deadly look and he grinned impishly in reaction. That damn wolf is walking the edge of a beat down as much as Zachary is!

"Maverick! She seems to be very sheltered by her parents. I believe Mr. Sutton is trying to do the honorable thing and not lead that little gal on." Mitch said nodding approvingly, leaning back to let the waiter take his plate.

"Exactly! Finally, someone who gets it! Nessie is a nice girl, even if she is a little crazy, she's not one-night stand material." I gestured to Mitch in gratitude and Mitch nodded in return.

"Well, then I guess you are better off just letting your brother and Castor Blood give her that necessary heartbreak. It's a life lesson that everyone goes through eventually." Fred nodded sagely, expounding as if he had all the wisdom about women in the world, wrapped up tight and put in his pocket.

I looked to the dance floor to see Castor tap Zachary on the shoulder to break in.

Oh, no, that won't do at all!

* * * * *

Crossing my arms over my chest, I waited impatiently as Castor escorted Nessie off the dance floor. I took her small hand in mine surprising her and quickly yanked her back out onto the floor without a word and wrapped my arms around her waist bringing her close to me. "What are you doing, Nessie?" I bent down twelve inches to whisper in her ear in irritation.

"What do you mean? I seem to be dancing with you, though you didn't bother to even ask!" She leaned back to glare into my eyes. "What is wrong with you?"

"There isn't anything wrong with me! Why are you out here making a fool of yourself with my brother and 'Castor'?" I ground out, irritated all the more because I could hear what suspiciously sounded like jealousy in my voice.

She gasped out loud shocked. "You are jealous!" Nessie exclaimed in a soft whisper.

"I am not jealous!" I lied. "I am just concerned about your behavior!"

"My behavior? You have been intentionally ignoring me since I came to Texas, and now you are angry with me because I am dancing?" She looked at me outraged.

Frankly, I couldn't blame her. I was acting like an idiot. What the hell was I doing? She could dance with whoever she wanted to! We weren't in a relationship, and I didn't want a relationship with her anyway!

"I'm not angry." Another lie. "I just don't want to see you get hurt." That was the truth. "My brother is a love them and leave them kind of guy and Castor is a vampire!" Well, at least half of that sentence was the truth.

"Devin, I am not stupid, I have heard things about your reputation; and in case you have forgotten, you are a vampire too." Nessie's voice was soft.

"Yes, but I would never hurt you, Nessie." I whispered realizing that I wanted that to be the truth also and it scared me to death.

* * * * *

As soon as the music ended Devin left Nessie on the dance floor and walked to his table to grab the bottle of whiskey. He could feel the wolf shifters, Zachary's and Fred's gazes follow him out of the dining room.

Heading toward the bar, he had an overwhelming desire to put some distance between himself and Nessie before he did something even more supremely stupid than dragging her out on that dance floor.

Why the hell can't I just leave well enough alone? I don't give a fuck who she dances with! I don't give a fuck if she even hooks up with somebody! He thought to himself in confused frustration sitting at the bar.

A pretty vampire with short spiky, punky, white-blonde hair, gave him a sultry, interested smile from behind the bar as she was drying glasses. She leaned down to place a glass in front of him, "I see you have brought your own bottle...sir." Her voice was breathy and sexy as she smiled flashing a bit of fang at him.

Devin gave her tall leggy body a heated glance. Here was something to take his mind off of Nessie and whoever she was getting wrapped up with.

* * * * *

Devin staggered over the fine, white-sand to the beach chair before falling into it to lift his third bottle of whiskey to his lips. His vampire body burned through the alcohol faster than a human's body would water, but he was doing his utmost to stay drunk. There was something to what Billy had said about vampires not being able to drink enough liquor to ever be really drunk again in their existence; and he was doing his damndest to prove him wrong.

It was cold, but between the alcohol and his vampire body, he wasn't feeling it. The villa behind him was blocking the majority of the wind, which was good enough for what he had planned.

His head lolled drunkenly against the back of the chair and the blonde vampire from the bar stared down on him. He could feel her hot hungry gaze rove over his body, though he was finding it difficult to bring her into focus with his own.

Of all the sexual encounters that he had in Peru not one of them had been with another vampire. He took another long drink then sat the bottle down in the sand next to the chair.

He motioned to her with his hands, slurring. "Come and get it."

* * * * *

Feeling restless and unable to sleep, Anisa put on a robe and left her room to wander down the smooth teak staircase; she thought that she would head to the library to find a book. She stopped just at the landing to peek around a corner when she heard voices. She saw three men standing talking to each other.

Fred was standing next to Mansuetus and Zachary in the lobby. They all three looked tired and Fred and Zachary looked worried.

"What do you mean that you can't find him? He's your master! You are supposed to be keeping an eye on him!" Mansuetus was asking Fred, and Anisa heard the frustration in his normally calm voice.

Fred looked at Mansuetus with irritation. "That's why we woke you up. You saw him leave the dining room a couple of hours ago with a whiskey bottle. He's all messed up about that little gal. I went to check on him in his room a little while ago and he ain't there. I woke up the other Boss," Fred motioned to Zachary, "and he wasn't with him either. We've checked the bar, but it is closed down, we even went back to the dining room to see if he was curled up in a corner there. We've checked all of the public areas. The only place we haven't checked is the individual rooms and suites."

"I'm getting worried Uncle Man!" Zachary said to him. "Do you think he could be sleeping it off in Mom's suite?"

"No. Kýrios would have called me by now to take him back to his own room. And at this point I am not waking them, Kyría will have a fit if she thinks that we have lost Devin. He is still transitioning, he is not to be left on his own." Mansuetus gave Fred an irritated look. "Have you checked Anisa's room? He could be there." Mansuetus said thinking of the possibilities.

"I doubt that very much. But I guess we can start there." Zachary told him worriedly.

Anisa quickly stepped down the stairs to join them. "He is not with me." She told them, her melodious voice skipping anxiously, surprising them with her presence.

"What are you doing up?" Mansuetus asked.

"I can't sleep." Anisa returned, then continued panicked. "What if hunters have kidnapped Devin?"

Anisa had been frightened about the existence of hunters ever since she had listened to her mother and Iris discussing them earlier and her imagination was running wild.

Mansuetus gave her an incredulous glance before replying, "Anisa, there is no conceivable way that hunters breached the security force around this villa and have only kidnapped one young vampire without alerting us to their presence." He tried to keep his tone reasonable, but knew he was failing. *Children, dramatic children*, he thought.

"Then where could he be?" She asked caught between worry and curiosity. "Surely, he wouldn't have taken a vehicle and left the villa, would he?"

"No. Security would have alerted the front desk if he had left the property. Let's check the outside of the villa. If we still can't find him, we will have no choice but to wake up Kýrios. Let's hope we find him. Kýrios has little patience for wild, young, vampires." Mansuetus muttered.

* * * * *

After checking the front of the villa and the garages with no luck in finding Devin, they headed out the back to the beach and split into pairs, with Fred and Anisa heading to the left and Zachary and Mansuetus heading to the right. They all quietly walked along the length of the villa cognizant of the fact that there were vampires sleeping in the suites beyond the beachfront patios. Luckily, the fading moonlight gave them an unobstructed view of the soft, white beach heading down to the water and they didn't see any shapes that could have been a prone body passed out between the villa and the ocean.

Anisa was shivering with the cold and Fred had removed his jacket to place it around her shoulders. As Fred and Anisa passed the third patio area, they heard a muffled scratching noise like the continuous sound of rocking chair rails moving back and forth over rough concrete in the shadow of the villa causing them to pause in concern and they crept forward silently, approaching the source of the sounds.

* * * * *

I threw my head back against the beach chair, grabbing her short blonde hair to roughly pull her head back and clutched her slender hip hard as she ground her pussy down around my cock, panting out in shallow groans. My drunk-high was wearing off quickly and I was rapidly becoming more sober than I wanted to be.

I moved my hand to her small breasts massaging them roughly through her shirt and bra as she moaned softly in response excitedly. I wished that they were fuller. The woman in my arms was too bony for my tastes, but she felt good sliding her wet cunt up and down my cock. Still, she wasn't who I really wanted to have in my arms right now.

I was becoming aware of the fact that she was straddling both myself and the beach chair, with her short skirt hiked-up around her waist and the feet of her extremely long legs planted firmly on the ground. I couldn't even remember how my pants had gotten unfastened and pulled down around my thighs or how this had all started; but I was willing to finish it. I slid my hand in between us to firmly stroke her clit and felt a shudder flow throughout her body causing my cock to twitch in response.

I was so thirsty, and my jaw ached like I had been in a fist fight and had been socked a half dozen times.

She pulled me tighter to her as the rhythm of her hips raced with vampiric speed and her pussy tightened around me. I clutched her to me driving her on with my hands as I sensed my jism gather in my balls. She rode me hard and fast as I felt her mouth caress the side of my throat and her fangs graze over my skin. I could feel the tremors of her body start in her belly and move to her pussy to clutch around my cock tightly and I thrust up hard and deep as she gave a little rapturous cry against my throat and sank her fangs into me.

God, it felt fantastic! She suckled at me as I thrust against her, holding her hips tightly as I thrust over and over while she came around me. Yet, I quickly realized, I was seeking a release that was not forthcoming. I needed something! I desperately continued to swiftly thrust into her, hanging on the edge of an orgasmic precipice, experiencing intense pleasure, yet unable to fall over the cliff and discover that ultimate relief.

She gently moved my head against her throat as she suckled me, running her hand through my hair tenderly, and I felt my own fangs with my tongue. I ran my lips against the curve where her shoulder met her throat, and she groaned in encouragement as I grazed my new fangs over her skin. She held me tightly against her as she rode me faster keeping time with my thrusts and as I felt myself finally start to stumble over that cliff, I bit down on her drinking her blood in and felt her explode around me, milking the cum out of my body in the most potent orgasm I have ever had in my entire life.

* * * * *

Anisa and Fred stopped in shock at the sight of Devin and a blonde vampire locked in a tight embrace feeding off each other. As Anisa let out a shriek of fury, they lifted their heads to look at them with glazed eyes as blood ran out of their mouths. Anisa launched herself at them spilling them and the beach lounger over into the sand, as her fists flew.

Fred yelled, "Tarnation!" and attempted to pull her from them as she punched the female in the eye and her other fist connected with Devin's nose with a decided crunch. As Fred took one of her elbows to his jaw staggering him, he could hear Mansuetus and Zachary running in their direction.

"Ow! Nessie! What the hell!" Devin said from the sand, tangled up in limbs as Fred tried to pull Anisa's flailing form off of him. Her foot connected with Devin's jaw snapping his mouth closed with a clap as she screamed in rage.

"You bitch! What do you think you are doing?" The female vampire screeched at her quickly rolling away from Anisa's wildly flailing fists and feet.

"You slut!" Anisa shrieked in return reaching to try to scratch her eyes out, only prevented from doing so by Fred who had his arms wrapped around her waist but was still struggling to contain her. "What the fuck do you think you are doing fucking my mate!"

The female vampire's eyes widened at this information, as she looked behind at Fred, who was barely holding the struggling, raging, Anisa from launching herself at her, to Mansuetus and Zachary who had just arrived. The female vampire was gone in a flash as Devin, who was covered in sand, the vampire's blood, his own blood from his broken nose, and still half inebriated struggled to stand and pull up his jeans.

Anisa pulled away from Fred and launched herself again at Devin, taking him back down into the sand, punching him in the throat and again in the face. Devin put up his arms trying to prevent her enraged fists from connecting with him. Fred once again tried to pull her off of him and finally succeeded with Zachary's help.

"Stop it Nessie! You are being crazy!" Devin yelled struggling again to stand up.

"What is going on out here!" Came a dark angry command as they all turned to see Nichola striding furiously out of a patio two doors down from them in black pajama bottoms and shirtless. Leila, who looked to be wrapped in a sheet, and holding a growling Princess against her, poked her head out of the door.

They could see Rom and Esmeralda coming from farther down, and Iris and Aleksei poking their heads out of the patio door in curiosity one patio down.

"You are a cheating bastard, Devin Sutton!" Anisa yelled at him struggling to pull away from Fred and Zachary.

"Nessie, stop!" Devin told her, suddenly, and for the first time, feeling her rage and heartbreaking pain run through his body; his voice sounded small, guilty, and tired. "We are not in a relationship. I am not your mate." His words rang hollow even to himself.

Anisa angrily pulled away from Fred and Zachary with a sharp jerk took two steps forward and lifted her leg to give a swift kick to Devin's balls that would have made an NFL kicker proud.

He dropped to his knees clutching himself with a sharp yelp, then fell over onto his side to curl up into a fetal position in the sand groaning and whimpering weakly. Every male watching flinched.

"You are right, Devin!" Anisa ground out furiously over his groaning body. "You are not my mate!" She turned to run crying, to launch herself into her mother's arms, yelling, "Momma!"

As Esmeralda shushed her crying daughter and walked her away, Nichola and Rom came over to stand over Devin's whimpering form as he rocked in pain. They looked at each other briefly before Nichola said down to Devin with a brief, pained, sympathetic expression, "Their feet are absolutely dangerous, aren't they?"

Nichola looked at Mansuetus, Fred, and Zachary shaking his head. "Get him carried to his room and cleaned up. If I am not mistaken, he has more than his own blood on him. I will be up to see him shortly and then I want to know what the hell has went on tonight." Shaking his head ruefully he walked back to Leila and Princess.

Soulmates

Now, I can finally feel her! I can feel her, and her heart is broken. She hates me.

Devin thought miserably, staring at the ceiling of his room as he lay on the couch with an ice pack held to his crotch, and one to his nose, which had been reset by Dene. According to the doctor, his fully transformed vampire body should be totally healed by the morning.

Devin didn't care. The misery and guilt made him feel like he deserved the ass kicking that Anisa had given him. Afterall, everything he had done up to this point was to keep from getting close to her, to keep from hurting her; and he had ended up hurting her anyway.

Nichola walked into his room, followed by Rom and Mansuetus. He could see Fred and Zachary's faces peek around the door curiously before Mansuetus shut it.

Nichola who had pulled on a grey t-shirt that was tight across his chest and shoulders, in addition to his black pajama bottoms ran a hand through his hair that was mussed up. Without all of his stylish and expensive clothing he barely looked older than Zachary. Rom too wore a grey t-shirt, and grey sweatpants, and with his long, straight, black hair running down his back and around his shoulders he also looked much younger than the attitude he usually exuded. They both sat down on the bed next to each other and fixed Devin with their intense vampiric gazes.

Devin was too miserable and in too much pain to be intimidated by them.

"So, how was it?" Nichola asked with a smile, surprising Devin.

"Which part?" Devin groaned out. "Feeding or getting kicked in the nuts?"

"Since my mate has kicked me in the testicles before, I am quite aware of how that feels. Obviously, I am speaking about the feeding. More importantly I want to know: did you lose control?" Nichola replied inquiring calmly.

"No and it was great for all of about 30 seconds until Anisa tackled us and started kicking our ass." Devin's initial laugh ended in a moan of pain.

"Women get very violent when you sink your fangs or other parts of your body into something strange." Romulus chuckled in a wholly knowing manner.

"What are you doing here anyway Rom? You should be pissed at me. I made your daughter cry." Devin stated bluntly, but miserably.

Rom smiled wryly. "I have taught my daughter how to manage herself."

"I am painfully aware of that fact." Devin stated adjusting his ice pack with a small sound of pain.

"Yes, and you still didn't try to strike her back, even to defend yourself." Rom stated candidly, as if he was proud of him.

"I would never hit her!" Devin said passionately.

"Good. But I am aware that things happen between soulmates and that women can be emotional over things that we men do not even find important. So, I am sure that you will probably make her cry many times over your lifetime, even if you don't know what you did to make it happen."

"I am not her soulmate." Devin said weakly.

Mansuetus stood tall, crossing his arms over his chest, and snorted in disgust as Rom gave out a short bark of laughter.

"You can keep denying that fact, but it is very plain to us that you are. The more you try to fight it the more miserable you will be and the more confused, and dangerous, your emotions will become. You are not old enough nor strong enough to try to resist a mate-bond; and no one, no matter who they are, can resist one forever." Nichola explained, striving for patience.

"Okay." Devin said abruptly. "Let's say I feel something. Whatever it is, it isn't love. Let's get that straight. It doesn't matter. I am a vampire, more than ever, after tonight. She's a human. I don't want to harm her. It is too dangerous for her to be around me. I won't put myself in a position to harm her." Devin breathed in deeply and then said in a soft miserable tone, "Besides, you heard her, I am not her mate."

"You are right, it is not love. Being soul-mated is deeper than that. It is something that most vampires strive for. It is also something that most never experience, no matter how long they live. The fact that you have a soulmate is an honor; and a gift to be cherished, regardless of the difficulties of the situation." Nichola told Devin. "As a new vampire, you are more blessed than you can possibly understand right now."

"Anisa is currently being driven by fury." Rom explained patiently. "Women say many things that they don't mean when they are angry. She is human, and we have protected her, so she doesn't fully understand the vampire nature even though she lives with two of them." He smiled. "Give her some time. The first thing you need to do is apologize."

"I am sorry that she cried, I am sorry that her feelings are hurt. But she needs to know that I am not sorry about the rest of it; it was great." Devin told them and they looked at him like he was insane. They all started speaking at once in panicked voices.

Mansuetus covered his eyes with his hand, muttering, "Younglings!" in disbelief.

"If you apologize like that, she will kick you in the balls again!" Rom exclaimed.

"Don't ever apologize to a woman with that type of an explanation. Never admit that you might have enjoyed any part of what she is angry about! Just tell her you are sorry and endeavor to never make the same mistake again! Otherwise they might murder you in your sleep!" Nichola exclaimed in concern.

Devin smiled devilishly at them in response.

"Oh, Imp!" Mansuetus exclaimed laughing softly.

Rom and Nichola looked at each other, shook their heads, and chuckled.

* * * * *

Devin walked into the dining room the next day to find Leila and Esmeralda having coffee. Both of them glared at him in silence as he approached their table and sat down.

"Good morning, Mom, Es." He said and motioned to the waiter, ordering a glass of porcine blood.

"I am not quite sure what to say to you, Devin." Leila's voice was stern as she briefly sipped her coffee. "Your behavior over the last several months has been atrocious! Drinking, gambling, and all of the women. And don't even think for one minute that you and Fred got by with running that moving poker game under everyone's noses in Peru! Nichola knew about it the whole time and took steps to keep you out of trouble! Now, you end up in an altercation with Anisa and some other woman in the middle of the night waking up everyone and making a spectacle of yourself! You are embarrassing your family! I did not raise you to be this type of man!" Leila finished furiously.

Devin knew that his mother was seethingly angry over his behavior and last night's escapades had pushed her to the end of her patience. He felt deeply ashamed for embarrassing her, because she was absolutely right, he did know how to behave better. He had been using his transitioning and Billy's death as an excuse for saying 'fuck you' to everything and everyone around him.

"I know, Mom. I am sorry. I am going to make it up to you." He told her sincerely.

"You need to make this right with Anisa!" Leila exclaimed.

Devin took a sip of the pig's blood that the waiter brought to him. He swore that he had drank a gallon of the thick pungent stuff over the last several hours. Mansuetus, Nick, and Rom said that it would help flush the whiskey from his system, take the edge off his emotions and keep the bloodlust at bay. It seemed to be working. He felt better, more like his old self and definitely more balanced since he had started transitioning.

"I am going to speak with her, Mom. But you guys understand that she and I have to work this out between ourselves." Devin encompassed both his mother and Esmeralda in his gaze.

They both nodded and Esmeralda finally broke her silence. "I do understand, Devin, but I will not tolerate you abusing my daughter." The beautiful blonde, blue-eyed vampire looked dangerous for a moment.

"I promise, I will do whatever it takes to keep from hurting her again." Devin told her earnestly.

* * * * *

"Anisa, may I speak with you for a moment?" Devin asked formally, approaching her, as Castor Blood escorted her and Iris into the dining room.

"I am getting ready to eat breakfast, Devin. Besides after last night, I don't think we have anything left to say." She stated coldly but Devin could feel the hurt and heartache throughout her small form, causing guilt and shame to well up in him because he knew he had caused her that anguish.

Castor gave him a cold look, as if Devin were encroaching on his territory, exuding power at him in warning.

Devin easily ignored him and his push of power.

"Anisa, I just need a few minutes of your time. I won't keep you long." Devin told her softly.

Castor glared at Devin out of his dangerous, light green eyes, under his sharply drawn tawny brows that perfectly matched his artfully messy tawny colored hair. "I don't believe that the lady is inclined to speak with you at the moment." His voice was clipped and dripping with disapproval.

"This is not your business." Devin said to him dangerously, squinting at him coldly. "You don't make decisions for her."

"And neither do you!" Anisa stepped in between them to glower up at him, her small hands fisted on her hips and her cerulean blue eyes snapping once again in fury. "I don't have anything to say to you, Devin. Right now I am hungry and am going to have breakfast." She told him angrily, turning and started heading for a table leaving the two vampires to glare and bristle at each other, only to turn back towards them and say sweetly, "Are you coming, Castor?"

Castor smirked at Devin in triumph and taking Iris's arm followed in Anisa's wake.

* * * * *

Devin sat with Zachary, Fred, Mitch, and Ric as they were eating breakfast, drumming his fingers on the tabletop, and glaring daggers at the table where Castor, Anisa, and Iris sat chatting. Anisa was lightly flirting with Castor and from the half-lidded, contemplative, seductive looks he was giving her he seemed to be immensely enjoying himself.

"I think we can take him, Boss." Ric said to Devin also glaring in the direction of the table. The wolf shifter, who was a scrapper, had started referring to him as 'Boss' since he had decided that Castor was infringing on Devin's 'territory'. It was typical pack behavior, one for all and all for one; and it indicated that Ric thought of Devin as part of his pack.

"Undoubtedly true." Zachary murmured, agreeing with Ric. "Except Devin has already been called out by Nick and our mother for his behavior. Getting into more trouble right now is not an option. We will have to figure out a way to distract Castor without violence so that Devin can get Anisa alone."

"Who says I want to be alone with her?" Devin asked angrily while he continued to scowl at the table, rapidly rapping his fingers on the tabletop in frustration as Anisa playfully tapped Castor on the arm laughing at something he had said.

The other men looked at him incredulously for a moment before they ignored him to continue plotting against Castor.

* * * * *

"Hey, Gramps!" Zachary said jumping up and heading to Aleksei as he wandered into the dining room obviously looking around for Iris, who the vampire frequently referred to as his ladylove.

The ancient vampire smiled at Zachary. The old vampire liked the brazen young human detective very much. He managed himself fearlessly amongst both vampires and the wolf shifters, and occasionally exhibited some preternatural traits that Aleksei found both unusual and interesting.

When Zachary found out that they were relatives, he had taken to referring to Aleksei as 'Gramps', and instead of finding it insulting, the old vampire who had long ago lost any close relatives, found it endearing, as the young human reminded Aleksei of one of his favorite sons who had been killed during the Vampire-Shifter war.

"Good morning! How are you, Detective? I see your brother is no worse for wear after his adventures last evening." Aleksei nodded to the table where Devin sat. He looked to where Devin's livid gaze was directed, to see Iris sitting with Castor and Anisa who was flirting outrageously with the young handsome vampire. "Ah! I see." Aleksei murmured as Zachary stood next to him.

"Houston, we have a problem." Zachary whispered conspiratorially, crossing his arms over his chest, and Aleksei chuckled softly in response.

"And you think I can help with this problem, Detective?"

"Sure do, Gramps. You see the wolves," Zachary pointed his reddish-brown bearded chin towards the table, "are advocating removing Castor from Devin's soulmate equation. Seeing as how Nick is wanting us to be friends and work toward a treaty with the European wolf-shifters, I think that would be a problem."

Aleksei chuckled softly in response. "I do believe that would anger Nikolaos. So how can I help?" The old vampire's voice held a tinge of excitement at being involved in the younger men's plots and plans.

"Can you see if you can distract Castor? Maybe get him away from Anisa for a while so that Devin can talk to her privately?" Zachary asked hopefully.

"I might be able to help you with that." Aleksei smiled with a nod.

* * * * *

Anisa stomped back to her room, each step bound in frustrated irritation.

Aleksei had spirited Castor away, demanding that he fully inform him on the hunter situation that he had left in Kiev; though Castor promised to come to her room to collect her when he was finished, and show her the library here at the villa, and maybe play a game of chess.

Up until that point, she had been trying ridiculously hard to torture Devin by overtly flirting with the exceedingly handsome and sexy vampire. Inexperienced in trying to make someone jealous, her efforts had worked much better than she had ever hoped as Devin had sat at his table watching her with steely eyes.

Surprisingly, Castor had responded immediately to her efforts. His determined light green eyes focused on her with an intensity like he was gazing at an exceedingly rare, luscious steak that he couldn't wait to devour. After Devin's neglect and actions from last night, her feminine confidence was suffering, and Castor's attentions were both thrilling and slightly frightening.

If she hadn't seen it with her own eyes, his fangs, and the blood as it dripped from his lips and flowed from his mouth, she would never have believed that Devin would ever bite someone. Yes, her parents were both vampires, but she had never seen either one of them drink blood from a human, or from each other.

She covered her heart with her hand as she remembered the hollow stillness in her soul and the ripping pain like a razor slicing open her chest, as she watched him both feeding from and fucking another woman.

Deep inside she was embarrassed to have totally lost it, but the pain that had pierced her at the sight of him in another woman's arms had been like a scalpel slicing through her soul. The pain and rage were unlike anything that she had experienced in her entire life.

And after putting her through such agony, he expected her to speak with him as if nothing had happened? That was not going to take place! She was done with Devin Sutton!

She was almost to her room when a hood was thrown over her head from behind and strong arms encircled her and she felt a rope quickly wrap around her body, then what felt like a gag came over her hooded mouth preventing her from screaming. She struggled as muffled sounds of distress escaped her. She kicked and fought as another person lifted and secured her legs and feet with a rope, then she was being lifted and spirited away.

* * * * *

"Boss! Pssst! Boss!" Fred hissed from over the banister from the second-floor landing above the open lobby, as Devin made his way through looking for Anisa. Devin glanced up to look at him and Fred motioned quickly for him to come upstairs with some urgency. Curious, Devin used his vampiric speed to run up the stairs. "Come on!" Fred said rushing to Devin's suite with Devin following closely in his wake.

As they entered his room, Devin saw Ric standing there grinning at him victoriously and then over Ric's shoulder he saw Anisa's hooded form lying on the bed. Devin stopped in shock.

"We got her for you, Boss!" Ric told him jubilantly.

"Oh, shit! What have you guys done!" Devin exclaimed panicked.

Upon Devin's outburst, Anisa's body started flailing around on the bed and he quickly ran over to her to pull the gag from around her hooded head.

She started squawking like an enraged chicken and her struggles tripled as he pulled the hood off of her head. "What the hell is wrong with you, Devin Sutton?" She yelled at him with blazing eyes, and her face looked sunburned in her fury.

"You two better get the hell out of here before I untie her." Devin growled at Fred and Ric.

Smiling in triumph, they quickly exited the suite closing the door behind them.

"Are you crazy?" She yelled at him as he struggled to untie the ropes that bound her struggling body. They had trussed her up like a calf during branding season.

"I am sorry, Nessie! I swear I had no idea that they were going to do this to you." He told her meekly.

"What the hell is wrong with your people?" She continued to holler.

Devin stopped pulling on the knot briefly. "There is nothing wrong with them! They think they are helping; especially since you won't talk to me, and you are hanging all over some other guy!" He yelled back at her, shocking her into silence for a nanosecond.

"I can talk to anyone I want to, Devin! And I don't have to talk to you! We aren't mates, remember?" She shouted her voice choking in anguish as her eyes filled with tears as she remembered his words from the night before.

She continued to struggle furiously against her bonds and Devin looked ashamed for a second before he continued to untie her.

"Listen, Nessie. I am sorry about last night. I never meant to hurt you in any way. I have specifically tried to stay away from you, so I don't hurt you. It's the last thing that I ever wanted to do." He mumbled as he focused on the knotted ropes.

"Just get these damn things off of me!" She told him stonily.

Both her anger and her sudden coldness flayed his soul.

He finally got the ropes off of her and she stood rubbing her wrists heading for the door.

"Would you please stay and talk with me Nessie? I really am sorry. I just want us to get past this." Devin told her in a sincere voice.

"I have a date." She told him nastily. "Castor and I are going to play chess in the library."

Faster than she could see, Devin was standing in front of the door to the suite, blocking her exit. It was like he was sitting on the bed one moment and the next he had materialized in her path.

"Nessie, Castor is dangerous!" He growled at her.

"How do you know? You don't even know him!" She scoffed at him, secretly thrilled by his jealous tone.

"Nessie! You are a human and he's a vampire. That means he's just as dangerous as I am!"

Devin's now red eyes glowed down into hers and she was sure that as he spoke, she saw a hint of fang in his mouth.

"I like him! He's been nothing but nice to me since I met him!" She exclaimed trying to push her way around him.

She suddenly found herself flat on her back in the middle of the bed and Devin was holding her down with his long, muscled body pressed tightly against hers.

"Nessie!" He snarled and this time she saw his fangs in conjunction with his red eyes, causing her some fear. "You are so naive! You really have no clue, do you?" He asked burying his nose in her soft silken hair to breathe in her luscious scent of chocolate, popcorn, and wild figs.

He whispered as his lips caressed the skin of her shoulder where her shirt was pulled aside, causing her to shiver in response, "He's like a fat spider, and everyone knows that you catch more flies with honey! Vampires are predators! Vampires hunt! We bait our traps with sugary words, sweetened kisses, and sex." His hands roamed over her succulent curves pulling her even tighter against his hard body as if he were trying to mold her to him.

"You stop this, Devin Sutton!" She hissed at him in anger, shoving against him trying to push him off; it was like trying to move a mountain.

"You know you have convinced everyone that we are soulmates…" He leaned up on one arm to look down into her wide, blue eyes.

"I was wrong, and they are mistaken!" She told him cruelly, bravely glaring up into his red eyes. Her eyes filled with tears as she felt heartache overtake her.

"I always thought you were wrong too, Nessie." He said gently but truthfully. "I was drawn to you, and wanted to badly fuck you," Anisa flinched at his harsh words. "Because I could never feel your emotions, I just thought it was sexual obsession, and probably bloodlust on my part. Another pain in the ass aspect of being a vampire. So, I stayed away, because I didn't want to hurt you. I like you and I didn't want you to be a victim to my vampire nature. I thought I was being noble; and after some of the things that I have been up to recently…you were the only thing I was being noble about." He smiled briefly at her and bent to kiss her quickly on the tip of her pert nose, as she glared up at him in silent outrage.

"After finally getting my fangs and feeding last night, I've done nothing but feel you. Your emotions are flowing through my body and through my mind like a cold, rushing stream that can't be stopped, washing away all of the muck that I have felt buried in and that I have been dealing with for months. Getting rid of all of those negative emotions, well, it's made me feel cleaner and more whole than I have in a long, long time.

I know you are furious, and hurt, and I am sorry for being the cause of that. I know that you believe that I cheated on you and from your perspective that makes sense; but you need to understand that I did not believe that we were soulmates.

From my point of view, I did not cheat on you; I was only doing what I have been doing for months; trying to overcome and control the feelings and desires that I have been experiencing throughout my transition. Granted, I have chosen some unsavory ways of coping; and I will admit, I haven't been handling it very well." His voice was calm as he gazed into her eyes and gently ran his hand soothingly up and down her arm.

Looking at him in silence, she realized that his eyes were back to their normal pecan color; she could see small flecks of gold which seemed to float in his irises.

"I can do better, Nessie." Devin told her as if he suddenly made a decision. "If you give me a chance, I can make it right between us. I promise."

Not All Creatures Are Alike

Devin's lips hovered above Anisa's as he breathed her in.

Anisa was suddenly nearly overcome by the scent of sweet coffee and pastries, and she could almost taste the mint on his lips. She breathed deeply as an ache started in the pit of her stomach. She watched in rapt fascination as his tongue darted out of his mouth to lick his bottom lip and then run over the sharp point of one of his fangs. She wasn't sure if he wanted to bite her or kiss her.

As he slowly lowered his mouth toward her lips, Fred burst into the suite, hollering, "Boss! That Castor guy and your brother are about to fight!"

Devin leapt clear of Anisa dashing out of the door much to her continued frustration.

* * * * *

Bored and looking for something to do, Zachary and Mitch were walking out of the lobby and heading toward the back of the villa. According to Aris, the villa housed a spa area for both men and women and they wanted to check out the steam room and the gym.

"If the gym is not that great, we can always go for a run on the beach!" Mitch was saying as they stopped next to the glass doors to look out to the secluded beach of the villa. "It might be a little cold, but at least the sun is out, and it isn't going to rain or snow on us!"

Focused on the dark Aegean Sea washing up on the pearly white sands of the beach, Zachary, who was nodding his head, started to reply when a sharp voice came from behind them.

"Where is Anisa?" If the voice could get any more demanding or cold, Zachary and Mitch would have been frozen to the marble floor.

Zachary turned to see Castor striding toward them in irritation.

"How would we know?" Mitch replied to Castor's question with a question.

"I wasn't asking you mongrel scum!" Castor sneered at Mitch. "I was asking the human!" Castor's voice spat out the word 'human' like he was saying 'piece of dog shit'.

Mitch made a rumbling noise deep in his chest that sounded just like an animal's warning growl.

"Dude, I don't know what the fuck your problem is, but you need to take it elsewhere." Zachary said steadily giving Castor a deadly look as Fred and Ric, looking decidedly triumphant, walked down the stairs and in their direction.

"Your brother needs to stay away from her." Castor warned stepping close to Zachary to glare at him out of cold, light green eyes.

Fred took off running back up the stairs as Ric came close with a deep growling sound of warning that sounded remarkably similar to the noise that Mitch had made. Zachary motioned to Ric with his hand, halting the shifter about four feet away from the three of them.

Castor barely registered his presence as he continued sneering, "Anisa's much too good for the likes of weak vampires, humans and mangy wolves."

"What my brother does or doesn't do with Anisa is none of your damned business." Zachary said calmly turning his back on Castor as if he found him to be more of an irritant than a threat. "Come on, guys." He said to the shifters as he took a few steps down the hall in the direction of the gym.

"Don't you turn your back on me, human!" Insulted, Castor snarled from behind him then grabbed Zachary in a full Nelson.

Inhuman growls came from the shifters, but before they could shift, Zachary speedily bent forward and stepped to the side bringing his leg behind Castor's pushing against his knees, grabbed Castor's legs and using both his own strength and the weight of both their bodies, he lifted Castor and fell back to slam him onto the marble floor, with his own body weight landing on Castor's chest, in a move that would have made a professional wrestler proud.

Zachary then smashed his elbow into his sternum, causing Castor to gasp as if the wind had been knocked out of him, then using his elbow as a fulcrum, he brought his fist down sharply into Castor's balls, causing him to yelp, then took that same elbow and rammed it into his teeth.

Zachary rapidly scrambled up and away from the bloody claws that were swiftly sprouting from Castor's fingers. Castor suddenly got to his feet, but his reaction time was more human than vampiric, and reached for him. Zachary quickly ducked out of his reach, instantly driving the knuckles of one hand up and sharply into Castor's throat, throwing him off balance. He then heard his brother's voice.

"Mitch! Door!" Devin yelled as Castor clutched his own throat desperately trying to draw breath.

Mitch threw open the door to the beach just before Devin hit Castor like a linebacker at top speed sending him flying into the Greek sunshine. Castor fell, landing on the sand, immediately curling in on himself like a sick and dying, poisoned spider, screaming in agony.

* * * * *

Aris, Nichola and Aleksei came running down the hall in response to Castor's screams followed by Anisa, Leila, Iris, and Esmeralda. Nichola rushed out the door and Anisa screamed in distress as she tried to head out the door after him to Castor.

Devin quickly grabbed her pulling her close, where she struggled to escape his grasp. He told her sharply, "He's in extreme pain and you are human. He's going to need blood. He's dangerous right now."

Nichola quickly came back into the villa with an unconscious Castor in his arms. He sent a furious glare at Zachary and Devin, paused before them, then demanded, "I want to know exactly what happened!"

"He jumped me." Zachary told him calmly crossing his arms across his chest.

"And got his ass handed to him." Devin said with an angry snarl.

66

"Mr. Tsoukalous." Mitch addressed Nichola calmly and respectfully. "He was deliberately trying to provoke both myself and Zach. He has a major issue with both shifters and humans. He was looking for a confrontation."

Nichola nodded sharply and walked away carrying Castor. Nichola ordered furiously over his shoulder. "Aris! You and the Doctor get that damned spray booth operational and send a donor to Castor's suite."

* * * * *

Aleksei sat down with Zachary, Devin, Fred, and the wolf shifters in the bar taking them in with a wise, knowing look. Zachary was coolly drinking a scotch on the rocks, while Devin silently sipped a glass of porcine blood in annoyance.

Devin was irritated with Anisa who was in a snit because her 'precious' Castor was hurt. Then Leila had given them all a look of extreme disappointment as she had left with the other women, still further frustrating him. Afterall, they weren't the ones who started the fight!

Fred, and the shifters, sat silently and broodily sipped whiskey.

The whole group of them gave off an air of moodiness as if they were suffering from an injustice.

"So, Detective, I am curious." Aleksei's eastern European accent was pronounced. "How did you walk away from a fight with a three-hundred-year-old vampire without a mark on you?"

Zachary smiled enigmatically at the old vampire, and Aleksei wasn't sure that he was going to get an answer.

"He has a black belt in Krav Maga." Devin answered quietly.

Aleksei raised an eyebrow, impressed. His black eyes sparkled in curiosity. These interesting young men were constantly surprising him.

"Dev too." Zachary told Aleksei with a small, twisted smile and a tilt of his head towards Devin.

"Was Nikolaos aware of these skills?" Aleksei asked intrigued.

"I don't know. Maybe. If Mom told him. I don't even know if she ever even talked about it with Uncle Man." Devin answered looking to Zachary curiously.

"I'm sure if he had known, he would have asked me about it. I don't believe

I have ever discussed it with Uncle Man since we started." He glanced back at Devin.

"Me either." Devin replied.

"When did you start?" Aleksei asked Zachary.

"About ten years ago when I entered the academy. It's a dangerous job; being a police officer." Zachary explained. "I talked Devin into taking lessons with me. I needed a sparring partner." Zachary smiled at Devin and his robin-egg blue eyes sparkled with mischief.

"Yeah, it was just an excuse to get to hit me." Devin replied with a grin.

* * * * *

Castor slowly lifted the lids of his eyes as he felt a presence next to his bed. He felt totally pummeled and drained of energy. Anisa leaned forward to grasp his hand lightly in between her own.

"It's okay. Don't try to speak." The smile that she gave him was tinged with worry. "Dr. Lambert says that you should be feeling better soon."

Castor gazed at her, then tried to smile reassuringly; but instead ended up grimacing. "I have fed, so I am sure that he is right." He rasped out, bringing her hand to his lips.

"Anisa." Came a smooth voice from behind them.

They both glanced to the doorway to see Nichola neutrally looking at them.

"Would you let me speak with Castor please?"

Anisa nodded her head, quickly gave Castor a sweet smile, and exited the room closing the door behind her to give them some privacy. Nichola walked over to sit in the chair that Anisa had vacated, leaning back to cross his legs fixing Castor with a stern look.

Several seconds went by before Castor finally blurted, "Whatever you have to say, Uncle, just say it!"

"So, I see you are getting along well with your cousins." Nichola stated sarcastically.

"They tried to kill me!" Castor cried out.

"That is not true." Nichola replied steadily. "Both of them know that sunlight doesn't kill; only incapacitates." He then glared at Castor. "But claws *can* kill. Were you trying to kill one of my sons, Castor?" Nichola's eyes gleamed a reddish amber in rage as he looked at the telltale signs of blood around Castor's nails.

"I was angry! He's just a human and took me down! I didn't expect it. I lost control!" Castor looked away in disgust.

"Thank the Gods then that the four of them were in control! You are lucky one of the shifters didn't take your head off your shoulders! You purposefully started this conflict! You have been pushing both of your cousins and the wolf shifters without knowing or understanding the backgrounds of any of them. You haven't bothered to try to get to know them or anything else other than provoke them!" Nichola's voice was scathing. "I expected you to share your knowledge in preparation for treaty discussions. This treaty is important to our community and our very existence! Instead through your arrogance and prejudices you are making enemies of those who should be your allies!"

Nichola stood to look down his straight nose at Castor in disgust. "Not all creatures are alike, Castor! You of all people should know that! Are you like those that we have had to put down in our own community? Intransient in your thoughts, thinking that you know better and unable to adapt?" Castor looked up into Nichola's furious, now deep red, eyes in shock. "Do you think that you are the only one to have ever lost someone to another species? Will you continue to behave like the hunters that you hunt? Blaming the whole of another species for your very own personal pain?" As Nichola's enraged power flowed over him, Castor flinched as if Nichola had slapped him.

Nichola's voice, which had been rising in volume, became very grave. "I expected better from you, Castor." Castor looked at him with stricken eyes. "I am extremely disappointed."

Nichola walked out of the suite closing the door behind him quietly.

* * * * *

"Well, we are quite the unwelcome people around here!" Fred exclaimed walking back into the bar, which is where the men had remained even though it was past dinner time.

Devin glanced at him in question as Fred set down at the table in disgust.

"Yessir! All they seem to care about is a handsome face and a tight ass! If you have those, then you can get away with anything!" Fred said then reached over and snatched Ric's whiskey to shoot it down.

"Hey!" The wolf shifter exclaimed in surprise.

"Are we talking about the Castor situation?" Mitch asked calmly.

Fred sat back in his seat in disgust. "Of course! What else?" He asked with furiously pursed lips.

"Okaaaay." Zachary said with a look to Devin who raised his eyebrows in response.

"So…how's Cassie?" Devin ventured gently, looking at Fred.

"I don't want to talk about it." Fred said bluntly.

They all stiffened and seemed to go on high alert when Castor walked slowly into the bar. He looked better than he had when Nichola had carried him away; at least he was conscious now, and up and moving around. Though he was a little peaked and obviously not one hundred percent yet.

He came to stand in front of the table and the other men prepared to defend themselves, looking at him with distrust.

Castor looked at all of them. "I apologize for my behavior toward you. I take full responsibility for causing our altercation this morning. I have been unpardonably rude to you all from the beginning and I sincerely apologize for it." Castor told them meeting all of their eyes steadily. "If you can forgive my behavior, I would like for us to start over. Afterall, we are family, and we have an important mission to accomplish."

Devin looked at the others who glanced back at him with shrugs of their shoulders.

"Why don't you have a seat, cousin, and join us for dinner." Zachary told Castor with a small smile, pushing a chair out from the table with his boot. "We are all feeling a little salty at the moment, so we have decided to eat here in the bar."

Devin looked at Fred, "Yeah. Some of us more than others."

Fred looked disgruntled.

"Salty?" Castor asked in bewilderment sitting down.

"Irritated." Devin told him. "Mostly with most of the vampires…"

"And companions!" Fred blurted out.

"And companions," Devin clarified with a smirk toward Fred, "in the dining room."

"Yes, the elders can be frustrating on occasion." Castor commented with a nod of his head thinking of Nichola.

"I don't know. Gramps is pretty cool." Zachary told him.

"Gramps?" Castor asked.

"Aleksei." Devin clarified.

"You call Aleksei Ostrovsky, Gramps?" Castor asked Zachary in awe.

"Sure. He's old and a relative. What else should I call him?" Zachary smiled.

"He's a relative? Since when?" Castor asked.

"Since the Large Council meeting in Peru. The Doc took DNA from volunteers so that those vampires who wanted to, could know who their family members were." Devin answered. "Turns out he is a long lost relative of Nick's! They share an ancestor or something."

Castor looked at him in surprise.

"Turns out the Doc is a genius." Zachary told him.

Fred crossed his arms with a scoff.

"Which one of you retrieved me from the sun today?" Castor asked suddenly, looking at Zachary and the shifters.

"Wasn't us. It was Nick." Devin told him with a look.

"Nikolaos saved me?" Castor was shocked. "How?"

"I told you Doc is a genius." Zachary said sipping his scotch and Devin waved over a waiter.

* * * * *

They were all eating exceedingly rare steak and drinking. They sat around the table making small talk, basically discussing the other vampires who they jointly knew, the companion act that was recently passed, the various hunter organizations that Castor investigated, and the activities and improvements that were occurring on the ranch.

"So, what is your problem with wolf shifters?" The Alpha suddenly asked Castor.

Silence reigned for a few seconds around the table.

Castor cleared his throat before saying quietly, "A werewolf killed my mother."

Zachary, Devin, and Fred looked at each other in stunned surprise, then back at Castor in pity. Ric and Mitch looked at each other briefly.

"But you understand that we aren't Weres, right?" Ric asked.

"But you create Weres!" Castor's voice was strained.

"We don't." Mitch said emphatically. "I don't know of a modern pack who would. It's a hell of a process to put a human through if it doesn't end up killing them. And for what? They are never able to fully attain wolf form, they are useless for breeding because both males and females are sterile, and they go insane three nights a month. Not to mention the fact that even Alphas can't control them anymore than we could a rabid wolf. They always end up being a danger to the pack; either through violence to pack members or exposure to the human community."

Castor was quiet as he focused on cutting up his steak.

"When did it happen?" Devin asked him softly.

"About three hundred years ago. I was fifteen. You see I am a bastard; my parents weren't married." He clarified, looking at the other men without shame. "My father Jonas Tsoukalous, threw my mother and I out into the streets when I was three years old." Castor paused taking a bite of steak.

"Sounds like he was a prick." Devin remarked. "We kind of know what that's like." He glanced at Zachary who pursed his lips in response.

"He was." Castor smiled wryly. "Occasionally my mother would squabble money from him, and I know that before Uncle Aris was a vampire, he gave her money for food and shelter. But, basically from the time I was three to fifteen, my mother and I lived in the part of Katerini known as tsingániki póli."

"What does that mean?" Zachary asked.

"Gypsy Town." Castor told him with a smile. "It was a slum. Prostitutes, thieves, all sorts of unsavory characters; and a lot of gypsies."

"So your mom was a gypsy?" Devin asked.

"Yes, and my grandfather was what you would call a gypsy king. A king because he had influence in the gypsy community." Castor twisted his lips slightly in an unreadable expression. "But he was no better, and in many ways worse than my father. He was the one that sold my mother to my father when she was thirteen years old, after all. Five years later she returned to his doorstep with me on her hip. I can tell you he wasn't pleased about that fact. He immediately put her to work. She told fortunes during the day, and he pimped her out at night. So instead of being stretched to provide for two additional mouths to feed; he managed to come out on top of the situation. He took every penny my mother scraped together for himself." Castor's voice was emotionless, instead of bitter as one would expect; he sounded like he was speaking about a stranger's life from long, long, ago.

"How did it happen?" Ric asked. "Are you sure it was a werewolf?"

"Yes. It was one of her tricks. He ripped her to pieces." Castor's previously impartial voice cracked slightly on the word *pieces*, then after a deep breath, he continued on in that same neutral tone. "My mother, despite her hard life, tried to be a good mother. She did what she had to do to feed us, and I always knew that she loved me."

The men were all silent for a moment.

"So what happened then?" Devin asked.

Castor looked at him in inquiry.

"Did you catch it? Did you kill it?" Zachary asked.

"Mansuetus had arrived in the area to assist my Uncle Aris. You see Aris was transitioning. Mansuetus has appointed himself as the keeper of all things 'Tsoukalous'." Castor smiled wryly.

"Don't we know it!" Devin injected, smiling also.

"Mansuetus was at Aris's home when I informed my uncle of my mother's death." Castor paused remembering his fright upon seeing his uncle in his transformed state and how the muscles of Mansuetus's arms had bulged as he had restrained Aris from attacking him. "My grandfather was furious with me for doing so. You see, Aris while only a second son, still had money, and my grandfather had hopes that he would continue to send money to my mother if he was not aware of her death."

"Well, it sounds like your grandfather was a fucking piece of work!" Devin muttered.

"Yes." Castor responded. "Since I had gone against his wishes, he decided that I would sell myself, to keep his money flowing." The other men looked at him. "What he didn't realize was that by that time, his drunken episodes and fists no longer frightened me. So I ended up on the streets rather than lining his pockets through the sale of my body. He and the gypsy people under him searched for me, but by the time my mother had been murdered, I was a mature child of the streets. I knew how to survive and hide.

It had been almost a month of me avoiding my grandfather and stealing to eat before he and his men finally caught me. Since I refused to sell myself, he drugged me and sold me. Unfortunately, he sold me to my mother's murderer." He looked up into the shocked and horrified faces of the men listening to him.

"I didn't realize that Mansuetus and Aris were searching for me also and were investigating the creature that was stalking the streets of tsingániki póli." Castor's eyes lost their focus as he paused, he could feel the man's hands on his body as they caressed him in the alley, while he had struggled mightily to remove his bonds and fought down the nausea from the drugs that he had been given. A shiver of disgust flowed through his body as he felt the man's filthy, smelly, cock rub against his cheek while the man painfully gripped his long tawny hair trying to force his cock into his mouth.

He remembered the shuddering and spasms of the man's body as his hands gripping his hair had transformed into claws. Then a burst of air as those claws were ripped from his hair causing a burst of pain to flow over his scalp as some of his hair was pulled from his head in those clutching claws.

He remembered the screams and snarls of what sounded like animals tearing each other to pieces as he had huddled against the wall of one of the buildings that made up the alley. Not daring to look at the bloody fight taking place only feet from him in the darkness of the alley, he had struggled mightily against his bonds. Tears of frustration and fright had rolled down his sallow, dirty, undernourished cheeks, as he panted in terror, gnawing on the knots securing his hands, only to look up into the light amber eyes of a large wolf no more than three inches from his face.

74

In his deepest memories, he could still smell the blood that was caked around its multi-colored mouth. Sure that the monster would bite his face off, he closed his eyes in anticipation of his own death.

Castor's light green eyes focused on the men's faces around the table as he found himself back in the present.

"Uncle Nikolaos saved me." Castor said simply. "Of course it was about killing the beast that was stalking his home territory much more so, than it was really about saving me. But here I am." Castor cut into his steak.

"That seems a little harsh and doesn't quite sound like Nick." Devin said skeptically.

"Well, the man you know now and the man he was then, are different. Time and probably your mother have improved him." Castor told him.

"He said something similar to me a few months ago." Zachary replied and Devin looked at him quizzically. Zachary muttered to him aside, "I'll tell you later."

Devin looked at Castor expectantly, "Well that's not it, is it?" Castor met his gaze calmly as Devin continued. "Here you are," he gestured around. "You look a little older than I do. So, did you continue to live in Gypsy Town until you transformed into a vampire?"

"No. Mansuetus arrived on the scene to find a dead werewolf, and me still tied up and huddled against the wall of the alley. He untied me and because I was still fighting the effects of the drug that I had been given, he was taking me back to my grandfather. But when we arrived at the hovel Grandfather called a home, we found his mangled corpse drained of blood and Uncle Nikolaos sitting in a chair by the fire." Castor remembered Nichola's blazing red eyes as they traveled over his undernourished teenage body frightening him with their otherworldly intensity.

"He is your nephew! He is your blood! He is now alone in the world! You now have a responsibility to him!" Mansuetus had declared to Nikolaos, as Castor had stood gazing down at his grandfather's drained and broken body emotionlessly.

"I know what he is." Nikolaos had stated looking at Castor briefly, before turning back to Mansuetus. *"Did you really think I would allow a man who would sell his own grandson for the sexual gratification of a beast to live?"* His gaze returned

once more to Castor, and he approached him to take his narrow chin in his hand to gaze down into his stunned and frightened light green eyes. He released him and turned back to Mansuetus. "You will take care of him. Feed him, clean him, clothe him, educate him. Keep me apprised of his progress." Mansuetus had smiled in delight at this instruction, before Nikolaos continued, "And if he cannot be tamed, if he is too lost for polite society, if he becomes a problem...in short if he does not make my bloodline proud, I will find a solution to his existence." Nikolaos had left the hovel, flying into the darkness of the night; leaving Mansuetus and Castor alone with his grandfather's corpse. Castor had trembled in fear at the lightly veiled threat.

Mansuetus had smiled kindly at him, wrapping a large arm around his slight shoulders leading him out the door, "Come, boy."

"So, Nick killed him?" Devin asked bringing Castor's thoughts back to the present.

"Yes, and took me in. I am thankful for that every day of my existence." Castor murmured pushing away his plate. He smiled weakly at them. "Thank you for sharing a meal with me this evening, but I am tired and should retire for the night." He stood up to leave.

"Hey, Castor!" Devin said stopping him.

"Yes?" Castor asked.

"Why don't you join us after breakfast tomorrow, and we can draft up a treaty for Nick's review? The spray booth is supposed to be completed by noon, so afterwards, I could show you how it works if you like." Devin offered.

Castor smiled at him, "I would like that very much."

Love, Sex and Vampires

Devin leapt up the side of the villa to grasp the marble railing of a second-floor balcony and pull himself over. Trying the handle of the balcony door, he found it locked. He tapped lightly on the glass of the door with a hard, slightly pointed nail, then listened for movement behind the door.

Not hearing anything, he tapped harder, then finally heard movement in the dark behind the glass. Soon, he saw Anisa, her long, wavy, golden-brown hair slightly tangled down her back, dressed in a thin, white, baby doll nightgown, sleepily rubbing her eyes on the other side of the door.

She groggily looked at him and yawned widely, before opening the door to say, "What are you doing?" Her voice ended in a squeak of dismay as Devin quickly stepped into her suite from the balcony, shut and locked the door behind him, and scooped her up into his arms to carry her to her bed.

"Never, ever, open the door to a vampire, Nessie. It isn't safe." He instructed, laying down with her on the bed.

"But it's you!" She whispered to him.

"I too am a vampire and now you are here in my arms and anything that happens beyond this point is your fault, because I am only following my vampiric nature and cannot be held accountable." He teased, smiling devilishly at her kissing along her shoulder.

"I was sleeping you know." She complained.

"And now you're not." He grinned, smoothing a hand down the side of her silky nightgown to end on the outside of her bare thigh. The sensitive vampire skin of his hand relished the ultra-softness of her warm, satiny, skin. "I like your nightgown." He murmured as he breathed deep of her scrumptious scent which was making his mouth water in anticipation of tasting her. He wondered if she tasted as good as she smelled.

He lifted his head from her shoulder to gaze down into her large, wide cerulean blue eyes; surprised that he could see her and the colors of the room almost as well as he would during the day. He bent to gently run his lips across hers lightly, then suddenly deepened the kiss, entranced by the soft, luscious taste of her plump pink lips. As he stroked his tongue over her bottom lip demanding entrance to her mouth, she opened her lips and wrapped her arms around his neck, and he groaned as he slowly plundered her sweet-tasting mouth with his tongue.

Slowly ending the kiss, he lifted his head to look down into her half-lidded eyes as he felt her heart pound against his chest.

"That's the first time that you have ever kissed me." She whispered in wonder.

"Not really. I imagined kissing you a thousand times since I met you." He told her and found that his voice was deep with need.

"Was it better than you imagined?" She asked in a breathy whisper.

"Oh, yes." He groaned out as he lowered his mouth to hers again. He could feel her small fingers comb through his chocolate brown locks gently and then smooth themselves over the muscles of his back as he ran the palm of his hand under her nightgown to brush over the soft, silken, skin of her belly and then up to gently cup the underside of her ample breast; causing her to moan softly and her heart to wildly thunder.

He gently pulled away from her mouth to kiss his way down to tongue and nibble at the stiffened peak of her breast through the thin silky nightgown, wetting the fabric. He could feel her trying to pull his t-shirt up his body and over his head.

He lifted himself up to help her, desperate to feel his skin against hers. Once she pulled the t-shirt from him, she rolled him over onto his back straddling his hips and lowered herself to kiss him wildly.

He gripped her hips, as she ground against his erection, slightly shocked, and then turned on, when he realized that her rounded, supple ass was bare, and she was wearing a thong. He groaned against the sensation as her pubic bone slid over the head of his cock which was straining against the thin fabric of his pajama pants. Between her satin thong and his pajama pants there was truly little separating them.

Her small hands moved over the hard, defined muscles of his chest and the washboard of his abdomen, kneading and caressing, as she continued to pump herself against him with tiny gasps and moans.

As Anisa slid down his body to pull at the string-tie of his pants, Devin suddenly grasped her hands. "Woah, Nessie. Go slow. I am trying to keep it under control." He whispered in an achy voice.

Smiling she leaned back and pulled her nightgown over her head, and he feasted his eyes on her pert, pink-tipped, generous, breasts. Entranced at how beautiful they were, he reached up to cup them, softly kneading them with his long fingers, and running his thumbs over her pebble-hard nipples, he didn't notice anything more until he felt her small, soft hands encircle his bare cock and start to stroke him.

"Oh, Jesus." He whispered, quickly trying to stop her with a pained moan. "Oh, God, Nessie you are killing me."

She removed her hands to take the loosened waistband of his pajama pants and pull them down his body. She then knelt in between his knees to move slowly up his body until her face was above his cock. He looked at her with intense eyes and she told him, her gorgeous blue eyes wide with a wild desire, "I want to taste you."

Knowing that she was a virgin he asked, "Have you ever done that before?"

She shook her head and his cock twitched in anticipation, making her eyes widen further still.

"I am not sure where to start." She whispered suddenly swallowing nervously.

"Kiss it, lick it, suck it. I promise you I am going to love it no matter what you start with." His voice was hoarse as he watched her lips lower to him.

She ran her soft, wet, dusty-pink, tongue over the ridge of his cock, tasting him gently and he groaned out suddenly clasping his hands behind the pillow that his head was resting on to keep from grabbing her head and thrusting his cock between her wet lips.

The muscles of his ass cheeks tightened as he involuntarily thrust himself slightly forward with another groan when she gently nibbled and licked her way along his length, causing his cock to tremble under her lips. He felt her grip his base close to his body, and then lower her lips around the engorged head of his cock, taking him into her mouth slowly as she sucked him in.

"God, baby, that, feels so good." He encouraged her thrusting himself slightly into her mouth.

She started to bob her head up and down around him, taking more of him into her mouth as she became more comfortable with the activity, until he could feel her lips meet her hand that grasped him.

"That's it, baby, suck on me, God that feels great." He spoke to her as she increased the speed of her ministrations. "Nessie, I am getting close," he panted out. "Baby, if you don't want me to come in your mouth, you need to stop." He suddenly told her which only caused her to suck him harder and bob her head faster.

Devin closed his eyes tight, moaning, "That's it, baby! God, you are wonderful." He unclasped his hands to gently run his hands through her silken, golden brown, waves. "Almost there." He whispered warning her in case she changed her mind; she sucked him even harder and suddenly he was over the edge and yelling out as he spurted into her mouth only to feel her swallow him down. She continued to bob her head, sucking around him, prolonging his orgasm, until he gave a groaning, strangled, laugh, and begged her to stop.

She pulled her mouth up and off of him, and he reached forward pulling her to lay with her back on the mattress, enfolding his arms around her and kissing her deeply, tasting himself on her lips. "God, Nessie, that, was perfect! You are perfect." He moaned into her mouth.

He looked at her lazily to see her blush up at him; pleased with herself.

He moved between her legs and pulled the thong from her hips and down over her legs, causing her body to tense. "Oh, no, baby. You don't think you are the only one with a talented tongue, do you?" He smirked at her teasingly as he kissed his way down her torso, pausing to suckle gently on her nipples as she relaxed and softly moaned, lightly running her fingers through his dark hair.

He moved his hand down her smooth naked body, pausing to stroke gently over her hairless mons pubis. He had never been with a woman before that was totally hairless and he was fascinated with her smooth skin.

"God, you are beautiful." He whispered running his lips over her trembling body, pausing to dip the tip of his tongue into her belly button, causing her to squirm and giggle. "Tell me if you don't like what I do to you, Nessie. You don't have to tell me if you like something, but if you don't like it, tell me. We will never do anything that you don't want to do."

"Okay." Anisa whispered shyly.

He kissed his way further down her body, taking his time so that she could relax and enjoy every bit of what he was doing to her. He could feel how tense and shy she was and was willing to take this as slow as she needed him to.

When he had finally settled himself in between her legs to gently spread her wide to his gaze, he gently ran the tip of his tongue over her. She jerked slightly in response, and he blew gently over her clit.

"Oh!" She exclaimed softly.

He smiled to himself as he dipped his tongue inside of her body. God, she was sticky and sweet! He had never tasted anything like her. He felt her fingers gently run through his hair, as small sounds of pleasure escaped her lips. He glanced up to see her slightly arched with her head thrown back, her eyes tightly closed and plump mouth parted in wonder.

Taking her clit in his mouth, he suckled and thrummed his tongue over her steadily, eliciting gasps and moans to pour forth from her lips. She gripped his head tightly to her.

That's it, my Nessie, ride my face. He thought at her never stopping the steady rhythm of his tongue.

"Oh, Devin." She gasped out in shock and desire.

That's right. I know you can hear me. God, you taste so sweet. So delicious. I want you to come for me, Nessie. I want you to come on my face and let me drink you in.

He gently inserted a finger halfway into her, to feel her muscles tightly contract around him. She groaned loudly as he continued thrumming her with his tongue and gently stroking her, while she grew tighter and tighter around his finger.

Almost there, baby. I can feel you. Come for me.

She exploded in his arms in orgasm with a cry of completion, and it was the most beautiful thing that he had ever experienced.

* * * * *

Devin lay with his arms wrapped tightly around her small, limp, body that was sleeping across his chest. His cock was hard and demanding that he fuck her; but he ignored those demands. He was in charge of his cock, not the other way around and he was determined to take it slow with her. As far as he was concerned, she deserved his patience after what he had put her through.

She gave a soft little snore against him, and smiling, Devin gently kissed the top of her head before settling back and closing his eyes.

* * * * *

Anisa floated down the stairs on her way to the dining room, feeling wonderful. Devin had left her room a few hours ago, telling her that he had work that needed to be done and he would be busy most of the day, but he would see her later.

She sat next to her mother, who sat at a table with her father, Aleksei, and Iris, smiling happily.

"You are in a good mood this morning!" Esmeralda noted sipping coffee.

"Yes." She said with a smile, pouring herself some coffee from the carafe on the table. Looking up at the waiter who was now standing next to her she said brightly, "I will have eggs benedict, hash browns, and fresh fruit. Could you also bring me a large tomato juice? Thank you." She smiled happily at the waiter, and he returned her smile with one of his own, before nodding his head to place her order with the kitchen.

"And hungry." Rom said to Es with raised eyebrows. His daughter hadn't been eating well for several weeks now, and her moods had run from moody to depressed to hopeful to angry for just as long; both he and her mother had worried about it.

"Yes, I am starving." Anisa said with a small laugh.

The four vampires glanced at each other, slightly stunned, and bewildered by the moodiness of young humans.

"Iris and I are going shopping later this afternoon if you would like to join us." Esmeralda ventured not looking a gift horse in the mouth.

"Oh, I would love to! Is Lady Tsoukalous coming also?" Anisa asked happily, thinking that this could be an opportunity to get to know Devin's mother better.

"No, she and Nikolaos are going to drive to where he was born later this afternoon. She told me she wasn't even sure if they would be back until tomorrow since he was being very secretive about it." Iris told her.

"Well, I am looking forward to shopping with you and Momma in any case, Lady Iris." Anisa replied enthusiastically.

* * * * *

Anisa was walking down the hallway toward the library, when she was grabbed and pulled into a dark closet. She gave a small shriek of fear that was cut off by a hand over her mouth.

"I have you in my clutches now, my pretty." Came an evil voice out of the darkness next to her ear, which would have been totally terrifying if it hadn't ended on a devilish chuckle.

"Oh, Devin!" She whispered as the hand was removed from her mouth, and she slapped him on the shoulder prompting a small grunt from the figure that held her tightly in his arms. "You scared me to death!"

"Not quite to death, I hope." He murmured slipping his hands down to firmly cup her ass pulling her against his erection. "I couldn't keep you out of my mind today, baby." He leaned down to kiss her deeply, causing her to moan against him.

"I have been thinking about you today, too." Anisa whispered against his lips.

wanted to see you for a moment. I have to go and show Castor how
_____ ₂ spray booth." He said in disappointment as he nibbled her earlobe,
causing her to give a little ticklish squeal.

"Why are you showing him how to use the spray booth?"

"Oh, because we are trying to make friends with him since we threw him
into the sunshine. He's trying, we're trying. You know how it goes. None of
us want to be on the wrong side of the big, bad, vamp!" He said cheekily.

"The big, bad, vamp?" She asked curiously.

"Yeah, Nick. He expects us all to play nice with each other and be ready to
meet with the local Alpha wolf shifter sometime tomorrow." He gave her a
quick kiss. "But I am looking forward to seeing you tonight."

"Well, I am going shopping with my mom and Iris in a couple of hours so
we might not be back until after dinner."

"Well, have a fun time." He told her obviously reluctant to let her go.

"Go on. Go play nice. I will see you later." She said laughing at him as he
poked his head out of the closet to look both ways, then turned quickly to
blow a kiss in her direction and step out into the hall to speedily walk away.

She poked her head out grinning as she checked out his tight ass while he
strode down the hallway toward the spa area of the villa. Feeling a bubbling
happiness throughout her body, she stepped out and headed in the other
direction toward the library.

Conquering The Sun and Friendship

"I don't believe you. It's a trick." Castor, dressed in a pair of red swim trunks and dark sunglasses, told them firmly and surprisingly without blame as he stood inside the open, but shaded, doorway to the back of the villa with Devin standing next to him. He was resolute, with his arms crossed over the sharply defined muscles of his chest and abdomen.

"Dude, not even my sense of humor is that cruel." Devin, who was also wearing a pair of dark sunglasses, but was more covered by a long sleeve t-shirt, jeans, and a cowboy hat, said to him exasperated, thankful that Anisa wasn't out here to see Castor's strong body.

She was already way too fascinated with the other vampire as far as he was concerned, and he could imagine the questions that she would put to him if she saw the exquisitely drawn, emerald-green oriental dragon tattoo on the left side of his chest.

It must have hurt like a son-of-a-bitch when he had it done as it was extremely detailed and probably took a long time to complete. It was as long and wider than Devin's large hand and ran close to one of his dusky nipples.

"Yeah, why would we trick you at this point?" Zachary said to Castor standing in the white sands of the beach, under the Greek sunshine, next to Mitch, Ric, and Fred. "Come on out."

"No, I won't. I understand the need for revenge, but I was wholly sincere in my apology to you." Castor told them in an apprehensive voice. "This is

85

not necessary to trick me in this manner. Before I do this, I would like to talk to Uncle Nikolaos to confirm your information."

Zachary huffed slightly, rolling his eyes in irritation, then gave Devin a purposeful look. "Cousin, trust us." He told Castor in a coaxing voice as the vampire shook his head negatively.

Devin shoved him out into the sunshine of the beach, and Castor yelled out in surprised fright, only to quickly recover as he didn't experience any burning sensations or pain.

"Oh…" He breathed out in wonder as he held his arms out and away from his body, looking up at the sun through the dark sunglasses. "Oh…"

"Told you." Devin said following him out into the sunshine.

"Oh…" Castor said once again, then looked quickly to the other men. "This is not a good thing."

"What do you mean that this is not a good thing? This is fucking great!" Devin exclaimed pulling his shirt off his body to stand beneath the sunshine with his arms outstretched.

"No, Devin, it is not." Castor told him. "Not all of us can be trusted to the luxury of sunshine. Think about it. Imagine what the monsters of our kind could do if they were able to move about freely under the sun." The others looked at him with sudden understanding. "We need to speak to Uncle Nikolaos about this. He cannot share this technology with all of our kind. Its use must be limited to only those of us who can be trusted to not arbitrarily commit murder."

* * * * *

"Wonderful, brilliant children." Aleksei said with a smile as Castor, the boys, the wolf shifters, and Fred, exited the conference room where he, Nichola, and Rom, as well as the other three members of the small council, via Zoom, were meeting to review the draft treaty. "That is our future, gentlemen, and I frankly am proud of it."

Nichola looked to Rom for his input.

"They are correct. You cannot allow the formula for the sun inhibitor nor the secrets of its equipment to be shared with all of our community." Rom spoke in agreement as he looked at Nichola. "How many systems are there in existence?"

"All of the hotels are being outfitted with them. There is one at the ranch, which is now operational, your residence in Utah and of course my Toronto residence." Nichola's voice was thoughtful.

"I understand that the technology of the sun inhibitor system is wholly owned by you, Nikolaos, and the decision to share it is your responsibility alone. But I must agree with the youngsters. Between the six of us," here Aleksei motioned to the large screen of the conference room showing Beutel, Peake, and Prince Khaldun, "I am sure that we can all come up with different members of our community who should not be allowed to indiscriminately mix with humans twenty-four hours per day."

Nichola looked to the others on the large screen monitor. Both Peake and Prince Khaldun were nodding in agreement with Aleksei and Rom.

"As much as I hate to make this unanimous, could you imagine what it would have been like hunting Earle if he would have been able to move unfettered in the sunshine?" The green-eyed German, Beutel, who normally went against the grain on any decision by the small council, shuddered visibly.

Nichola sighed deeply in disappointment, thinking about Latour. "I agree. If any vampire would like to temporarily experience the sun; they will have to register at one of the hotels for a treatment. At least in this way, those who have learned to mix with humans without incident will be able to experience it and if there is a problem, we will know who has accessed the technology and where." He nodded to Mansuetus who sat in a corner of the room. "Make it happen, Mansuetus."

"As you wish, Kýrios." Mansuetus stood, nodded, and exited the room.

* * * * *

Devin and the other five men morosely walked along the white, sandy beach.

"It was the right thing to do." Castor was telling them.

"Maybe. But Nick was excited about this," here Devin stretched out his hand toward the sun. "He thought it would help change the community for the better."

"It still might." Zachary told them both, turning and dexterously walking backwards to face them while he spoke. "Sudden change is never good though. Let's see how other vampires react to having that type of freedom before allowing everyone to have it haphazardly. You got to keep the humans both clueless and safe."

"Are you speaking about yourself?" Castor snarked, smirking at him.

"Dude, I live with both vampires and wolf shifters. I am hardly clueless. Besides, I can keep myself safe." Zachary returned his smirk.

They turned quickly upon hearing a rapid, playful, high-pitched barking headed their direction.

Running toward them at top speed, over the fine Greek sand, her silverish wheat-colored, long hair floating around her small body like Fabio riding a horse in a beach scene on the cover of a romance novel, came Princess, her tail wagging wildly as she approached them. Following sedately about half a football field behind her were Leila and Cassie, both dressed in tantalizing bikinis and billowing swimsuit wraps.

The men stopped to wait for them.

"Look, Fred! It's your woman!" Ric whispered to Fred, who immediately scowled and crossed his arms, glaring in Cassie's direction.

"Hey, rat dog!" Devin said bending to pick up Princess as she bounded up to them.

"Your mother is a very seductive vampiress." Castor murmured in a sultry voice, his gaze lingering over Leila's exposed curves as she walked over the beach.

"Dude! Keep it in your pants!" Zachary exclaimed giving him a small shove.

"Yeah, it is not cool to be openly perving on your buddy's mom!" Devin told the bewildered vampire with an irritated tone; like he shouldn't have to be telling him the bro code rules.

"Besides, she's like your aunt! Nasty!" Zachary grimaced in both disgust and disapproval.

* * * * *

We were all sitting in the bar drinking, trading barbs, and telling outlandish stories later in the evening. It had been a while since I enjoyed a night in all male company without feeling the need for any female distractions. Even Castor had grown on me throughout the day. I was starting to realize that he was so intense because he had been raised by, lived with, and was trained by Nick and Mansuetus, and though I loved Uncle Man, living like Castor must have for the past three hundred years was not something that I would have ever wanted for myself.

I definitely appreciated my mother more than ever after knowing a little bit about Castor. Even though I was now a full vampire in every sense, I decided I liked my humanity, and wanted to keep a hold of it as long as I could.

I watched as Zachary laughed at some of the stories that the shifters were telling and envied my brother for a moment as I drank my porcine blood; and not for the first time over the last several months, I was glad he was here with me.

I listened smiling as the wolves were telling Castor, in great descriptive detail, about hunting predators on the ranch. Castor looked so awed and envious at the prospect that I was considering inviting him out for a visit.

I felt a buzzing in my pants and pulled my cellphone out to see that a text notification had come through from Anisa, which caused my heart to skip a beat in anticipation.

What's your favorite color? Anisa had texted.

I smiled devilishly and texted back, *Whatever you are wearing...*

Lol! We are going to get something to eat. See you later?

I smiled as a sudden image appeared in my head of her smiling at her phone. *Can't wait. Text me when you are on your way back.*

K. Came her text, followed by a picture of a pair of 'smooching' lips.

Chuckling, I was suddenly surprised by the small bubble of joy that welled up in me. I realized it was the same feeling that I had been carrying around inside me ever since I'd made the choice to just stop fighting the overwhelming desire to be with her. After all of the recent pain, I realized that I really liked the happiness that Anisa had brought to me.

I hadn't felt contentment like this since before I had started my transformation into a vampire. Breathing deeply at this feeling that had lodged itself in my heart and pebbled my skin, I realized that I had never felt this particular exhilaration before in my life. It wasn't love...couldn't be love... but this joyous feeling was a definite result of being with Anisa.

"Hey, who wants to play some poker?" Fred asked.

"Gramps, you in the mood to lose some money?" Zachary asked with a gleam in his eye.

Aleksei gave him a little challenging grin and looked at Fred, "I will play."

"You in Boss?" Ric asked.

"Yeah, I'll take your money if you insist!" I threw down a gauntlet with a laugh, and while the others moaned and talked trash, I smiled and sent my Nessie a pair of smooching lips in return.

A Long Night

❧

The men sat around a large table in the bar area of the villa playing seven card stud poker. Fred, whom everyone knew had a tendency to cheat, was positioned as the dealer, while the rest of the men sat with drinks, poker chips, and a few of them were smoking cigars.

"You know those things will kill you, Gramps." Zachary told Aleksei trying to read him as he called Aleksei's bet.

Aleksei smirked in response revealing nothing as he drew on a cheroot.

"I'm out." Mitch said throwing in his cards looking around. "I wonder where Romulus is?"

"Feeding, I am sure." Castor said throwing his cards in also. "I'm out."

"I didn't know that he still fed on humans." Devin remarked tossing chips in front of him. "I will call and raise you fifty."

"I'm out." Ric said tossing in his cards.

"Many of us subsist on a combination of human blood and animal blood. Few of us have the ability to feed off emotions, like myself, Nikolaos, and your mother." Aleksei commented. "I call."

"I thought that was an age thing." Devin remarked.

"Well, it is." Castor replied lighting a thin, Partagas cigar, then blowing the blue-gray smoke above their heads. "But not all of us develop the same abilities at the same age and mates seem to draw off of each other's abilities."

"It depends on many factors. Not all vampires are born, some are made.

Not all vampires ever grow old enough to totally subsist off of emotional energy, fly or shapeshift. We each have different gifts and strengths. I have always suspected that it is a bloodline aspect. Even before the doctor developed his test, I have always felt a connection to Nikolaos and his bloodline; so frankly I wasn't too surprised to find that we are related. He and I have much of the same abilities." Aleksei murmured looking in speculation at Zachary who was studying him intently in return.

"I fold." Zachary said after a moment.

Devin looked at Aleksei with a smile as he turned over his cards. "Three kings. Let's see those cards, Gramps."

Aleksei slowly smiled in return laying his cards down. "Flush."

"Damn!" Devin sat back in annoyance.

All of the other men around the table gave out groans of irritation.

"That is the last four hands!" Ric exclaimed in disbelief.

"There is probably a lesson to be learned here, since Uncle Nikolaos would not like it that we were gambling in any case." Castor purred with a slight smirk seemingly happy to be breaking one of his uncle's rules.

"While the cat's away…" Devin smiled at him devilishly.

"What's Nick's issue with gambling anyway?" Zachary asked generally as he watched Fred shuffle the cards.

"Nikolaos saw many humans gamble vast fortunes and estates away over the centuries. Many families have been devastated through gambling." Aleksei murmured.

"Well, wait until he finds out how much Mom likes the one-armed bandits in Vegas!" Zachary chuckled.

Glancing at his cellphone briefly, Devin got up and walked into the lobby then returned shortly with a concerned look on his face. "It's almost eleven o'clock! Don't you guys think that the girls should have been back by now?"

* * * * *

Anisa's eyes fluttered open, and she could see a smooth, polished, grey concrete floor from where her cheek rested upon its cold surface. The light around her seemed sparse and it hurt her eyes to try to bring everything into focus. Her body ached and she felt battered beyond belief. It was as if someone had picked her up and slammed her onto this floor over and over again.

There was a throbbing pain in her head, and she slowly reached a trembling hand up to the spot that hurt the most probing gently feeling a wetness that she instinctively knew was blood. She tried to sit up by pushing herself up on arms that shuddered like windows in a hurricane, only to roll over to her side as nausea overtook her and she power-vomited up the dinner that she had with her mother and Iris.

She continued to heave, the muscles of her entire body clenching in one painful spasm after another, until there was nothing left in her stomach, and her body felt void of all moisture: finally closing her eyes in pain and exhaustion.

"Jesus! This one has puked all over the place!" Came a concerned echoing voice around the area and in the dim light, and cold and clammy floor of the concrete, she was reminded of a dank, damp, cave.

"Let her lie in it! The filthy little blood whore!" Answered a hate filled voice.

A young man dressed all in black from the ski cap on his head to his black Reebok tennis shoes yanked open her cell door with an unoiled screech. Barely able to move, she looked up into his face that was partially hidden by large, black-rimmed glasses that gave him a studious look. He looked at her in pity, grabbed her arm and dragged her weakened, unresponsive body away from the vomit to the other side of the cage and proceeded to clean up the vomit from the smooth, sealed, concrete floor.

"Why are you wasting your time with that?" Came the cold angry voice.

"We are supposed to be taking care of them! Sonchus wanted them all alive! We have already fucked up enough this week!" The young man answered furiously.

"What does it matter? They were all blood whores from the villa or monsters that deserve to die!" A horrible hateful voice came from beyond her mottled, fuzzy vision.

Anisa heard heavy booted feet against the concrete come stomping her way, to deliver a swift steel-toed kick to her midsection that caused her to gasp for breath and to simultaneously heave dryly, curling in upon herself, as pain rolled over her body once more.

"Knock it off! Or you can explain to Sonchus why she died!" The young man in black ordered.

Anisa tried to control her heaving, shaking in reaction to the pain and nausea sweeping through her body. She felt a presence kneeling next to her and tried to focus her fuzzy gaze on it.

"I am sorry, little one. Sonchus will figure it out when he arrives. If you are innocent, I am sure that he will let you go." She heard a soft tender voice coming through a long tunnel as she felt a smooth hand brush her blood-soaked hair from her face before she once again lost consciousness.

* * * * *

"Anisa is not answering her phone!" Devin told the others, voice extremely concerned, as the phone rang through to Anisa's voice mail for the third time.

Aleksei's face also grew anxious as he took out his cell phone to start dialing it, lifting it to his ear to listen. He closed his eyes in concern as the connection to Iris's number also went to voice mail.

Devin quickly left the bar heading into the lobby yelling "Rom!" at the top of his lungs.

The black-haired, black-eyed, vampire suddenly appeared as if by magic in the lobby half-dressed and looking decidedly disheveled, a smudge of blood on the corner of his mouth. "What?" He asked alarmed at the intense look on Devin's face.

"Have you heard from Es?" Devin asked quickly.

"No. Why?" Rom asked growing nervous.

"Call her please. Neither Anisa nor Iris is picking up their phones. I have a bad feeling." And he did. Something was not right and there was a growing tightness in his chest, and a steady throbbing pain in his head was making itself known. "Where is Mansuetus?" Devin looked to Zachary who walked into the lobby followed by the others.

"Here." Mansuetus, who had heard Devin's panicked shout for Romulus and had decided to find out what all of the commotion was about, said as he was coming down the stairs.

"Dev, maybe they went to a movie, or a club?" Zachary told him seeing that his brother was starting to look pale with panic.

"Who did the girls take with them for security?" Devin asked Mansuetus ignoring Zachary, while a sharp uncomfortable feeling flowed over him, as he watched Rom disconnect his phone, then hit redial in frustration to call Esmeralda again.

Aris joined them in the middle of the lobby to answer. "A limo driver and another general security guard. Lady Esmerelda requested a limo, the itinerary included shopping and dinner, so I am sure that they will be back very soon. A driver and a guard are standard for guest security while taking a trip into Katerini. These are just precautions insisted upon by Lord Tsoukalous because Katerini is relatively safe, Master Devin." Aris told him trying to allay his fears.

Rom stopped dialing his phone closed his eyes and stood very still, like a stone statue, barely breathing. Everyone went silent watching him.

"I...don't...I...don't...feel her." Rom said deep in concentration. His eyes snapped open, glaring redly at the other men. "I can't feel Es."

"I will call the guards." Aris told them finally concerned, quickly walking back to the front desk to make those calls.

* * * * *

"Mama." Anisa whispered still unable to focus her eyesight. "Mama." Painfully, she tried to sit up, feeling for something to hold onto. Her dainty, dirty hand, which was stained with her own blood, wrapped around the cold steel bars next to her; and she used them to weakly pull herself up, her breath hitching in her lungs at the extreme pain in the muscles of her core, into a sitting position leaning heavily on them.

Slowly as she hugged herself against the steadying cool metal of the bars, her eyes were able to focus on the limited light around her. It looked like she was in an old concrete bunker; it's high rounded ceiling dimly lit by naked bulbs, like something out of an old, world war two movie. Her imagination ran amok in fear, and she expected any moment to see a man dressed in a gray, wool, SS uniform to come walking from the pitch-black hallway, his

95

high, black, polished boots clicking menacingly against the smooth concrete floor, leading out of the dimly lit cell area.

She strained her eyes to look into the cells on either side of her. Huddled in a dark, shadowy corner on the other side of the cell next to her, she saw an even blacker figure. "Mama?" Anisa whispered louder.

"I am not your Mama, child." A low, hissing voice came from those shadows. The huddled figure unfolded, spreading the darkness, and slowly crawled toward her.

Anisa shrank away from the bars, as quickly as her injured body could move, to sit against the back wall of her cell in fear, as the figure pulled itself steadily forward across the concrete floor of its cell.

Her muddled mind could not comprehend what she was seeing, as an alien creature pulled itself from the shadows into the murky light.

The creature crawling toward the bars in the next cell was bright red and looked to be covered in smooth, scaled skin. It had a large, square jaw, long, pointed nose with a hump along the ridge, and yellow reptilian eyes with elongated pupils. The being, which was anything but human, had long reddish-brown hair that fell past its shoulders.

It looked like a humanoid snake and the way it had slithered toward the bars and the way it leaned fluidly to grasp them with claw-tipped hands prevented her from seeing it below its waste and she didn't know whether it had legs or a tail.

It looked at her curiously with a coldness that was totally alien.

She bit down on her fist in panic to prevent herself from screaming out in fear. She knew that if she screamed it would bring her captors back to her cell and after the small amount but debilitating physical abuse that she had already received from them, she was reluctant to draw unwarranted attention to herself.

"Fear not, child." The creature told her in a hissing whisper. "I am in no position to harm you." The creature's long, lava-colored, forked tongue flicked out of its mouth as if tasting the air. "Sssss." It suddenly hissed out in wonder. "Not a child. A young woman. A young vampire maiden." Its tone had changed from cold and alien to one of decided interest as it peered at her through the bars.

"What are you?" Anisa whispered around the fist in her mouth, unable to banish the quivering fear from her voice.

"I am Ssytis." He told her softly, drawing on the s in the word, looking at her intently in the gloom. "I am a Naga."

"I have never heard of a Naga." She told him. Speaking to someone else was helping her to control her terror of the situation she found herself in. "Did you see when they brought me in here?" She asked.

The creature nodded his head, his gaze unblinkingly intent.

"Did you see if they brought in two other women with me?" She asked moving closer slightly, trying to keep her voice as quiet as possible.

The creature shook his head negatively, his focus creepily never wavering from her.

Disappointment coated her features and Ssytis took note.

"Do not despair young woman." He told her and she thought that he meant to make his soft hissing and alien voice to be comforting. "This facility is larger than it seems. They may yet be here."

She removed her fist from her mouth. "My name is Anisa."

He watched her, nodding slightly to acknowledge her name.

"How long have you been here?" She asked needing to speak to keep the terror from taking over.

"At least five cycles, maybe more." Came the quiet reply as the creature slid tiredly down to lean against the bars and then into the corner closest to her. She realized that he had exchanged one corner of his cell for another.

"Cycles of the sun?" She asked confused and at his nod continued. "So five days." She was thoughtful for a moment. "Have you seen anyone other than myself and the guards here?" She looked at the cage on the other side of her, since her eyesight now seemed to be back to normal, to see that it was empty.

"Yesss." Came the tired reply as she heard him shift his body against the bars and the wall.

She looked curiously back in his direction and saw that he did indeed have legs that were covered in torn, dirty, canvas pants. For some reason this helped to alleviate even more of her fear. "Well, do you know who it was?" She asked curiously, needing him to keep speaking to her.

"Male bear-shifter." He told her, closing his eyes. He looked exhausted and ill.

"What happened to him?" She asked.

"They removed him. Anissssa." He rolled her name on his tongue, caressing the s. "Go to sleep. You need to rest while you can."

She knew she shouldn't, but couldn't help herself from asking, "Do you think the bear shifter is okay? Do you think he is alive?"

"No." Ssytis told her turning away from the bars and her. Leaning his back against the bars his voice continued in its whispering hiss. "Nothing that screamed like that could possibly still live."

* * * * *

Devin walked quickly down the teak stairs of the villa, expertly sliding his nine-millimeter Beretta into his shoulder holster, flanked closely by Zachary and Fred who were also armed. The wolves and Castor eagerly awaited them in the lobby.

"Where do you think you are going?" Mansuetus demanded sharply to the group.

"I am going to take a car and I am going to find my mate." Devin's voice was cold, determined, deadly and brooked no interference. He looked back up the staircase as Romulus descended the stairs.

Rom wore tight black pants, black knee-high boots, a flowing, long-sleeved black shirt, and black, long, open vest that came to the top of his thighs. His long, straight, black-hair was pulled back and small, gold hoops shined against the swarthy skin of his ears. He carried a knife on each hip, one in each boot, and was putting an especially deadly looking katana into a scabbard on his back in between his shoulder blades.

"That pirate looks familiar." Zachary murmured.

Rom gave Zachary a half smile and slapped him briefly on the shoulder in reassurance, then turned to Mansuetus. "Don't try to stop us, Mansuetus."

"Romulus," Mansuetus said, and it was obvious that he was trying to diffuse the situation. "Nikolaos is on his way back."

"He left hours ago, it will take him hours to get back." Romulus told him reasonably in return.

"You can't lead a search party full of armed vampires and wolf shifters through Katerini without attracting the attention of the local authorities!" Mansuetus motioned to the other men who were armed to the teeth and had the looks of a rag tag platoon. "Besides, you don't even know where to start." Mansuetus told him trying to remain reasonable.

Romulus pulled out his cell phone and pulled up his tracking app. "Both Anisa's and Esmeralda's phones are downtown." He caught Mansuetus's shocked gaze. "What? I am a vampire, who has a vampire mate and a human daughter. I am absolutely keeping up with where the hell they are located." He started to head out of the villa.

"Wait!" Devin said suddenly and looked at Aris with suspicion. "There is no fucking way that Nick doesn't have trackers on all of the vehicles."

Aris glanced at Devin in irritation, huffed once, then walked around behind the desk of the lobby, logging into a computer. "Yes, there is a GPS tracker on each vehicle." Aris acknowledged defeatedly, realizing that there was no way they would convince the men to wait for Lord Tsoukalous. The men looked at Aris, who returned their look sternly. "You will promise to hold me blameless if you find the ladies in a compromising position."

"Oh, my God, Aris!" Rom exclaimed dangerously. "They are not out feeding from or fucking humans with my daughter in tow! Is the limo with their cell phones?" He held up his phone to show Aris the map location of Anisa's and Esmeralda's cell phones.

"No." Aris said softly lifting his eyes from the computer screen to stare at Romulus in horror as he realized that the limo was no longer in the city where the cell phones were located.

"Devin, set up this system on your cell phone so we don't lose track of the limo." Rom immediately said taking charge and Devin went around the desk with Aris to get it done. Looking at the others Rom said, "We will go to the location of the girl's cells first. One of them could be there and hurt. Then we will go and track down the limo."

"Fine!" Mansuetus suddenly exclaimed. "I am also going."

"Good," Rom replied. "You are driving the other Humvee."

* * * * *

Devin, Zachary, and Castor sat in the back while Mansuetus drove, and Aleksei sat in the front passenger seat as they followed the Vee driven by Rom.

"How did you know?" Zachary asked him quietly.

"About Anisa? I don't know. I know that something is wrong with her, I can feel it. I could feel pain earlier, but I don't anymore. Still, there is something wrong with her." Devin replied.

"No. How did you know about the GPS tracker installed on the limo?"

"I lived with Nick and Mom day in and day out for months, and frankly the dude is a stalker. I caught him installing a tracking app on Mom's cell phone one day. He asked me not to tell her about it because he said, and I quote, 'She will be terribly angry with me.'" Devin smirked mimicking Nichola's calm voice. "Which, knowing Mom, is kind of an understatement." He looked at Zachary out of the corner of his eye to see him nodding his head in agreement. "Nick explained that he needed a way to track her if she ever went missing. He sounded really sincere, but frankly, I thought he was just being old and paranoid. After seeing Rom pull up his cell phone tracker, I knew that there was no way that Nick didn't have every vehicle he owns installed with a tracking system."

"Seems like he always plans for any eventuality." Zachary observed.

"Yep; and as soon as I get Anisa back to the villa, I am putting a tracker on her phone too!" Devin's voice was stern.

* * * * *

Since it was now after midnight, Eleftherias Square in Katerini, Greece, was almost deserted, which ended up being a lucky occurrence for the group. As they all followed Rom, who was using his tracker app on his phone to find Esmeralda and Anisa, like Sherlock Holmes used his famous magnifying glass to find clues, Devin decided that Zachary was right, Rom did look exactly like a damn pirate, and if there had been more people out, he would have drawn a lot of attention.

Surprisingly, the only ones who wouldn't have stood out were Mitch and

Ric who had shifted into their wolves. Eleftherias Square was known for its large-breed stray dog population, so Mitch's sandy-brown wolf, and Ric's pitch-black wolf, fit right in; though the local dogs that the group came upon naturally gave them a wide berth. The wolves tried to sniff out the ladies' scents, but it wasn't easy to pick them out of everyone who had walked there today.

Rom turned down an alleyway behind a clothing store and they ended up in an area of the buildings where merchandise deliveries were made. They looked around seeing stacked wooden crates, tarps, and a few dumpsters but nothing else.

Frustrated, Rom said to the others as he looked down at the screen of his cell phone, "This is where the cell phones are!"

Aleksei suddenly stepped forward and stood still for a moment. "I smell blood." He murmured in concentration trying to pick the scents out amongst the dumpsters and general waste strewn about in the loading area.

"Human?" Rom asked suddenly standing next to him, trying to pick smells out of the layered scents of the alleyway also.

The wolves raised their muzzles in the air on either side of Rom and Aleksei. The others watched them as they tried to locate the faint smell of blood on the slight breeze flowing through the alley.

"Damn it! I can't tell!" The old vampire suddenly burst out in frustration.

Mitch's wolf ran a dozen feet away to stand on his hind legs placing his front paws against the side of one of the blue, rusted dumpsters with a sudden whine.

Zachary swiftly opened it and then climbed in to dig around briefly, "Good God! Aunt Iris!" He exclaimed in grief.

Aleksei leaped in beside him and pushed him back to pull Iris's limp black-haired body close to him, "Oh, moy golub', what have they done to you?" He whispered in anguish.

Iris's still, broken, body was covered in blood, though not all of it seemed to be her own. It appeared that she had been stabbed several times and her body had several cuts, scrapes, and her face was battered where she had been brutally beaten.

"Give me room!" Aleksei ordered, and the others stood back, while he gently picked up her body out of the waste of the dumpster to suddenly leap straight up into the air to float down to the concrete of the delivery area. There he tenderly laid her down, straightening her limbs to assess the damage, then gathered her close to his own body.

Aleksei held her tightly in silence against him with his head pressed firmly against her chest for several long seconds, as the other's looked helplessly on. "She yet lives!" He exclaimed suddenly, biting deeply into his own wrist, and pressing it to her mouth. "Swallow, my love, swallow." He commanded her and the others felt the residual power wash over them from that command and found themselves swallowing in response.

Even those of them who had been on the receiving end of Nichola's power were overwhelmed at feeling Aleksei's ancient energy for the very first time.

Rom leaned forward to grasp Iris's throat and massage it to ease as much of the old vampire's blood down into her body as possible.

Both Mitch and Ric approached Iris to sniff at her, whining to each other.

"Yes, my friend, she smells wrong." Aleksei told them worriedly, watching her face as he kept his wrist pressed to her mouth.

"You understand them in this form?" Devin asked in awe as he knelt next to the old vampire and gently held Iris's cold, limp hand looking down on her poor ravaged body. Like this, the usually flamboyant, fun-loving vampire reminded him of a broken doll, and his heart ached.

"Yes. Those of us who are able to transform can communicate with our shifter brethren. After a time, we who are 'other', are much more alike than we want to admit." He remarked softly, looking over Devin's head to Mansuetus he ordered. "Call Dr. Lambert. Tell him that I am bringing Iris to him. She will need several bags of saline and as much blood as he can manage. She will need the blood intravenously as I believe that she has been poisoned." Aleksei's voice was grave.

"I will get the car." Mansuetus said starting to turn around.

"No." Aleksei ordered. "I will fly her back. It will be faster and less conspicuous than a speeding car down the roadways."

Iris groaned weakly struggling against Aleksei's wrist and he removed it, sealing the wound with his saliva.

"Can you speak?" Rom asked urgently. "Where are Es and Anisa?"

"Es…" Iris's voice was a pained croak.

"Yes, Aunt Iris." Devin said gripping her hand tightly. "What happened to them?"

"Hunters." Iris managed to get out before she once again lost consciousness.

* * * * *

"Fucking hunters!" Castor ground out in hatred after Aleksei had quickly gathered Iris into his arms and instantly taken flight into the dark sky, heading towards the coast. At his pace, the only way anyone would see him is when his flying form passed in front of the brightly twinkling stars.

"Search the rest of this alley! They had two security personnel with them! If we don't find their bodies here somewhere, we have to assume that this was an inside job and call Aris to secure the villa!" Zachary ordered suddenly.

Everyone spread out in a space that was only wide enough for a delivery truck to drive through. It ran the length of several back entrances to stores sharing the same building; they looked behind the crates, wooden pallets, under tarps and opening the other dumpsters that belonged to the connected businesses.

Ric growl-barked sharply from the far end of the alley next to the delivery truck entrance, causing the others to run towards him. He was sniffing a small dark stain on the concrete next to the corner of another dumpster.

"Vampire?" Rom asked him, his head and nose full of the slightly off scent of Iris, and the black wolf moved his head from side to side.

"Human?" Devin whispered in sudden fear. Ric whined once in response.

Devin stood up swiftly, pushed open the dumpster and leapt inside. Under a tarp he found a uniformed body of one of the security guards.

Thank god, it's not Nessie! He thought to himself, sagging slightly as relief flowed over him like a running stream; then straightened as guilt over his personal relief crashed into him like a breaching wave.

Turning the man over he saw that he had died due to a gaping knife wound in his throat that had allowed his blood to flood the bottom of the dumpster.

He looked familiar.

"Mansuetus." Devin called softly and the big man joined him in the dumpster. "Do you know who it is?"

"Limo driver." Mansuetus told him sadly.

Devin and Mansuetus got out of the dumpster.

"I found a phone." Castor said coming forward.

"I have the other one." Rom said presenting it to Devin. "It's Anisa's."

Devin took it from him and smiled briefly to see that her background photo was a picture of himself that she must have taken when he wasn't aware of it. He had a sour, disgruntled look on his face as he had gazed in the direction of the camera, and Anisa.

He breathed deeply and tears stung his eyes as he tried to calm the fear he was feeling. He had spent so much time being an asshole to her and now just when he had just started to get his shit together it looked like he was going to lose her! He held his breath trying to dispel the fear from his system. He was worthless to her if he couldn't keep it together.

Rom grasped his shoulder as Devin silently gazed down at the phone. "Don't worry. We will find them. They left Iris for dead. If they had killed them, they would be here; so they must still be alive."

"I am calling Aris. We have two missing women and one missing guard. He needs to know that this abduction is looking more like we have had a security breach at the villa. There may be more hunters still there. They could all be in danger." Mansuetus walked away, his phone to his ear.

Fred suddenly looked concerned and started dialing also.

"We've got to find that limo." Devin said to Rom in a determined voice.

* * * * *

Anisa stayed still and quiet against the cold concrete, pretending to be unconscious, as she woke to hear booted feet softly walking toward her cell. She heard a key slide into the metal lock on her cell door, turn, and then the sound of the door being pulled slowly open, screeching softly on its unoiled hinges. She watched through squinted eyes, booted feet walk quietly over to her unmoving form to stand next to her for several seconds.

She tried to prepare her body for more violence and could feel every muscle tighten, like an old-fashioned garage door torsion spring only waiting for the right moment to break free and decapitate someone.

"That idealistic young fool." The cold voice of her earlier tormentor suddenly whispered over her in disgust. "You live with them and that makes you just as culpable for their crimes. The fact that they haven't killed you and let you run free must mean you are special. Let's see what makes you so special, little blood whore."

Anisa felt strong, rough hands grasp her, pulling her small body into the air and she came up swinging, connecting with his mouth, pain numbing her hand as she sliced her knuckles on his teeth. Grunting, the man with the cold, hateful voice, backhanded her against the wall, where she slid down the wall to slump on the floor, blood dripping from her nose. He grabbed her shirt pulling her to her feet by it and ripped it down the front, sending buttons flying through the air with the speed of plastic bullets.

Grasping her throat, he slammed her against the cell wall, causing her to grunt out in pain, and held her there squeezing her throat tightly to cut off her breath as he reached under her skirt to rip her thong from her body. She clawed desperately at his hand, her short, but sharp, nails digging into his skin deeply, trying to draw breath as she heard him unbuckling his pants and pulling them down to press his body against hers, slobbering against her cheek.

Unable to draw a breath, she was starting to see black spots before her eyes when she felt his hand fondling her roughly under her skirt as he tried to wedge his body in between her fiercely kicking legs. Her world was going dark when she gave one final struggle against the oncoming blackness, and she desperately reached up to thrust her thumb nails into his eyes in an attempt to gouge them from their sockets.

He cried out slamming her viciously against the wall, bouncing her skull off the concrete with a sharp crack, as he stumbled back against the bars of the next cell, his hands to his eyes, only to feel the strong, red scaled, claw-tipped hands of the creature in the cell grab him by the throat and grab his penis and testicles in a tight hold.

His movements suddenly halted, and he pleaded, his voice laced with terror, "Stop."

Ssytis leaned into his ear through the space in the bars, his hissed whisper like a lover, "Do you like to rape little girls?"

"No." The man's tone was begging as he looked at Anisa who was struggling to force air back into her lungs and to unsteadily pick herself up from the floor where she had fallen in a painful heap.

"Give her the keys." Ssytis ordered lowly, tightening his grip around the man's throat and crotch causing him to gasp and clutch at the claws gripping him. Ssytis then ran his long, red, forked tongue over the skin of the man's ear and face, drawing in his fear and causing the man to shudder and squeal in terror like a pig in the slaughter chute, his voice no longer cold, emotionless, and filled with hate. "Now." Ssytis ordered in a low hiss as he squeezed his large hand around the man's crotch tightly, digging his sharp reptilian claws into his pubic hair and drawing blood.

"God, please." The man begged and tears ran down his face as he held his arm out to Anisa. Around his wrist a springy plastic bracelet held a set of keys.

Anisa looked at Ssytis who met her eyes with his bright yellow unblinking snake gaze and slightly nodded to her; she quickly stepped forward, her hands shaking with emotion, to grasp the bracelet and remove it from the man's arm.

"Help me." The man begged her as she started to walk out of her cell. "I gave you the keys. Please tell him not to. I am sorry." His dirt brown eyes, like the bottom of a moldy, muddy pond, pleaded with hers.

She looked at him with a hatred her gentle nature had never thought she would feel before and turned her back to him, immediately hearing the sound of tearing flesh, blood splashing on the concrete, a quick high cry of horrified agony and terror that was immediately cut off by gurgling and whistling sounds as if someone was choking on their own blood, followed finally by the thud of a large, falling piece of meat hitting the concrete of the cell with a wet squelch.

She refused to turn around to view the carnage behind her and painfully made her way through the door of her cell and around the outside to Ssytis's cell door. His large, ruby red, scaled form, stood tall, at least two feet taller than she, and looked down at her, clutching the bars of the cell door tightly with his dripping, gory hands. She looked up into his cold, yellow-gold, reptilian eyes, feeling no fear, and inserted the key into the lock turning it and then opened the cell door.

Without any barrier between them, he stepped sharply forward moving his eyes over her as if taking a visual inventory of her injuries. He nodded once as his yellow eyes returned to gaze down into her cerulean blue eyes.

"Good girl." His voice hissed gently.

* * * * *

"Fuck!" Devin yelled in frustration when they found the abandoned limo on the bare, uninhabited, northern outskirts of Agios Dimitrios.

Zachary and Mansuetus methodically went over the limo looking for clues. They found Iris's cell phone in the back and some bags of clothes which made sense since the women had went into town to go shopping.

"Pop the trunk, Uncle Man." Zachary told Mansuetus who was in the front seat. When the trunk opened he went around to find a stained tarp in it. "Look familiar?" He looked at Rom.

Rom looked at the shifters who had changed back to their human form. "This is definitely blood, but it smells strange. Can you tell if this is human or vampire?" He asked giving them room.

Mitch looked over his shoulder after a few minutes to say, "Both. More vampire than human though."

Rom's faced was closed to all emotion as he watched Ric suddenly pull his clothes off in frustration, and immediately change into his pitch-black wolf. Sniffing the ground like a blood hound he followed an invisible trail about forty feet back down the roadway. Transforming back, he said, "They were transferred to another vehicle here. It's impossible to track it any further, the concrete holds no tracks."

Rom's face flashed briefly with despair.

Mansuetus came around the vehicle to stand looking at Rom. "Aris just texted. It looks like they have captured at least one hunter posing as a worker at the villa. We are needed."

"Do you have keys for the limo?" Rom asked quickly. "We have got to clean up this mess. We will be dealing with the authorities soon once the body in the alley in Katerini is discovered and identified."

"The keys are in the limo. I will drive it back. Aris has already retrieved the driver's body and taken it back to the villa." Mansuetus told him quietly.

"I will drive the Humvee back." Devin said suddenly to Mansuetus, and Zachary, Castor, and Fred immediately joined him as Ric and Mitch followed Rom back to the other Vee. Starting up the vehicle, Devin put it in drive, to start the hour trip back to the villa. "Nick should be at the villa by the time we return." He told the others in a cold voice as he drove down the road. "And I need you guys to keep him out of my way," Devin's voice was dangerous and determined, "because I am doing whatever it takes to make that motherfucker tell me where the hell they have taken my mate!"

* * * * *

"We need to escape while we can, Anissssa." Ssytis told her softly, looking around a corner of the hallway to make sure that it was empty of threats.

"I have got to find my mother. I can't leave her here." Anisa told him. "Please help me find my mother." She pleaded in a small whisper. "I am going to look for her whether you help me or not, but I have a better chance of getting her out of here if you help me."

"Nagas and Vampires are enemies. I have helped you enough!" Ssytis hissed out and she could hear the dread in that sharp hiss.

"You wouldn't even be here if I hadn't let you out of that cell." She whispered, looking up at him in determination.

"I saved you from being raped! You owed me!" He countered quietly glaring down with his yellow, reptilian eyes at her, putting his scaled nose almost against her own.

"And you are scary as hell! I could have left you locked up in that cell!" She returned whispering harshly, angrily staring up at him, with her fists clenched by her side, fearlessly holding her ground.

He made a face at her showing his small, pointed teeth and long fangs, that if it had been on a human she would have called a grin. "Fine! Stay behind me, stay silent, and if we run into anyone stay out of my way because

I intend to murder anyone we come across. Remember in this facility, no matter how innocent they look, they are your enemy."

They made their way down the dimly lit hallway. It was like the facility was under a power outage and the only lights that were lit were emergency lighting. Anisa opened doors quickly looking into each room, as they walked quietly, unlocking the doors with the keys that she had taken from the now dead guard, which she had thoughtfully secured to her own wrist using the plastic bracelet. Many were cells, but there were other areas that looked like mini-operating rooms. Unfortunately, they didn't come across anyone: enemy or fellow prisoner alike.

"God," Anisa whispered in frustration. "Where could they be?"

"Shh." Ssytis motioned for silence as they heard footsteps coming from one of the rooms that remained unchecked.

* * * * *

They filed purposely into the villa to find Nichola waiting for them, a worried look aging his usually youthful, handsome, but passive face.

"Where's Mom?" Zachary asked.

"With your Aunt in her suite." Came his reply and Zachary ran up the stairs.

"Where is the hunter?" Devin and Rom asked simultaneously.

"Secured. We can use him as a trade." Nichola was trying for a reasonable tone.

"Where is he?" Rom asked dangerously.

"Do you really believe that is how hunters operate, Uncle Nikolaos?" Castor asked quietly as Nichola faced off with Rom.

Devin reached out with all of his senses while the others were starting to argue with Nichola. He found a wildly pounding, fearful heart coming from the opposite side of the villa and silently left the arguing trio to head in that direction.

He texted Zachary: *Do WHATEVER IT TAKES to keep him busy!* Then he opened a heavy, teak, door to the room where he knew he would find that frightened beating heart. As he let himself in, he found Aris sitting in a folding chair beside the door, looking ill with grief and something else.

109

There was also a young man, really just a boy, with a short crop of dishwater blonde curls, glaring at him out of basilisk eyes, who was tied spread-eagled across the top of a table.

Devin looked around the room, quickly realizing why they were keeping him there. This heavy, solid, teak door was the only access and there were no windows in this thick-walled storage room. With a vampire as a guard, he would be dead before he could be rescued and from the boy's defiant look, he was aware of it too. He knew his time on earth was short.

Eager for any news whatsoever about Anisa, Devin glanced at Aris unconcerned by his presence. "He tell you anything?"

Aris shook his head negatively, looking at the floor in guilt.

"And you are sure that he is part of this?" Devin demanded, looking at the young man who could be barely older than eighteen if that, with deadly eyes.

The boy met his gaze with a fanatical glare declaring, "And I ain't telling you a fucking thing either, you monster!" The boy's defiant voice was in Cockneyed English, surprising Devin; but the surprise didn't prevent him from tasting that bit of fear underneath.

To Devin that fear tasted delicious; and he could work with it.

"Well, that answered that question." Devin gave Aris a cold look. "Why don't you take a walk, Aris."

"Master Devin…" Aris began weakly.

"This is partly your fault, isn't it, Aris?" Devin suddenly asked in a deceptively soft voice and Aris blanched at the direct question.

Aris's guilt over the matter had only grown since Aleksei had arrived with Iris's unconscious, brutalized body and that guilt was so palpable Devin could taste it in the air.

"Take a long walk, Aris." Devin told him simply and Aris stood up to leave the room. "Oh, and Aris?" Aris looked back with culpable, conflicted eyes. "Avoid the lobby. It would be helpful to do a perimeter sweep instead."

Aris swallowed his guilt. He knew that his Uncle had requested him to keep this young villain safe in the hopes of a trade with the people who had abducted the ladies; but he didn't agree with him. Aris knew what would happen if they didn't find the two missing ladies as soon as possible; there would be no ransom, no trade. If they ever found their dead bodies it would be a gift.

This boy knew where they were being held, and if he didn't, he had still been part of the plot to kidnap the ladies in any case. He had made sure that Aris had assigned the newest guard to the limo, by telling him that the regular guard was ill when he had requested him for the assignment. It had been a lie and Aris had not confirmed the information of his illness with the Villa Security Chief.

Instead he had taken this boy at his word.

The boy who he hired as part of the kitchen staff just one month before, without fully vetting him, because he was attracted to him.

The boy, who had so sweetly been sucking his cock only that morning. Which, now, after everything, seemed such a long time ago.

Even if no one else realized it at this point, as far as Aris was concerned, this whole thing was his fault. Everything that had happened was on his head because he had allowed his lust for a beautiful young man to cloud his judgement.

Aris nodded once and Devin shut and locked the door after him.

When Devin turned around, he smiled at the boy and made sure to show his fangs.

"Yeah? Like I am supposed to be afraid of them? That poofter you just closed the door on, has been sinking his teeth into me for the past week! I suppose you want me to suck your cock too?" The boy's brave scoff was laced with fear.

Devin had suspected something of the sort by Aris's behavior.

Devin slowly, purposefully, reached behind him to remove his small, razor-sharp, knife from his back waist sheath, turning it gently so that the overhead lights flashed off of the blade, making sure that the boy was able to see every movement. He walked slowly toward the boy, smiling widely. He put as much evil intent into his countenance as possible and found that it was an easy task as he thought about what Anisa might be suffering at the hands of these mortals. As far as Devin was concerned, these hunters were no longer misguided humans to be cared for or even feared, but only animals to be wiped out.

* * * * *

Ssytis grabbed Anisa and pushed her flat against the wall of the hallway, next to him, as the footsteps approached the closed door. Ssytis stood frozen and silent next to the door waiting for it to open.

As the door was pulled open the young man with the black-rimmed glasses stepped through, muttering under his breath, "Stupid bastard should have been back by now!" then gave out a terrified screech that was cut off by Ssytis squeezing him by the throat and holding him against the wall next to the door with his feet dangling. The man's eyes bulged from his face that was quickly turning a mottled red.

"Stop, Ssytis! We need to find out where they are." Anisa commanded.

He looked at her in cold irritation but loosened his hold letting the bespectacled man slide down the wall to have his weight supported by his booted toes.

"Where are the women that were with me earlier?" Anisa asked sharply.

The man looked at her in bewilderment. "How are you up and moving around?"

Ssytis gave him an impatient look and grabbed the man by the crotch giving him a strong squeeze with his clawed hand, to which the man gave a sharp, quick bleat and started blabbering.

"One is in the room, the other one was killed. But it was an accident! We didn't mean for it to happen, the drug didn't work on her as well as it did the other, and she fought us like a wild cat. We were trying for containment..." He stopped speaking suddenly as Ssytis squeezed his throat again.

Leaning close, face-to-face, cold reptilian gaze to human, Ssytis said softly, "Quiet."

"Oh, God!" Anisa whispered covering her mouth in horror as she realized that her mother might be dead. She rushed into the room to find an unresponsive Esmeralda cuffed by her wrists and ankles to a hinged standing table. She looked dirty, beaten, and bruised, but not too damaged.

Almost overwhelmed in relief to find her mother still alive, Anisa was lightheaded as she bent-over to work the leather cuffs from her mother's ankles, glancing around for something that would make the table lie down so she could reach her wrists.

Suddenly from the hallway she heard the sound of ripping fabric and flesh and a high-pitched traumatized screaming.

Ssytis walked into the room, his hands wet in blood and gore once again, as the screams went on and on, and easily reached up to pull apart the leather cuffs of Esmeralda's wrists.

"My God! Why didn't you kill him like the last one? His screaming is going to alert the others!" Anisa told Ssytis in panic as he scooped up her mother and tossed her over his shoulder like a rolled-up piece of spare carpet.

"You are so murderously, blood-thirsty, my little vampire maiden." Ssytis's hissing voice sounded approving. "According to him they were the only two on duty for the next few days. They are awaiting their leadership to arrive sometime in the next forty-eight hours. We will let this one suffer." Ssytis hissed out, walking through the door not even acknowledging the young man clutching the gaping wound where his genitals had once been attached to his body, his shocked, tortured, horrified screams were dying down in volume as blood flowed between his fingers, the pool of blood steadily widening around him.

Anisa gaped at the man in horror for a brief moment than ran to catch up to Ssytis's retreating form.

"How do you know he was telling the truth?" Anisa asked skipping to keep up with his strong, red-scaled, long-legged body.

"Because human men take great stock in their single penises and will do anything to protect them. Including betraying all that they hold dear." Ssytis told her, stopping in a room next to an exterior door, to grab a set of vehicle keys that hung on the wall.

"You have some sort of sick thing going on about that don't you?" Anisa accused him, feeling ill at the faint, dying sounds of screams from behind them.

"They were both owed for the similar act that they performed on the bear-shifter." Ssytis explained, his voice dripped with loathing and disgust. "But with him they took him piece by small piece, laughing as they did so. Secure in the knowledge that he was unable to shift, heal, or defend himself due to their drug. I listened to his shrieks as they held him down to carve on him for more than an hour until he finally bled out. If I would have had the luxury of time, I would have done the same to them." His voice at the memory was full of repulsion and hatred.

She swallowed down the bile that was fighting to come up, along with the overwhelming sympathy that she unexpectedly felt for Ssytis for the horror of what he must have witnessed only one cell away.

Then a thought suddenly popped into her mind in bewilderment. "What do you mean by single penises?" She asked confused as they exited the building, and he handed her the car keys to an old two-door jeep.

He placed her mother gently into the back of the vehicle then went around to the passenger side of the car and got in.

"Until these drugs wear off I will be unable to complete my transformation to either my human form or my true form. But when I do, I will show you what I mean by single penises. You drive."

* * * * *

"Well, should I drink you dry?" Devin asked the boy, making a long, gradual, shallow cut on the skin of his arm, causing the boy to hiss in pain. Devin bent and leisurely licked the cut, healing it with his saliva.

"Go ahead, you fucking monster!" The boy yelled out and fear gushed from his pores. "Just get it over with, cause I ain't telling you shite!"

"Oh, I see now why Aris liked you so much." Devin said slurring his words through his fangs and the sudden mouthful of saliva as he drank in the boy's extreme terror and blood from the wound he had made. "You're delicious."

Devin sliced down along the other arm.

"Fuck you, vamper! Fuck you!" The boy screeched out, fighting valiantly against his bonds; as Devin also licked slowly down the wound along that arm, letting out a hungry moan. Devin then used the small razor-sharp knife to shred the boy's shirt. "Jesus, just kill me!" The boy fearfully shrieked out over the sound of shredding fabric.

"But you taste so sweet. So sweet." Devin murmured, carving into the boy's chest. "Yes, taking your life quickly would be such a waste!" He leaned away from him to purposefully dip his finger into the blood running from the stinging, shallow cut he had made, bringing it slowly to his lips.

The boy looked at him in horror, directly into Devin's bright, blood-red, eyes, as Devin slowly sucked his blood from his claw-tipped finger. Rolling his tongue around and beneath his claw to get every drop of blood like one would lick to get to the juicy center of a tootsie-pop.

"Yes, I think I will turn you." Devin said suddenly as if that was the best idea he had ever had in his whole life. "If I turn you, I will be your Master, and you will be compelled to obey me. You will tell me where your friends have taken the women, in fact you will love me so much as your Master that you will beg to tell me everything I want to know about the hunter organization. You will plead to be allowed to please me and as I cut out your humanity only to heal you over and over, I will allow you to please me on your knees." Devin's voice was low and seductive, as he licked over the cut on the boy's chest, slowly sealing up the narrow cut as the boy quivered in disgust making a stuttering 'n...n...n...n...n' noise.

Devin looked up to lock his gaze with the boy who had lifted his head to watch in horror as Devin licked along his chest.

"And the best part?" Devin's voice was a purr of ecstasy. "I can cut and feed from you every day, for the rest of eternity, and if you ever displease or disappoint me, I can turn you over to your hunter friends to do with as they please." Devin made another shallow cut from his breastbone down to his navel and then gave him an evil smile fully baring his bloody lips and teeth as if in preparation to give the boy the best gift ever.

The boy stared at him and started screaming in terror. "No, no! Please no! I will tell you where they are being held! I will tell you where Sonchus is! I will tell you anything that you want to know! Just don't turn me! Do not turn me!"

Safe?

~◦◦◦~

D r. Dene Lambert looked down on Iris, exceedingly careful to show no emotional reaction to the fact that his former master and vampire lover was lying deathly still and quiet in bed. He methodically checked the saline and blood bags that he had just replaced.

"Well?" Aleksei Ostrovsky, Iris's current lover asked impatiently.

Dene faced the old vampire, his face an expressionless mask. "Her wounds are knitting well, but she has been infected by a foreign substance. I have taken samples, but I do not know what that substance is as yet."

"So is it poison?" Aleksei asked coldly.

"Yes, poison is a good term for it. There is an injection mark here." Dene pointed out a small, bruised area along her hairline, which sported a puncture mark directly behind her right ear.

"Will she be alright?"

"I can't say for sure, but she seems to be out of danger for the time being. Flushing her system intravenously with both saline and blood was a good call. But as with all poisons, I am sure it has taken a toll on her body. Whether her vampire body will totally repair itself in time without further treatment or she will have lasting damage is another matter entirely and quite unknown at this point; at least until I am able to identify the substance that she was poisoned with. Then I can develop an antidote." Dene answered him coldly, clinically.

"You wouldn't allow your past to..." Aleksei began.

"Aleksei." Dene found himself saying more sharply than he had intended. He breathed deeply, schooling his features, then continued. "I am a doctor before anything else. I will do my best by her."

Aleksei nodded to him, sitting on the bed to grasp Iris's hand and gaze down sadly at her.

Dene left the room as Leila came flying down the hall towards him wordless like she didn't trust her own voice and instead gave him an apprehensive, questioning look as she gripped his hand tightly, unconsciously exhibiting her vampire strength.

He said simply, "She's recovering," then winced slightly at her grip, nodding towards the door of the suite and Leila quickly released him to enter the room.

Dene hung his head as he walked towards Nichola's office suite, where his small lab was housed.

Not watching where he was going, his mind full of too many conflicting emotions, he almost walked straight into Cassie who was holding Princess close to her breasts in apprehension. She gave him a frightened searching look and he stopped to briefly cup her youthful, pretty face gently before moving toward his office.

"Fred called. We may be in danger. They believe that there may be people amongst the staff that are involved with this." Cassie told him softly, looking at him with worried eyes.

He grimaced slightly to learn that she had been speaking to Fred. "Bring Princess and come into the lab. I have some tests to run. I don't want you out here alone." He told her leading the way and then locking the door behind them.

* * * * *

"You are sure?" Nichola asked Aris. "Positive?"

"Yes, Lord Tsoukalous." Aris responded his eyes downcast, which immediately made Nichola suspicious.

"Is he the only one involved?" Nichola asked, power laced his voice washing over Aris's body causing him to wince.

"There is another that is missing, he was assigned as additional security to the ladies on their outing." Aris cringed again as he heard an inhuman growl from deep within Nichola's chest. "But there could be more. I cannot say for certain at this point."

"Do you have anyone that you trust?" Nichola's question was harsh.

"Of course, my lord." Aris responded immediately.

"Keep everyone in a suite that you are unsure of, under guard. Vampire only perimeter sweeps inside and out every fifteen minutes until the others return." Aris nodded without meeting Nichola's eyes, knowing that they would be red with rage. "Question our prisoner for further information, but do not harm him. We will use him for a trade for the women." Aris started to speak, but then nodded and left to do his bidding.

Nichola glared at Aris as he walked away. There was more to this story than he was being told; but until the others returned he needed to focus on protecting his family. Nichola walked to his suite to retrieve his weapons and make a phone call.

* * * * *

Zachary rushed into Iris's bedroom to find his mother and Aleksei sitting vigil on either side of Iris's bed.

"How is she, Gramps?" He asked quietly.

"Much the same. But out of immediate danger." Aleksei responded in a funeral whisper as if in mourning.

"Was she poisoned?" Zachary asked bringing a chair to sit next to his mother reaching over to grasp Leila's hand tightly to comfort her.

"Yes. Though the doctor doesn't know with what yet. He is still running tests." Aleksei told him emotionlessly.

"Is she going to…" Zachary stopped himself suddenly as if saying the word could make it a reality.

"Not if I have anything to do with it." Aleksei said, bowing over Iris's hand in prayer.

Zachary's cellphone buzzed with a text notification. He looked down at it briefly, then raised his head to look at Aleksei. "They have captured a co-conspirator." Zachary told Aleksei a slight inflection to his voice.

Aleksei raised his head sharply, "What?"

Zachary motioned with his head to the hallway and Aleksei followed him, leaving Leila to sit with Iris. Zachary closed the door after them, and Aleksei looked at him expectantly.

"Nick and Aris captured him. He is employed here at the Villa. Devin is going to question him now, but that won't last long. He is asking that we keep his actions quiet and Nick off his back as long as possible." Zachary looked at Aleksei with meaning.

"Because Nikolaos will not want the prisoner tortured." Aleksei stated.

"Yes. He wants to use him to trade for Esmeralda and Anisa."

Aleksei scoffed. "If your mother was missing, he would draw and quarter him and go to war."

"Most likely. But he could be correct in his thinking to keep him as a hostage and used for a trade." Zachary ventured.

"You are much like him, Detective." Aleksei gave Zachary a slight smile as he grasp his shoulder with affection. "He too wishes that logic and civilized behavior would govern all actions, it makes him a good and stable leader for our kind. Unfortunately, fear and rabid hatred are what drive hunters; and not just toward we vampires, or other creatures that could be seen as a danger to the human race, but anything that is not fully human; no matter how benign. This zealous loathing has always governed them; it always has and always will. There is no reasoning with the mad hatred they carry." Aleksei headed down the hallway toward the staircase and Zachary followed him.

"What do you suggest our course of action be?" Zachary asked.

"When war comes to your doorstep you do not use your words to stop the death and bloodshed it brings. You use whatever weapons are at your disposal to fight off the offensive. Then you return the attack with extreme prejudice. Peace is only achieved with a fanatical aggressor when peace is the least offensive avenue open to them and even then sometimes they still choose death. The hunters have been killing our kind for long enough, it is time we take the fight back to them. Nikolaos knows this, now we must make him remember it." Aleksei walked down the stairs to the sound of raised voices in the lobby.

* * * * *

"Enough of this, Nikolaos! They left Iris for dead! They have Esmeralda and Anisa. We need to make that hunter tell us where they are, then we need to rescue them!" Romulus was yelling as the phone behind the lobby desk was ringing. Due to the security measures, and Aris guarding their prisoner, no one was manning the desk.

"If we attempt a rescue, they will just kill them outright!" Nichola emphasized in a cold deep voice. "Torturing him will just convince them that we are as bad as they think we are!"

"Uncle!" Castor interjected loudly as the ringing continued. "There is nothing to prove to these hunters. They are going to kill them regardless! It is what they have been doing for the past two hundred years! I have watched it happen too many times! If we know where they are, we could get lucky and save them, but if not we still need to destroy this nest! We need to know where they are located, and we need to use whatever methods it takes to obtain that information."

"And who will do this? You, Castor? Do you hate these humans so much to use torture? You have never tortured anyone before. It does something irreversible to you! You, Romulus? You vowed to never walk that path!" Nichola's voice rose in frustration as the phone kept its incessant ringing. "Or do you want me to do it once again?"

"Uncle, you know what the hunters are like. You know what they will do to them. What they are probably doing to them now. You know that we must end this nest, not only for the safety of vampires, but all supernatural creatures." Castor, flanked by Mitch and Ric, said as Aleksei and Zachary joined them.

"We have got to show them that we are not what they think that we are." Nichola told him.

"They do not care, my friend. They took Anisa. It is easy to see that she is a human. And she is not the only human that they have assaulted in the past. No one who associates with us can be truly safe. They are not out to protect the human race from us; they are out to exterminate us and anyone who stands in the way, human or other, are dead too!" Aleksei calmly entered the conversation.

Rom looked at Nichola meaningfully. "And Nikolaos, I do not ask you to perform this service. They are my mate and my child. I will do it. Just tell me where he is."

"He's down the hall and to the right." Devin said staggering drunkenly toward them from the other end of the main hallway, covered in blood.

"What have you done?" Nichola erupted.

"I did what needed to be done to save my mate. Don't worry he is alive. I know where they are at, now we just need to go get them." Devin said flippantly coming up to the group and Nichola rushed him to hold him against the wall of the lobby in a brutal grip.

"This is my house! You had no right…" Nichola started only to find himself in Aleksei's unbreakable grasp.

Uninjured and unfazed, Devin pushed himself away from the wall with disgust facing Nichola's rage head on. "Security in your house sucks!" He told Nichola brutally and Nichola's eyes widened in surprise. "Anisa is my mate! *You* have no right to tell me that I cannot help my mate! If it was my mother that they had captured, that boy down the hall wouldn't have survived *your* torture; and we all know it! It is the same reason why you don't take part in hunter operations worldwide and why you want my brother to join Castor's team!" Castor and Zachary looked at Devin in surprise. "You need steady hands and clear minds to do what is going to need to be done in the future, Nick. It is why we are here;" Devin gestured to Castor, Fred, Mitch, Ric, and Zachary, "it is why you want us to convince the wolf-shifters to ally themselves with us and you don't attempt it yourself; because despite your control, deep down we are still more human than you are."

* * * * *

The men in the lobby smelled the blood first; then they saw Anisa and Ssytis, who was carrying Esmeralda's body, enter the villa.

"Naga!" Nichola growled out and would have launched himself forward if Aleksei hadn't still had him in his grasp. The others stepped forward aggressively.

Anisa stepped in front of Ssytis to protect him, raising her hands towards the vampires, and the giant snake man looked down on her diminutive form in surprise behind her. "Stop!" She ordered the others. "This is Ssytis, he is my friend, and he helped me, and mama escape from whoever was holding us captive. You will treat him well under our laws of hospitality; we owe him a life debt."

Devin and the other men took in Anisa's blood matted hair, bruises, and ripped blood-covered clothing in shock.

"Nessie!" Devin ran to her, pulling her close to hold her tightly in relief and she leaned into him exhaustedly with a tired, broken sob. "God, baby, I thought I had lost you." He told her in a breaking voice.

Aleksei released Nichola and walked forward to stare up at the Naga. "I thought you were dead." He stated seemingly in shock.

"Alek." Ssytis nodded his head at the old vampire. "I am surprised to see you alive also."

Rom came forward, looking at the Naga with wide-eyes, and held his hands out to Ssytis to take Esmeralda's unconscious body. Ssytis carefully handed her over to him. Rom nodded his thanks and then called for someone to get the doctor as he headed upstairs. Devin lifted Anisa's small form into his arms, cradling her gently against his chest and followed him up the stairs.

"You look terrible." Aleksei said to Ssytis softly as Nichola approached slowly looking up at him in wonder then looked to Aleksei. "Why are you in between transformation?" Aleksei asked the Naga much to Nichola's surprise.

* * * * *

Ssytis walked around the suite that he was taken to, interested in the sumptuous luxury that he found there. Surprisingly, he felt no apprehension about being housed with a bunch of vampires. He remembered Alek from the Vampire-Shifter War, when the peace treaty had been negotiated between the various species. Ssytis at the time had led the Naga faction and the quiet, unusually aged-looking, vampire had led the Vampire faction. Both sides had lost much in that bloody war, but the vampire had constantly held himself with both honor and integrity throughout negotiations and it was a quality that Ssytis had respected and admired, because he unfortunately saw so little of it amongst the younger males of his own species. That total lack of honor is what had caused the other supernatural tribes to band together against them, and almost drove them into extinction, which finally brought them to the armistice table.

He had been surprised when the little vampire maiden had declared him safe passage, refuge, and the owner of a life debt. From what he remembered about vampire law that would mean that he was safe amongst them as long as he lived. Despite some of the issues that he had become aware of over the centuries throughout the vampire world, her knowledge of the law regardless of her youth and human status, spoke to the old vampire's continued influence amongst his people.

Ssytis wished he had been so successful with his own. It had been at least two centuries since he had visited the last remaining Naga stronghold in the known world, if it could be called a stronghold at all. His brethren had never been that numerous before the war and their numbers hadn't recovered since.

He walked into the bathroom and turned on the shower to watch the steam rise throughout the room. His body temperature was low; had been low ever since he had been tranquilized like a mindless animal. Whatever type of drug they had used on him had prevented him from fully transforming into his human-looking form or returning him to his natural Naga body and it also had prevented him from regulating his body temperature. It was why he had been so lethargic when they had first brought Anisa into the cell area that they had been keeping him in.

Their attention to Anisa, his lack of response and movement within the cell, and the fact that they had few people at the facility had caused them to almost forget about his presence. They had not remembered to administer the drug to him in more than twenty-four hours; allowing his body to further process the drug and returning some of his strength to him.

When they had captured him, he quickly realized that the hunters had no idea what they had captured. Though he wouldn't have expected them to know. For all intents and purposes even the supernatural world thought that his race was extinct.

The fact that they had been able to capture him at all, caused him much chagrin. It took more energy and thereby heat to remain in his human form and with the wintry weather he had taken to sleeping in his Naga form. He didn't hibernate like many snake species, but chilly weather did affect him, and he slept more in order to conserve more energy. That and the fact that he was almost two thousand years old probably didn't help his increased need to sleep much, he admitted to himself; though if another creature had told him that, he would have been extremely offended.

He was sure that one of the sparse staff of the small hotel at the base of Mount Olympus where he had been living at, must have seen him in his natural form and alerted the hunters. He remembered truly little of the actual capture, except for a stinging bite in the side of his human form's neck while he was walking back to the hotel after dining that evening. He had tried to shift before he had lost consciousness.

He had been looking forward to finding his bed with his full belly, and admittedly, he had imbibed a little too much ouzo that evening. He had also been disgruntled because the waitress that he had been pursuing for sexual sport had declined his invitation to join him after her shift, explaining sweetly that she had a betrothed. Hence, the additional ouzo consumption.

In the old days he would have just snatched her as she left the establishment at night; but kidnapping women, even if it was to give them the most satisfying sexual experience of their lives, was frowned upon in this modern age and very quickly brought in the local authorities.

Still, the cold and his lonely, drunken horniness aside, he should have been paying more attention to what was going on around him and maybe, they wouldn't have got the drop on him the way that they had; or at least he would have put up a decent fight and killed a few of them in the process. He knew better at his advanced age and was concerned that he had gone soft like many other species. This modern age of plenty could take away one's edge for survival if you weren't careful.

The hunter's lack of knowledge about his species was probably why they hadn't maimed him in the same way that they had the bear-shifter. They knew about bear-shifters; Ssytis was an unknown, and as an unknown he warranted additional study in a fully intact manner. His capture had excited them, and their leader, Sonchus, had directed that Ssytis remain unharmed until he had an opportunity to study him directly.

As Ssytis stepped into the shower he leaned forward bracing himself on the shower wall to instantly shiver in reaction to the hot, steaming water that flowed over his scaled body. He was still so cold.

After several minutes of standing under the water, watching as the bloodstained water circled the drain, he picked up a bar of soap to bring it up to his nose to inhale the fresh bergamot and citrusy floral and herbal scent with a soft, tired, sigh. He proceeded to finish washing the rank blood and gore from his body.

* * * * *

Anisa lay in the bathtub in Devin's suite, soaking the aches and bruises of the previous night while Devin knelt behind her painstakingly, and gently, washing the blood from her golden-brown tresses. She moaned, half in pleasure, half in pain, as his long fingers lovingly massaged her scalp.

Once she was totally clean, he helped her from the bathtub, gritting his teeth as he inspected the bruising on her abdomen, her swollen lip, and the slight bruising under her eyes; then wrapped her in a large bath-sheet to carry her back into his bedroom to tenderly start the process of combing through her wet hair. He didn't speak to her at all, or demand information, as he combed her hair, he just let her be and she was thankful for that. She wasn't ready yet to discuss what had happened.

He left briefly to retrieve some articles of clothing from her room, and had returned to dress her in a warm, long-sleeve nightgown and then tucked her into bed placing a finger beneath her chin to kiss her lips gently. "I am going to check on your mom and Aunt Iris." He stepped away from the bed and she suddenly grasped his hand stopping him.

"I was so happy to learn that Iris is alive." She said softly.

"You are all alive, Nessie. That's all that matters. You are all alive and everything is going to be okay." He quickly bent down and pressed his lips against her forehead. "Try to get some sleep. I will be back to check on you later."

* * * * *

Devin met Dene in the hallway giving him a look when he realized that they were both heading in the same direction: the Naga's room.

Things To Live For

I had finished drying off my scaled skin and was struggling to get out of this in between state I had found myself in, and I didn't care what form that took whether my true form or my human form, either would do at this point, when a knock came from the door to my suite.

Breathing deeply, I buried my frustration with my inability to transform, wrapped a bath sheet around my hips and opened the door to find the boy who had hugged my vampire maiden, and a strange man, who I sensed was neither a vampire nor a human, standing in my doorway. The boy carried a large white terrycloth garment in his arms and the man carried a black medical bag. I stepped aside to allow them to enter.

"I thought you might want something to wear until we could send the seamstress up to take your measurements for some clothing." The boy said and handed me what turned out to be a large, oversized robe.

I dropped the bath sheet to reveal my hemipenes and the boy's eyebrows raised in either surprise or admiration. Probably both. Afterall, I myself was quite proud of them, they were long, firm, knobbed, and slightly curved when erect, and over the centuries I have had much occasion to pleasure a vast variety of females without complaint. The strange man's face remained stoically impassive at my male display as I put on the robe.

"I am Dr. Lambert, and this is Devin Sutton, Anisa's mate." The man said and I almost smiled at the slight stress on 'Anisa's mate'. "I am trying to figure out what the poison is, that you and the ladies have been exposed to and would like to ask you some questions, take your vitals, and take a sample of your blood if you would consent to it."

"Will you be able to help me return to my natural form?" I asked him.

"If I can figure out what you have been given, it will be a huge step forward to curing you all. I have got two unconscious vampires and you are finding yourself in this," he gestured to me, "what I have been told, in between condition. The only one who seems to be functioning normally, at least physically, at this point is Anisa. I have been informed that you were present during her incarceration. If you could give me some insight as to her initial reaction, that would be helpful also." The doctor told me.

"Why don't you ask her?" I asked.

"I will but…"

"I have asked him not to examine her until after he has examined you." The boy interrupted to tell me.

"Why?" I asked now irritated.

"Because she has been through a lot, and the more information that we can get from you, the less that we will have to make her relive." Devin told me and I could tell from his pained voice that his concern was wholly upon Anisa.

"Ah, I see." I looked at him in understanding. "You believe that she has been raped." He flinched at my words. "She was not. At least not while she was in the cell next to mine."

"Her body, everywhere on her body," he emphasized, "is covered in bruises and scratches." He told me.

"There was one man who did abuse her and would have raped her. But she bravely fought him, and I was able to reach him through the bars and end his existence. It is how we escaped." I explained and he suddenly sat down on the end of the bed, breathing deeply in relief, to cover his face with his hands. I walked to him and grasped his shoulder in my clawed hand gently. "She is lucky to have someone who cares for her." I murmured but knew that the sound of my hissing was less than comforting for most creatures. Surprisingly he looked up at me and smiled.

"I am her mate." He said simply as if that explained everything.

"Dr. Lambert, if you really want to know what poison we have been exposed to, you need to infiltrate where we were being held. There should be no one there for at least another two days." I said to the doctor then looked down at the young vampire. "You should leave directly after the sun descends."

He smiled at me, and I was reminded of an imp with a secret, then he nodded, and left the room, leaving me with the doctor and his ministrations.

* * * * *

The sun was up and bright when Devin headed down the stairs looking for Zachary. He found him with Castor in the bar looking decidedly tired as Zachary leaned his head upon his hand on the table, dozing lightly.

Devin gave him a small shove to the shoulder to rouse him. "C'mon. Let's go check out the hunter's headquarters. Dene needs to know what type of drug everyone was exposed to and Ssytis says that there isn't supposed to be anyone there for the next two days. Now is the time to get in there and find out what they gave to the girls."

"Aren't you tired?" Zachary asked him grumpily.

"No. And you can sleep on the way there and back if you want. It's at the foot of Mount Olympus and it is a two-hour drive from here." Devin said. "Where is Fred and the wolves?"

"Probably curled up somewhere." Castor told him.

"Not Fred, he rarely sleeps." Devin responded.

* * * * *

"I miss you being around, Fred." Cassie told the cowboy softly as he sat next to her on the sofa in his room.

Princess was curled up sleeping softly on Fred's lap and he was gently running his rough, work-hardened fingers through her long, silky fur. "Why'd you come here, Cassie?" Fred asked, never taking his eyes off of the small dog.

"I told you. Princess missed you this morning." Cassie said sweetly.

"Listen, Cassie-girl," Fred murmured "I like you. A lot. But the Doc he likes you a whole lot too. In order for this to work, between the three of us, he should buy into it."

"Fred, Dene just wouldn't be comfortable with all of us in the same bed and I wouldn't be either." Cassie started.

"I'm not talking about that. I'm talking about sharing. Sometimes you are with me, sometimes you are with him. You know he wants you all to himself and I won't hide just waiting for you to creep up my back stairs when you want your boots knocked." Fred told her bluntly.

"It's my choice, Fred. I don't want to be exclusive with anyone. I just got free." Cassie told him in exasperation.

"Then you need to tell that to the Doc. I am not asking for you to stop seeing him and only see me. I wouldn't be no good for a one-on-one thing anyway. I have a brand-new vampire I have to look after. Things are probably going to be wild and woolly for a while, especially now that he is mated. I get that you just got free, Cassie-girl. I really do get it. So, I wouldn't ask you to tie yourself to only me, but you got to let the Doc know that you are going to be with me too. Otherwise it will just blow up in your face." Fred reached over a hand and grasped Cassie's in her lap, stroking his thumb over her soft skin.

"He may not want to see me anymore anyway, not after this morning." Cassie said sadly.

"Well, you will have to make up your mind on what to do in that case. If you don't want to be tied down to one man, then you don't want to be tied down to any man." Fred told her with an accepting shrug of his shoulders. "But if he thinks that you are his girl, and his girl only, and you encourage that belief, then I can't take you to my bed, no matter how much I want to, because that's the same as cheatin'."

Cassie rolled her eyes at him. "Like you don't cheat!"

"Cheatin' at cards is not the same thing as cheatin' on the heart. One is a game, and the other is not." Fred picked up Princess's sleeping body and sat it next to him on the sofa and leaned over to give Cassie a sweet kiss on the lips. "I may be a cowboy, Cassie, but I am not an idiot. I know you don't want an exclusive relationship right now in your life, it's too soon after what you went through.

So you're probably thinking that I am trying to get you to choose me in some sort of power play when I tell you that I can't take you to my bed; but I am not. I have had women cheat on me, because I thought that they were mine and I don't like it. I like the Doc and I won't do that to him. But you and me, we are friends, so I am just going to tell you straight. It may not be me that you cheat with, but if you let the Doc think that you are his exclusive gal, when you know in your heart that you ain't, eventually you will end up sleeping with someone else and then he is going to be hurt when he finds out." Fred said putting his forehead against hers to gaze into her blue eyes.

She sighed. "I have already told him this morning that he and I are not exclusive."

"And what did he say?" Fred asked.

"He just asked if I was talking about you and only you."

"And what did you tell him?" Fred inquired surprised.

"I told him yes." Cassie said softly, leaning in her slight body to give Fred a small kiss.

"And?" Fred questioned, his hands were itching to touch her, he wanted to run his fingers through her silky light-blonde hair and over her soft skin; and though his cock was uncomfortably hard in his jeans, he needed to know that doing so wouldn't violate his own personal code.

"He just looked at me, nodded and went back to working in his lab."

"He didn't say a word?" Fred asked incredulously, panting slightly his lips millimeters from her own.

"No, and frankly, I don't need his specific permission, Fred!" Cassie told him getting frustrated.

Fred quickly leaned her back on the couch, to push his strong, hard body against hers and she wrapped her arms around his neck, "No ma'am you don't!"

* * * * *

He is sweet and gentle. I have never had a man touch me like this before, without the violence. I push those thoughts from my mind as he slowly unbuttons my shirt, parting it to kiss each inch of exposed skin.

I start trembling, not in fear, but in need as his lips caress my nipple

131

through the white lace of my bra. I move my hands through his straight, straw-looking hair to hold his head to me, surprised at how soft it actually is compared to what it looks like. He reaches underneath me and unfastens my bra, then stands up to pull me to my feet, surprising me.

Everything with him is a surprise.

He wraps his hand tenderly behind my neck pulling my face up to his and whispers, "Cassie, I want to make love to you, but if you ain't ready yet, we will wait."

I gaze up at him, amazed at how pretty a man's hazel eyes can be and let a soft smile curve my lips as I whisper back, "I think I am ready." But even I hear the nervousness in my whisper.

"We will go slow, and we will stop anytime you want." His soft voice is full of that Texas twang that I find so charming and I find myself feeling a foreign fullness in my lower belly. "Trust me?" Fred asks me, and that fullness threatens to take over my heart.

"Yes." I tell him as he leisurely removes my shirt and eases my bra down my arms baring my breasts to his gaze which turns hot.

"You are beautiful." He whispers, caressing my skin with his calloused fingertips like a priest would lovingly touch a cross.

I reach up and undo the buttons of his shirt, "I want to see you too, Fred." I tell him clumsily attempting to pull the ends of his shirt from his jeans.

He grins at me, pulling the shirt from his waistband and removing it. He sits back down on the couch with a flop, and Princess jumps up to give him an irritated look then leaps on the floor to spring up onto a chair across the room, circling three times to settle down for her early morning nap.

"Help me with my boots," he tells me holding a leg up and I can't help but give him a bewildered look. "Put your leg up and over mine like you are mounting a horse." I do so and find myself facing away from him and grasping the heel of his boot pulling it to remove it, hearing him unbuckling his belt behind me.

Understanding flows through me as I quickly do the same for the other boot and then grip the bottom of his jeans and I can feel him lifting himself up behind me as I pull them from his body.

I turn to look at him standing between his spread feet.

Surprised, I ask, "No underwear?"

Grinning wickedly, he shakes his head 'no'. "Let that flow through your mind when you see me later." He teases.

"I am sure it will." I reply with a slight giggle, blushing, surprising myself. I am over one hundred years old, and Fred always makes me giggle like the teenage girl that I still look like.

I let my eyes rove over his body. He's all lean defined muscle with a small sprinkling of straw-colored hair just over his heart on the hard muscles of his chest, those wispy hairs bisecting the eight-pack of his abdominal muscles on their happy way down to his extensive, thick, uncircumcised, hard cock. The muscles of his long legs were also lengthy and lean; and it was quite evident that he had ridden horses his whole life.

He remained quiet as I looked my fill, and I met his twinkling eyes, "You are beautiful, Fred." I told him sincerely causing a pleased chuckle to escape his lips.

He leaned forward wrapping his strong arms around my hips pulling himself against me while I stood in between his legs. He placed a small kiss on my bare stomach just below my breasts. "Men aren't beautiful and even if they were, I am nowhere near as beautiful as you are." He slowly unzipped my long skirt sliding it down my legs to expose my white lace underwear. He placed his lips and nose against the mound of my sex and breathed deeply causing me to gasp in surprise. "Mmmmm. You even smell beautiful."

"Oh." I breathed out as he slid my panties down over my hips barely moving his head away only to return to kiss the curls of my mound. I held his head against me to hold myself steady as the shivers returned.

"Climb up here and put your knees on either side of me." He instructed sliding to the edge of the couch cushion, and I did. He leaned back bracing my hips. "Now lean forward and brace your hands against the wall behind the couch." He told me, and as I did, I felt his mouth against my netherlips.

"Fred!" I exclaimed as I felt a hot liquid feeling between my legs.

"Delicious." He whispered against me then thrust his tongue into me to drink of my juices.

The feeling was almost overwhelming as I involuntarily bucked against his mouth, but he held me tightly in place as his tongue lapped at me. My nipples were hard and aching as he reached a hand up and along my rib cage to massage my breast and to tweak my nipple. I was feeling a tightness deep within me when Fred suddenly stopped, and I embarrassingly couldn't prevent my disappointed moan.

"Not this first time, my sweetheart, this first time I want to reach it with you at the same time." He sighed sliding back up onto the couch to sit up straight so that I was straddling his hips and cock.

I looked at him bewildered on what to do next as he took himself firmly in hand.

"Now slide down on it."

I gazed into his hazel eyes in nervousness. Every time before, I had never been in control. Never felt like this. Never wanted it.

"It's me, sweetheart, take it as slow as you need to." His voice was gentle, but I could hear the desire lacing through his tone.

I lowered myself onto him, wincing in fear as I felt the head of his cock part me. He guided me with a hand on my hip as I gripped the couch on either side of his head and I slid down, inch by inch, over his length, never taking my eyes from his. His lips parted in passion, and he breathed out softly in a small moan as I took in his complete length. I breathed out feeling a deep need within my belly.

"God, you feel so good." His words were a groan. "Now ride me."

* * * * *

Her movements were unsteady and unsure, and I supported her by gripping her rounded hips in my hands as she tentatively moved up and down on my cock.

I cursed the existence of those pieces of shit; the companion Him and the vampire, Latour, and over the past several months had wished them back to life just so I could kill them all over for her.

I was very aware of the gift that she was giving me after all of the abuse at their hands and was determined that this would be good for her. But God, she felt great, and I found myself involuntarily throwing my head back

134

against the back of the couch and gripping her ass tightly as she moved on me with more surety.

"That's it, sweetheart, ride my cock." I whispered to her in encouragement as I felt her soft lips against my collar bone and her hips move faster.

I felt her wet pussy tighten around my shaft, hearing her moan slightly and knew if I didn't get out of my head, I wasn't going to last long enough for her to come.

Closing my eyes, I thought about the first time she let me hold her hand, and how skittish, how afraid, she was when we first brought her into our family. I thought about how sweet she had been when she had found me crying about the Boss one evening out by the shooting range; how she had held me while I cried out the grief. How she understood my loss. I thought about the first time I had watched her in the sunshine when she was out playing with Her Majesty, the Princess, how the sun had shown against the blonde of her hair, bringing out the lighter highlights, and how pink her cheeks were as she ran laughing with Princess playfully snarling on her heels. And I thought about how she and I both loved that little dog.

"Fred, Oh, God, Fred." She panted out softly in wonder, pulling my thoughts into the present, as her passion mounted, and her hips thrust against mine.

"Yes, sweetheart, are you ready?" I asked, and involuntarily thought about how this was going to be the first time for her, the first time this wasn't forced, the first time that she wanted it, and she was going to gift this first orgasm to me; then I bit the inside of my cheek till it bled because that thought damn near caused me to spill inside of her, and after everything that she had given me, I was not going to disappoint her in this.

I reached in between us and rubbed a gentle circle around her clit, and she screamed softly and came apart in my arms. I held onto her tightly while the involuntary movements of her hips and the fluttering of her pussy around my cock caused my eyes to cross as I exploded inside her with a sharp cry of my own, drenching her pulsating channel in cum.

Both of our orgasms were still shuddering through our connected bodies when I pulled her face to mine, "Thank you, sweetheart." I murmured against those sweet pink lips and then covered them with my own to kiss her deeply.

* * * * *

Cassie lay curled up sleeping in peaceful exhaustion in Fred's bed, Princess snuggled up against her back, as he lay on his side watching her sleep with tender eyes. He smiled softly as both she and the dog gave out little snores.

His sharp almost vampiric hearing picked up his posse coming up the stairs and he quickly but silently put his hat on and grabbed his jeans, shirt, boots, and gun belt, then stepped naked into the hallway to quietly close the door behind him.

He had thrown on his shirt and pulled on both socks when they all came around the corner and stopped in shock.

"Fred!" Devin admonished. "What are you doing naked in the hallway!"

"What if Mom sees you?" Zachary asked scandalized.

Fred shushed them. "Nobody is going to see me if y'all don't yell it to the world!" He whispered to them quickly pulling on his jeans.

"Jesus, commando!" Devin exclaimed, but quietly.

"Hey, I go commando too!" Ric exclaimed.

"That's not surprising." Castor murmured sarcastically.

"And way too much information this early in the morning." Zachary countered with a shake of his head.

"Got to let them baby makers breathe!" Ric replied with a grin.

Fred was quickly buttoning up his shirt and buckling his gun belt around his hips when Mitch leaned over to sniff him.

"Fred, you smell distinctively like…"

"If you say it I am going to shoot you." Fred told him in warning and walked them back down the hallway and away from his door.

"We are heading over to the hunter's hideout." Devin told Fred.

"I figured that we would do that today. I have been listening for you." Fred answered him. "No time like the present to get a messy job done."

"So…smells like you and Cassie are an item now." Ric said in a dreamy voice leaning in to smell Fred deeply.

Fred punched him in the arm.

* * * * *

"Just where do you all believe that you are going?" Nichola said looking up from where he had been going over security tapes with Aris and Mansuetus behind the desk.

"Ssytis says that there will be no hunters in their headquarters for the next few days and Dene needs to know what the hell they were given or he's not sure that he can cure Iris and Es." Devin told him. "So, we are going to go and see if we can collect information for him."

Nichola glared at them and started to speak when Castor stepped forward saying reasonably, "Uncle, this is exactly what my team and I would be doing if this had occurred in another area. This needs to be done while it is still relatively safe."

Nichola's glare did not lessen and then he said, "Fine. I will be going with you." The younger men looked at each other in surprise as Nichola turned to Mansuetus. "Make sure to alert Rom and Aleksei that we have gone. As for Leila, you know what to do."

Mansuetus nodded briefly then said, "My life for hers."

A New Evil

~~~ ❧ ~~~

Nichola had been driving for more than an hour in almost total silence as Zachary and the wolf shifters napped. He finally broke the silence by addressing Devin, "So, you have accepted that Anisa is your mate?"

"Yes." Devin's voice was blunt and hard as he was harboring resentment toward the other vampire for his manhandling of him the previous evening.

"Good. It is better to accept it than to continue to fight it if it is so." Nichola focused on the road ahead. "I owe you an apology for my behavior earlier." Nichola's voice was quiet. "But, even so, you are a young vampire, and your actions could have gone extremely wrong. You could have lost control and taken a life. You lose something of yourself with every life you take." Nichola's voice was bitter.

"I understand what you are saying, Nick, but what choice did I have? You should have gotten that information out of him before we ever returned to the villa. It was only luck and the presence of Ssytis that got Anisa and Es back safely. If he hadn't helped her escape, and we weren't able to rescue her, they would both most likely be dead." Devin responded.

"You are young, and have little control…" Nichola began.

"You are wrong. I have a lot of control. I am not fighting my condition, in fact I have wholeheartedly embraced it and have probably consumed several gallons of pig's blood since I got my fangs. I am not taking the chance of harming my human mate." Devin told him bluntly.

Nichola's countenance betrayed his frustration with Devin's logic. "As for existing, functioning, animal blood suffices. But, you could have been overwhelmed. After interviewing the hunter and learning what you did to him, I am incredibly surprised that your 'session' did not end with a corpse. At our core, we are predators! Our natures are such that violence makes us crave more violence, and human blood is the most addictive of substances." Nichola stated just as bluntly.

"You are speaking about temptation. I was extremely tempted." Devin admitted thinking back to the exhilaration that had coursed through his very cells as he had licked the blood from the hunter's wounds and the overwhelming need to take more. Devin sucked air deeply into his lungs and then continued. "I was tempted to drain the little bastard dry after I got what I wanted from him. Still, temptation and control are two different things and I have never been one to relinquish my control no matter the temptation."

"That's because you are a cold-natured control freak." Zachary murmured sleepily from the back.

"So you are awake?" Devin replied his lips twisting distastefully at his brother's statement.

"Yep. Mom is sending me shotgun texts wanting to know why you aren't picking up your cellphone and telling me to call her. Now." Zachary said and they immediately heard another buzzing notification. "Nick, Mom says she doesn't appreciate you shutting her out and if you don't call her right now she is getting in a car and coming after us."

"Call her." Nichola told Devin tersely.

Devin pulled out his cellphone, put it on speaker, and dialed Leila's number.

Leila picked it up in the middle of the first ring. "What do you all think that you are doing?" Leila's yell came through the speaker, waking the wolves and Fred, and they all winced.

"I psychí mou…" Nichola said in a soothing voice.

Leila cut him off. "Don't you I psychí mou me, Nikolaos Tsoukalous!" The men in the car raised their eyebrows at her furious tone. "We just discussed this last night! You are not to be putting yourself in danger! You gave me your word! Turn around and come back right now!" She demanded. "If you don't, I am getting in the car and coming after you!" Leila's furious voice was threatening.

"You will not!" Nichola snapped angrily. "I forbid it!"

"Excuse me? You what?" Leila's voice was low, dangerous, and indignant.

Nichola breathed deeply, letting his breath escape slowly through his pursed lips, gripping the steering wheel tightly in both hands; causing a small squeaking sound on the leather covered wheel as he twisted his hands slightly in irritation.

"Glykó." His voice was soft, but Devin could see that he was struggling with his composure. "I need you there in case the villa is attacked while we are gone, as Aris is unsure that he has ferreted out all of the traitors. There is no danger for us. Go to Ssytis's room and ask him yourself.

Leila, you must protect them as the other women are in no position to protect themselves. I am trusting you to do this." There was a long pause where neither of them spoke, then Nichola continued smoothly. "Can I depend upon you to defend them, agapitós?"

Several long seconds went by before she finally, reluctantly, answered, "Yes. But if you get yourself killed, Nichola, leaving me like this, I will never forgive you."

* * * * *

"Is that true?" Fred asked worriedly from the back after Devin disconnected the call with his mother. "Is the villa in danger?"

"I do not lie to my mate." Nichola told him emphatically before continuing. "Nothing is one hundred percent risk free in this life, but most likely the villa is not under imminent danger. Though there is a reason why I employ security." Nichola replied.

"No vampire residence is fully free from danger from hunters, ever." Castor told Fred. "Though it is exceedingly rare to have them attack a residence directly. It is the same reason why terrorists rarely attack military bases; a vampire's residence is a hard target due to the defenses. Usually hunters attack outside of the residence as they did last night. Even though these particular hunters infiltrated the villa, you notice that they chose to do the most damage by waiting for an outside opportunity, when their actions would have been the most successful and garnered the most damage.

What makes hunters so dangerous is the varying methods of those attacks. Guns, bombs, and now kidnapping and poison. They are extremely creative in their methods used to harm us. It is time for us to get just as creative in defending ourselves." Castor's voice held a suddenly understanding tone. "Hopefully, the wolf shifter tribes will agree to our alliance against them."

"Exactly." Nichola concurred quietly.

* * * * *

"I'll go." Zachary said as they sat in the car looking at the square industrial building partially hidden in the trees across the street.

"The fuck if you will." Devin told him quietly.

"None of you can do it." Zachary told him. "Even though you all can walk about in the daylight now, I hate to tell you this, but you all seem a little bit off. Even Fred. If I encounter anyone, I will just tell them that I am lost and need directions." He looked around at them all with a perceptive eye.

"No way." Devin said again.

"Keep your Bluetooth earbuds on, we will listen through Devin's phone. Once you get into the building and it is clear, let us know and we will join you." Nichola told Zachary and Devin glared at him as Zachary left the car to jog across the street. Nichola ignored Devin to address Fred. "Fred you are staying in the car. If anyone pulls up while we are in there you will alert us."

Fred nodded.

* * * * *

Zachary met them in the entrance of the building. "What's up with the lights?" Devin asked as he entered the dimness of the hallway.

"I smell blood and death." Mitch said in a gravelly voice, obviously holding back his wolf, as they moved down the hall.

"Ssytis left a couple of bodies lying around." Zachary told them in a detached voice as they came upon the last man that Ssytis had killed. The pool of blood around the body was wide.

"What's that?" Devin asked to no one in particular, walking over to look down at a small, fist-sized chunk of flesh, laying near the body. He recoiled, swallowing heavily once he realized that it was the man's cock and balls. "Jesus! What the fuck is wrong with that Naga?"

"According to Aleksei, this particular Naga has an extremely strict sense of honor and justice; he believes this Naga could be more trustworthy than many vampires." Nichola's expression held supreme doubt. "Still, the Naga are brutal and terrifying beasts with enormous strength." Nichola stated coldly motioning to the corpse. "They slaughtered many of our own horribly during the war. I hate the fact that we owe him a life debt!"

"Brutal or not, as far as I am concerned, for what he did for Nessie and her mom, he's my best fucking friend." Devin stated looking down the hall.

"There's another body in a cell down the hall almost just like this one. Except it looks like he killed that one pretty quick. Better than what this poor bastard experienced by dying slowly due to blood loss through emasculation." Zachary was using his Detective's voice, which was cold and detached. In his previous position as a San Antonio Homicide Detective, he had become desensitized to the horror of seeing some pretty gruesome crime scenes; or at least that was what he wanted the world at large to believe.

"I think I am going to be sick!" Ric whispered; the normally playful wolf shifter looked sweaty and pale.

"Knock it off! Pull it together." Nichola commanded them all sharply. "Spread out and collect as much as you can. I want laptops, hard-drives, files. Anything that holds data. If you see anything that could be a drug of some sort, I want it."

The others spread out and Nichola heard Devin say to the others, "If you find a locked door, let me know. I have a set of keys that I took from Anisa."

Nichola raised his phone to his ear. "Fred, be ready to bring the car here on my signal." Disconnecting the line, he joined the others in the search.

* * * * *

"Nichola, the local pack alpha and his mate are here. I have shown them to their suite." Leila, who was standing calmly flanked by Ssytis and Mansuetus, told Nichola as they walked into the villa carrying their treasure trove of hard drives, files, and vials of drugs that they had confiscated from the hunter's hideout.

The Naga, who stood eight inches taller than Mansuetus, making the big man seem small, was standing bare chested and footed, wearing a pair of borrowed black sweatpants that were too short for him. The large creature was still in his in-between state and was standing proudly with his arms crossed on his red scaled chest.

Devin walked up to him carrying some luggage. "I think we found your things at their hideout."

The Naga looked at him and took the luggage. "That answers a question I had. Obviously, they were alerted to my presence by the hotel staff where I was staying. I think I will make a return visit when your doctor cures me of my inability to shift into my true form." His voice was cold and deadly.

"Leave your thoughts of revenge for another time, Naga." Nichola told him. "That place rivaled some of the concentration camps I have seen. This is a new threat for all of us." He turned to Devin. "Get the drugs to Dene for testing and the files and other items to the conference room for review. Do you think that you have enough skill to connect the hard drives that we have taken? Or should I bring someone in?"

"No problem, I got this." Zachary told him carrying a large box and walking past him to the conference room.

* * * * *

"I apologize for not being here to greet you properly this morning, Vuk. We have had some trouble with a group of hunters; though our trouble does tie-in with why I extended my invitation to you." Nichola told the middle-aged looking, dark-haired, blue eyed, and extremely handsome alpha-wolf shifter holding his hand out warmly in greeting.

"No apologies are necessary, my friend. Your mate has been very gracious to myself and my Luna." The alpha returned warmly with a very white, toothy smile gripping Nichola's forearm.

"Allow me to introduce Mitchell Matheson, Alpha of the Diamond Wolf Ranch, and Maverick McAllister, his Beta. Their pack lives on my sons' ranch in Texas." Nichola indicated Mitch and Ric. "Gentlemen, this is Vukasin

Vasileiou and his Luna Louve. Vuk is the Alpha of the Skoteinó Fengári Pack here in this area of Greece. He will also be attending the shifter conclave next month in Skopje."

The two alphas squared up to look at each other and power flowed throughout the air. Mitch was much younger and larger than the Greek alpha, but suddenly he nodded slightly to him and smiled, holding out his hand. The power surge in the air died, and the smaller, older, alpha gripped his forearm like he had done Nichola's.

"My vampire friend tells me that you are looking to expand your pack and hopefully find mates for you and your Beta." Vuk commented with a smile.

"I am, but unfortunately, something tells me that we are going to have to take care of a threat to your area first before we can move on to more pleasant things." Mitch told him.

Vuk looked at them inquiringly.

"Come to the conference room my friend and I will show you what we have discovered." Nichola told him. "Let my mate take your Luna to relax in the spa. This is not a conversation nor a sight for women." He said leading the alpha wolf away with Mitch and Ric following.

Leila gave Nichola's retreating form a pointed, disgruntled look before she smiled charmingly at Louve, a lovely brown-haired, blue-eyed woman who appeared to be in her late forties. "I am sorry about that, sometimes Nichola's manners are from the distant past."

Louve smiled in return, meeting her eyes with understanding. "My dear, no apologies are necessary, I am unfortunately used to it myself as it is a distinctly Alpha trait."

* * * * *

"I hate to use you as a guinea pig, Ssytis." Dene told the Naga sincerely, holding up a syringe.

"Just do it." The snake man told him with irritation. "I can't survive outside this villa in this in-between state as I can neither fully defend myself nor camouflage myself. If I die at least it will be helpful knowing that you would be one step closer to helping the women."

"What are they to you, though, Ssytis?" Dene asked wiping the injection site on the Naga's exposed hip with alcohol. "You don't even know them."

"They are women, doctor. All women are wonderful. They are the carriers of life and the givers of pleasure. I am surprised that you do not know that by now." Ssytis said baring his teeth in a freaky-looking grin as he looked over his shoulder at the doctor who held the syringe at the ready.

Dene gave him a slight smirk in return, "You might feel a burn." He said and pushed in the needle through the Naga's thick skin, flinching when Ssytis hissed slightly.

* * * * *

"Well?" Aleksei asked as Dene entered Iris's room to check on her.

"He is resting, but we should know soon. Has she regained consciousness at all?" Dene asked approaching the bed to look at Iris, lifting her eyelids to check her pupils which were still responsive. He checked the IV bag which housed human blood, and then proceeded to check her other vitals.

"No." Aleksei told him, holding Iris's hand. "What now?"

"We wait to see how Ssytis reacts to the antidote." Dene told him calmly and moved to leave the room.

"Do you still love her?" Aleksei asked softly causing Dene to pause halfway to the door.

"I suspect that I will always love her." Dene said not looking at the old vampire. "But, I also realize, that she doesn't love me. I understand that and still I wish her nothing but happiness." Dene turned to look at Aleksei. "You make her happy in a way that I never did; and for that I am glad."

* * * * *

Dene was walking out of Esmeralda's room, leaving her in much the same state as Iris; neither worse nor better, when he saw Devin coming down the hallway to his own room, where he had placed Anisa.

"Have you checked on her yet?" Devin asked him as Dene headed in his direction.

"No, I am heading there now." Dene replied.

"Why do you think that Anisa's in better shape than her mom and Aunt Iris?" Devin asked.

"Anisa's blood panel showed little of the poison. I do not believe that she

145

was injected with it at all." Dene told him. "If that had been the case, she would have died."

"That doesn't make sense." Devin stated.

"It does if she only ingested it." Dene told him.

"But why inject it into the vampires and not Anisa?" Devin asked Dene.

"Maybe the vampires didn't react quickly enough to the initial dosage? There are signs that Iris and Es both ingested the poison and received it via injection. That's why they are both terribly ill. But, according to Anisa, she vomited several times which should have rid her system of most of the poison. She, other than her physical abuse, is doing well. Maybe in order to subdue the vampires the hunters ended up having to inject the vampires too?

But the main questions are: where did they eat dinner, and who in the restaurant was involved with these hunters? If they ingested the poison during dinner, which we have to deduce because of Anisa's initial reaction, it was when they were in Katerini. We need to find out how far this conspiracy goes and how much danger are we all in because of it." Dene explained.

"What was the poison?" Devin asked opening the door to his suite.

"A compound made of Ackee, Belladonna and Cassava. I have created an antidote and administered it to Ssytis about a half hour ago. I will check back with him as soon as I am done here with Anisa. He should know by now whether it has worked." Dene told him.

As they entered the room, Devin and Dene stopped in shock to see a barefooted, handsome, tall, broad, muscular man with long, thick, straight, red hair, and piercing yellow eyes, who was dressed in a tight red tee-shirt and a pair of form fitting blue jeans, sitting in a chair next to a smiling Anisa who was sitting up in bed amongst several supporting pillows.

"I believe that your antidote works quite well, Doctor." Ssytis's voice was a deep baritone and did not hold a hint of a hiss.

* * * * *

"Doesn't he look well?" Anisa asked Devin, who sat next to her on the bed, excitedly after Dene left to make and administer the antidote to Iris and Esmeralda.

Devin eyed Ssytis from his position next to her.

"Yes, he looks…great." Devin replied reluctantly and Ssytis smiled at him knowingly. "Though I am not sure that you are up for visitors."

"I am feeling much better!" Anisa exclaimed happily. "Still a little battered, but I am so much better!"

Devin smiling at her eternally cheery outlook, took her hand in his, "I am very glad." He told her warmly.

"So, I heard some of your conversation, young vampire. The women were poisoned where they ate yesterday? It seems that this villa is under surveillance by the hunters, and they have local help. I find that disturbing, seeing as how Tsoukalous is highly involved in the success of the town and surrounding area." Ssytis stated.

"Is that why you weren't staying here in Katerini?" Devin asked. "Because you believed that the whole area is under Nick's jurisdiction?"

"To put it bluntly, yes. Though we are no longer at war, my kind are few and avoid the rest of the supernatural world, preferring to blend directly with humans or to reside within a Naga community." Ssytis told Devin. "We prefer humans to even our own kind in most cases."

"Why?" Anisa asked innocently.

"Because there are no female Naga." Devin supplied and Ssytis raised his eyebrows slightly in surprise at his knowledge and gave him a small smile.

Devin had went out of his way to get as much information out of Nichola and Aleksei as he could about the Naga, what they were, and, since he knew that Anisa would be determined to befriend him because he saved her, any possible threats that Ssytis might pose toward Anisa.

Anisa looked confused for a moment. "But, how do you have babies? Or are you created like made vampires?" She asked Ssytis.

"We have children with human women." Ssytis told her. "We cannot create others via a transfer of bodily fluids like vampires. Our male children are not born human, unless they are female, and in that rare case they are totally human. Only males are born Naga and they always gain the ability to change to their full Naga form when they reach physical maturity. Our birthrates are low as it takes a special type of woman to nurture the seed of a Naga and in time bear a child." Ssytis's voice with Anisa was gentle.

She looked at him stricken. "I had never heard of a Naga before I met you. But I am not ignorant, I grew up in the vampire community. Does your low birthrate mean that your race is dying?"

"I am not comfortable with that term." Ssytis said softly. "The Naga, the Vampire, the various species of Fae, are all almost immortal. All of us have low birthrates. Shifters are mortal, though their lifespans are far beyond that of a normal human and their birthrates are higher than all of ours. I would like to think that our low birthrates are Nature's way of insuring that we do not overpopulate the earth." He smiled briefly at her.

"You said that you are almost immortal. Are you very old?" Anisa asked innocently.

"Anisa, that's a rude question." Devin softly admonished, though he himself was curious.

"Nonsense." Ssytis told Devin with a smile at Anisa. "I like her curiosity. I am incredibly old, child." Ssytis told her as if he were telling her a secret. "Alek and I are contemporaries. He and I, along with many others now dead, negotiated the end of the Vampire-Shifter War."

"Oh. You have seen so much history!" Anisa said in awe.

"A fair bit. Unfortunately, not all of it pleasant." Ssytis replied, though smiled at her response.

"I have always been fascinated by our history, but Mother always tells me that I am not to bother Aleksei with my questions." Anisa told him with irritation.

"You may ask me anything, Anisa. We have fought back an attack on our persons together and have made it through to the other side to survive. That makes us comrades." Ssytis told Anisa with a gleam in his eye that Devin did not care for.

"That's wonderful." Devin told him and his tone said otherwise, then looked at Anisa in concern. "But you need to rest, so visiting hours are over."

Ssytis took the hint gracefully with a smile and stood.

"No!" Anisa protested. "I'm not tired." But she belied the statement with a yawn.

"Nessie, you know that you are going to want to go and visit your Mom and Aunt Iris later this evening. I want you to rest until then." Devin told her reasonably.

"But I am bored! I don't want to stay by myself. I don't like it when I wake up and no one is here but me." Anisa told him in a small fearful voice.

"I am not going anywhere, Nessie. I will stay here with you until you go back to sleep." Devin told her looking pointedly at Ssytis.

"I will see you later, Anisa. I am going to find Alek and discuss what should be done about these hunters so that they are no longer a threat to you and this area." Ssytis smiled at her heading for the door. "Listen to your mate and get some rest."

My Little Mate

❧

D evin removed his boots and lay down next to Anisa gently enfolding her in his arms. He settled back as he comfortingly stroked up and down her arm, trying to ease her to sleep, as she laid her head upon his shoulder.

"You haven't asked me any questions about what happened to me last night." She stated curiously, her voice soft and unsure of what his reaction would be. She sensed that his silence on the subject covered a murderous anger.

"I figured when you are ready to talk about it, you would let me know. I don't want to drag up horrible memories for you when you should be focusing on recovering. I just don't want you to have to deal with it. Besides, I have been doing enough investigating on my own." He told her softly.

"You have?" She asked him, lazily stroking her hand up and down his tee-shirt covered chest.

He covered her hand with his own, stopping her movement as his body started to respond to her. She was in no shape to deal with his lust, and he wanted her to rest.

"Yes, just before you returned early this morning, I was interrogating a hunter that had infiltrated the villa under the disguise as a worker. I don't know what the hell Aris was thinking, well, I guess I kind of do, but he didn't vet him or one of the security guards who he hired for temp work based on the guy's recommendation." Devin started to tell her.

"There was a hunter? Working here? Are we safe?" Her questions came out in a frightened squeak.

"I am not going to talk to you about this if it's going to upset you, Nessie." Devin began. "You being upset is not going to help you recover any faster."

"No. No, I am okay. I want you to tell me, Devin. I need you to tell me." She told him in a strong voice. "Don't shut me out. After last night…well, I am stronger than you think."

He sighed deeply, unsure if he should continue. He didn't want her to worry or to frighten her needlessly after she had been through so much already. He wanted her to be able to rest and heal. Every time he looked at her now, he felt the overwhelming need to protect her, from both physical and mental threats. After last night's fiasco, he felt like a total failure in that department and was just thankful that he was going to get another chance. She was his and he was going to take better care of her whether she wanted him to or not.

"Please. What do you mean that you know what Aris was thinking? Was he in on it?" She asked softly.

"God, no! He feels terrible about the whole thing. He was attracted to the guy, so he didn't do a proper background check before he brought him into the villa. If I put my anger aside, looking at it objectively, I can understand why he would feel that the guy was innocuous. The guy is so young, barely an adult, and looks so innocent. You wouldn't have even thought that he would be a danger to anyone.

But, overall, Aris was thinking with his dick and didn't do his job right. It almost got you guys killed." Devin's voice was laced with anger and no small amount of fear at what could have happened. "The hunters have obviously been watching the villa for a while now and have learned a lot about Aris; there could be no doubt that the guy was chosen to infiltrate the villa based on what Aris likes. They dangled him like bait and Aris bit.

That helped set up the hiring of the other guy for security based on the kid's recommendation." Devin paused. "The security guy was one of the bodies we found, so he is out of the way. Still, Nick, Aris and Mansuetus are reviewing all hires made in the last six months."

Anisa sat up quickly, then groaned sharply in pain due to her bruised abdomen and ribs.

"Careful." Devin said quickly sitting up to brace her.

"Do you mean to tell me that you went to the hunter's hideout?" Anisa asked sharply. "Why would you do that? You could have been killed!"

"Ssytis told us that there wouldn't be anyone there and he was right." Devin told her concerned that she may have reinjured herself.

"I don't care you could have been…" Anisa not quite yelled.

"I know baby, but we weren't. Everything went fine." Devin told her.

"What was the point then if you 'knew' no one would be there?" She fixed him with her cerulean blue eyes incensed that he should take such a risk.

"Because we had to find out what the poison was that they had given you guys. We didn't have a choice. In order to cure Ssytis, your mom and Aunt Iris, Dene needed us to get that information. How do you think that Ssytis was able to return to his human form? We collected a bunch of other disturbing information too, Nessie.

More than we ever thought is going on with the hunters. They are some really sick fuckers! I mean really sick. From what we gathered, they have been doing experiments on anything that they can capture alive that is supernatural. They are trying to find new ways to kill us all. To exterminate anything that is not purely human. We found shifter bodies in various stages of autopsy. But, not just autopsy, Nessie. They were laid out like you would a frog in biology class.

This new hunter leader, Sonchus, he's a sick freak! He is the one that has been pushing for more 'creative' ways of killing us, way beyond the basics of knife, gun, or stake. According to what Mitch and Ric were able to sniff out, and the files that we collected, those autopsies were not conducted on corpses. They did that to the shifters when they were alive. To test regeneration properties of distinct species.

So far, they have been doing this to lone wolf types, like Ssytis. Those supes who exist alone or in small family units. The big packs, or vampire communities, have been exempt for the moment, we think because they didn't want to draw attention to what they have been doing. According to the hunter I interrogated, this infiltration of the villa was a first foray."

"I can't believe he just volunteered all of this information to you." Anisa told him.

"He didn't. It took some persuading." Devin told her evasively, not meeting her eyes.

"You tortured him." She gasped with horror.

"I did what I had to do." Devin told her harshly meeting her eyes with his.

"Did you kill him?" Anisa's whisper was laced with dread.

"No, but I wanted to kill him in a most brutal way; and with a deep-seated ache that was almost impossible to overcome." Devin's eyes glazed over at the thought; then he focused once more on Anisa. "And if he didn't tell me everything I wanted to know, and then some; I would have, Nessie and I wouldn't have felt bad about it one bit." Devin continued in that same cold, blunt voice.

"That's not who you are, Devin." Anisa told him softly cupping his face with her small hand and looking up into his pecan-colored eyes.

"Isn't it, Nessie? I think that's exactly who I am now. I am willing to do anything, anything at all, to keep you safe from harm. I am thankful to Ssytis for saving you from being raped; but I regret deeply not being the one to rip that guy apart myself." Devin's voice was cold and deadly.

"Don't say that Devin, it was horrible." Anisa told him leaning against his shoulder and wrapping her arms around his waist. "You can't lose your humanity like that."

He held her in return.

"I am not human anymore, Nessie." Devin told her with a shiver remembering how much pleasure he had received from drinking the hunter's blood.

"But I am human." Anisa whispered, her voice full of grief on Devin's behalf.

"I know, Nessie. I know." He told her sweetly as he stroked up her back gently, pressing his lips to the top of her head where it rested on his shoulder. "I am glad you are human. I wouldn't change you for anything. Lay back down and try to get some sleep." He moved her gently back to the mattress giving her a gentle kiss on the lips.

"Devin," Anisa's voice was small and unsure. "Would you make love to me?"

He raised his eyebrows in surprise and felt a flame of lust take hold of him and his cock immediately grew rock-hard. "Don't tempt me." He said in a soft gravelly voice that was covered in velvet, then cleared his throat. "You are covered in bruises." He continued getting a hold of himself.

"Oh." Her voice was laced with disappointment and a little hurt. "That's okay. I'm sure that I am not at my most attractive right now."

"Baby, that's not it at all. I don't mean it that way. You are beautiful and I ache to make love to you." Devin stroked her cheek gently, reassuredly, looking deeply into her eyes. "I just don't want to hurt you. Besides, you know, your first time should be all rose petals and champagne and that type of stuff." He told her with a soft smile, holding her gently against him.

"Devin, my first time almost happened on the cold, filthy concrete floor of a prison cell." Anisa looked up into his eyes sincerely.

* * * * *

He looked down on me with an intensity that was almost overwhelming. I wasn't sure what to expect from him. I wanted him to make love to me. I wasn't feeling desire, but fear. I just desperately wanted Devin to wipe away this fear and the memory of that man's hands on my body. I just wanted him to replace it with a memory of him. Him and him only.

Is that what you really want, Nessie? Are you ready for me?

Hearing his eager voice in my mind, I picked up images of him touching me, his hands clutching me to him as he thrust himself into me with abandon just before he sank his fangs into me. I realized that those rough pornographic images were his thoughts. Those thoughts made me catch my breath in anxiety.

He put his forehead against mine and then kissed me so sweetly, careful not to mark me with his fangs which were now present. Unfortunately, even though I knew that he would never intentionally hurt me, I couldn't help but tense up.

154

He smiled patiently down into my eyes and then held me close to whisper into my ear, "Let's wait, baby. I don't mind waiting for you."

I breathed a sigh of relief.

* * * * *

I quietly left my suite, checking back briefly to look tenderly at Nessie's slumbering form, before closing the door. I was feeling a little bit like a cad for sending those thoughts to Nessie. But, in the grand scheme of things, she was not ready, and I knew it. Not to mention that she was more injured than she was letting-on and no matter how much I craved to sink my cock into her tightness, if I did so now I really would be a cad and a horribly selfish one at that. I never imagined when I first met her months ago that saying no to fucking her would be this difficult, nor so physically painful. I adjusted my rock-hard cock in my jeans before walking down the hall toward the stairs.

God knows if I can keep this up for too much longer, and to think I was just bragging to Nick about how much control I was in. Obviously, when it came to wanting my little mate, my control was a lot softer than my cock.

Nothing But Trouble

⚜

"This is video footage of one of their 'experiments' in action, gentlemen." Zachary told the men in the conference room, and the others of the small council via Zoom, in a professional and detached voice, starting the video from the desktop's console.

The video was grainy and jerky and obviously taken with a cell phone. There was a slender, dark-haired, black-bespectacled man who looked to be in his late forties or early fifties. He wore a long white lab coat, and he was moving his hands reverently over some surgical instruments that were spread out on a metal standing tray; the type that you would see in an operating room.

On the modified surgical table, a young man was naked, strapped and straining. His arms and hands were restrained down along slender hinged supports, as well as his legs. His bound form had been made to look like Leonardo Di Vinci's Vitruvian Man.

The scientist was speaking as the videographer took in the scene, then focused on the young man's terrified face as he tried to escape the restraints of the table.

"Subject 23 is a known faun shifter, approximate age 25 to 35, though as we know age is always debatable, and the subject is uncooperative. He was collected west of Mount Olympus in the Lofos, Elassona area here in Greece. Due to the presence of a major thoroughfare and the uncooperating manner

156

of the subject, it is not currently known whether there is an established settlement of faun shifters in the area or whether the subject is a lone shifter. There will be an investigative team sent to the region to determine if there is a settlement.

The compound, which was administered forty-eight hours ago, has rendered Subject 23 unable to shift into his supernatural form. This purpose of this test is to determine whether the new compound has prevented shifting as well as impeded the shifter's natural regenerative abilities." The scientist's tone of voice was exactly what you would expect of a lecturing professor in a college classroom.

The videographer followed the scientist as he selected his first instrument. The scientist looked at the camera briefly with a barely recognizable, cold, detached hatred, before saying coldly, "We will be starting with the number fifteen blade scalpel for our first incision."

The videographer focused the camera as the scientist made a small, thin incision fileting the skin of the shifter starting at his shoulder and angling to the center of his chest. Blood flowed from the wound. The scientist reached across the shifter to make another incision from the opposite side. Then the camera focused on the shifter's wild-eyed face as he started screaming in terror, "No! God, no, please!"

The men around the table flinched as it went on and on.

"Enough!" Vukasin said in barely controlled disgust, horror and a growing rage. Zachary stopped the video just as the scientist, who had peeled away the first layer of skin from the abdomen of the shrieking shifter, was heading for body parts further south. Vukasin fixed his eyes on Ssytis to say in a pleading voice, "Please tell me Naga, that this is one of the men that you slew upon your escape from the compound!"

Ssytis looked at the Alpha only to shake his head in disappointment.

"No, unfortunately. I killed a younger version of him, probably his son or other relative. Though I guarantee you that one was no innocent, due to circumstances, he died relatively quickly. But this bastard? I would have taken my time no matter the risk." Ssytis's eyes gleamed dangerously.

* * * * *

Devin was sitting at the bar as the others filed in after the *'Hunters Are Bad, and Here's Why',* show and tell with Alpha Vukasin, sipping a glass of porcine blood with an empty, green-colored bottle sitting in front of him.

"So, how was Anisa?" Zachary asked looking at him with concerned blue eyes as he sat next to him at the bar.

"She's okay. She's finally resting." Devin's voice held a hint of 'don't go there, brother'.

"Hey, where's your vamp girlfriend?" Zachary looked around the bar with a grin, trying to poke Devin out of his sullen mood.

"That's not even funny, Bro." Devin muttered. "I haven't seen her since that night on the beach."

"Well, don't you think that is weird? It's been a couple of days since she's been working in the bar." Zachary asked.

"It depends. She bailed as soon as she saw Uncle Man that night and I don't know if Nick requires the vampire staff to live here at the villa or not. For safety reasons, that's usually the plan at his hotels.

Vampires have to live on site, and humans have a choice, but he makes it worth their while because staff housing is just as nice as guest rooms and, of course, it's free. But the villa is not as big a place as the rest of the hotels and to my knowledge there is no separate area of buildings where the staff live. I would guess that Aris would have reassigned her somewhere else after the other night to keep her out of Anisa's sight. Maybe that's why we haven't seen her around." Devin told Zachary taking a sip of his blood.

"Well, who's bartending then? I want a drink after that briefing with the Alpha." Zachary looked around the bar area for either a bartender or a waiter.

"I have no idea. I went behind the bar and got this myself." Devin told him indicating his own glass and Zachary got up and went behind the bar opening a bottle of whiskey and pouring himself a whiskey on the rocks.

Fred and Ric sat at the bar and Zachary pulled out more glasses and filled them a couple of fingers each, doing a little jig and flipping the bottle while he did it.

"You think you are auditioning for *Cocktail*?" Devin smirked at his antics, as Fred and Ric gave Zachary large grins.

"Well, I have had a lot of women tell me that I look like a young Tom Cruise, of course, my eyes and ass are nicer, and I am definitely taller." Zachary smirked in return. "Seriously, I am feeling really off since that blood-infested briefing." He swallowed in disgust. "I need a fucking distraction because it's going to take a lot of fucking liquor to wipe those images from my mind. It's bad enough finding the remains of those poor tortured bastards without having to look at the photos and watch the videos that those psychos took." He drank his whiskey down and then poured himself another shot immediately. "At least we burned their operations in Mount Olympus down."

Zachary's eyes squinted in remembrance of watching the orange-red flames flowing out of the windows of the front and licking the sides of the concrete building. He had watched the flames eating the evidence of the evil that the building had housed, along with the others as they had sat in the car across the road.

Zachary then looked up to see Mitch sit down with Vukasin, Nichola, Aleksei and of all people, the Naga, at a table. He pushed his bearded chin in their direction indicating them to Devin.

Devin looked over his shoulder at them, "Looks like the old dogs are getting along well." He stated taking another sip of his blood.

"Yeah, Vuk is going to sponsor the alliance at the conclave next month." Ric told him.

"I would hope so, the evidence we gathered was pretty damning." Castor said coming to stand next to Devin's chair, leaning close to tell him, "He told us that he has his beta checking in on some of the lone wolves in the area. There are not a lot, but there are a few, and they usually check in with him every month or so. He said that he hasn't heard from a couple of them for a while. But since they are not a threat to his leadership and not technically pack, he hasn't given it much thought." He looked at Zachary behind the bar. "Hey, Zach, since you are playing bartender, would you mind grabbing another green glass bottle like this one." He picked up the empty bottle in front of Devin and waved it at Zachary.

Zachary looked around behind the bar then shrugged his shoulders.

Devin gave him a put-upon look, got up walked behind the bar, and over to a backroom door off the far end of the bar. "I am sure they have some in the back." He told him entering the doorway followed by Castor.

They looked around for a few minutes finding numerous crates of several types of liquor, and a few bottles of cow's blood in blue bottles. Devin lifted a blue-bottle showing it to Castor and they both scrunched their faces up at each other.

"You know we are kind of blood snobs, right?" Devin said with a snicker as he put the bottle of cow's blood down and continued to look.

"Well, if cow's blood is all we have it would be fine, but there is no way that the villa doesn't have any porcine blood on hand. It's become immensely popular among our kind." Castor told him continuing to look at the various bottles.

"Maybe my mom has been guzzling it? She seems to like it too." Devin said with a short laugh imagining his mother on a pig's blood binge knowing that it would never happen; she was too prim and proper for such behavior.

"I doubt she's drinking it as much as you have been." Castor said with a snigger.

"It helps me keep from wanting to open up somebody's vein." Devin said sardonically.

"You should give it a try. There are blood donors here. I will join you and walk you through it if you would like. It's quite satisfying, in a couple of separate ways." Castor told him with a suggestive look.

"Nope. Not interested." Devin smiled at him continuing to look for the green bottles of porcine blood. "Besides, I don't think Anisa would be understanding." He slid Castor a knowing look; he was aware that often blood donors ended up being sexual partners during the act. He knew that everything was consensual, but it was still too new to think that blood frequently equaled sex and he wasn't sure how he felt about it. Also, he knew how Nessie would feel about the sex part and he knew that he didn't want to hurt her like that again.

Especially since he was still not having sex with her. He didn't want her to think that she wasn't going to be enough for him. Besides, since he had decided to stop fighting the soulmate bond, the thought of sex with anyone other than Nessie just wasn't all that appealing.

"How is that going by the way?" Castor asked Devin, though he didn't look at him directly as if the answer didn't make any difference and he was only making small-talk.

"Better now that I am not fighting it. When she isn't making me extremely horny, her presence actually brings me a lot of peace." Castor gave out a sharp bark of laughter as he searched, and Devin continued. "I like her, I mean I always have liked her, but I like this connection we have a lot more than I thought I would. It's not nearly as intrusive as I always believed. Being connected with her emotions in such a way…it's indescribable." Devin didn't meet the other vampire's eyes.

"I have been told it gets better and stronger, the longer your connection." Castor told him with something like envy.

"Do you ever think about…?" Devin let his question hang.

Castor chuckled bitterly. "What would I do with a mate? I kill vampire hunters for a living."

Devin moved a few boxes of various bottles around. "You get paid to hunt hunters?" He asked curiously looking over at the handsome, tawny haired, green-eyed vampire.

Castor nodded at him from further down the narrow storage room full of liquor. "The small council finances all of mine and my team's activities. Still it's not something that I would want to put a mate through. Don't get me wrong, it's an exceptionally good living, I want for nothing, and after three hundred years am wealthy in my own right, but I am nowhere as well off as you and your brother are, after your inheritance from William Burke. You are in a position to take care of a mate in a safe environment." Castor smirked slightly, holding his hands up to indicate the current situation. "Well, kind of. My life is dangerous like this all of the time. Yours hopefully won't be." He stood on a step stool to look at the boxes on top of a tall shelving unit.

"Did you know Billy?" Devin asked surprised.

"Not well, I met him a few times in London. But I liked him. He irritated Uncle Nikolaos to no end. He was brazen and American, and everything I have always imagined a cowboy would be." Castor smiled then walked to the very back of the long storage room. "Hey, maybe they are storing it in the walk-in refrigerator?" Castor asked walking over to the door and opening it.

"God, I hope not. Chef Joe says it's much better just bottled and room temp." Devin said coming up behind Castor who was standing in the doorway looking down on something. Devin looked around his shoulder to see what he was looking at and said, "Fuck!"

* * * * *

Devin yelled across the bar, "Nick! I need you and Uncle Man to come here."

Nichola who had been mid-sentence with Alpha Vukasin looked over at Devin in irritation. He took one look at Devin's face and realized that something was seriously wrong. "Please excuse me Vuk."

Nichola and Mansuetus quickly walked over to the bar's storage room and saw the light at the back of the long narrow room from the open walk-in refrigerator and headed that way. Both Castor and Devin were kneeling next to the bloody body of the vampire bartender that Devin had been intimate with a few nights before, which was now prone and lifeless on the floor of the refrigerator.

Nichola immediately knelt next to her and listened hard against her bloody chest. From the amount of blood surrounding her on the floor it looked like she had been stabbed several times and then left to bleed out.

Nichola looked at Mansuetus who looked shocked in grief. "Secure Leila and the Luna!" He commanded sharply and suddenly Mansuetus was gone with a preternatural speed, mimicking that of a vampire.

"Nessie!" Devin exclaimed in a worried whisper and also sped away.

As Devin hit the top of the second-floor landing he heard Castor sounding the alarm in the bar and quickly entered his suite to find that Anisa was no longer in the bed and instead saw a dark-garbed male figure standing next to it. Devin launched himself at him.

As Devin rolled around on the floor with the man, exchanging sharp blows, grappling for a handhold, he barely dodged a syringe that the man must have been holding and it buried itself next to his head in the plush carpeting of the suite. Suddenly, crashing glass poured over him and the man slumped on top of him, and Devin smelled human blood in the air. He looked up to see a panting, wild-eyed Anisa standing over them clutching the remains of a lamp that had been on the end table in the suite, tightly in her hands.

He stood up to embrace her tightly only to hear a moan from the floor and he turned sharply to deliver a swift kick to the human's head, pulling his kick at the last moment, and knocking the human unconscious instead of breaking his neck. He snatched the remains of the lamp from Anisa's shaking hands ripping the cord out of it and proceeded to tightly secure the man's hands behind his back.

"Where were you baby? Are you hurt?" He asked her struggling to keep his voice calm as he pulled the cord forcefully.

"I was in the bathroom. I am fine. I didn't even know anything was going on until I heard you two fighting out here." She told him in a quivering voice, as her small body started to shake and shiver in reaction to the violence that she had mete out.

He held her tightly against him, but only briefly, then grabbed her robe from the end of the bed tossing it at her. "You aren't to leave my side until I can get you into a secured area!" His voice was rough, and Anisa could feel both fury and fear through their connection. Devin knelt next to the unconscious man grasping him by the hair to growl out dangerously, "I should just end this fucker now!"

Anisa watched his fangs lengthen in his mouth in anticipation of the man's death.

"Oh, please don't." She begged him in a whisper not wanting to witness anymore death as she put on her robe.

"No." Devin said struggling valiantly with his emotions. "No, you are right. We need information from him." Devin grasped a leg and easily began pulling the unconscious man out the door. "Come on. Stay with me, baby. Careful of the glass. Do you have some slippers?" He asked Anisa over his shoulder solicitously as if this was just another day and they were heading for a stroll on the beach.

She suddenly knew that Devin was intentionally trying to keep himself calm to prevent her from freaking-out. She appreciated his efforts, but she was definitely heading in the 'freaking-out' direction.

She slipped on a pair of open backed tennis shoes that were next to the door and proceeded to follow him. He nodded approvingly at her actions. "Good. Keep an eye out for any other strangers until I can get you down to the bar."

"Aren't you going to pick him up?" She asked looking up and down the hall, as Devin pulled the hunter down the carpeted hallway ahead of her.

"Fuck no! I hope he gets carpet burn and breaks some fucking teeth on the staircase! It's the very least of what I want to do to him right this moment!" Came Devin's growl as he pulled him along.

* * * * *

They passed several armed security men, all vampires, who were coming up the stairs to secure the second and third floors of the villa.

"Would you like us to take him for you, sir?" One of them asked Devin.

"Nope. This bastard is mine." Devin replied with a growl. "Make sure that you check on the ladies convalescing and then carry them to the bar if they are unharmed. Don't you dare leave my side, Anisa!" He ordered as she started to head in the direction of her mother's room. With a wide-eyed look of terror at his back she continued to follow him.

As they arrived at the bottom of the stairs Devin barked out to Aris. "Aris, we are going to need cots or roll away beds set up in the bar area."

Nichola walked out of the bar to ask. "What are you doing Devin?" His voice was concerned as he saw Devin dragging the unconscious man behind him into the middle of the lobby.

"This villa is not secured." Devin announced coldly. "Exhibit A: We have a trussed-up hunter, a.k.a a former employee, down the hall. Exhibit B: We burned remains of another hunter who had made his way onto the villa's security detail, when we torched their hideout this morning. Exhibit C: We have a dead vampire in the cooler! Exhibit D: I have here by the leg." He gave the man a vicious kick in the ribs causing him to give out a small painful yelp and moan despite still being partially unconscious.

"This one was lying in wait to kill my mate in *my suite*. I put to you, Nick,"

Devin continued with a huge amount of sarcasm. "How did he know that Anisa was in my suite? This villa is not secured. We still have a mole here and we need to get our family into a central location to keep them safe! This fucker," Devin shook the man's leg roughly, "is going to tell me who the fuck it is or he's going to come to know that the shit they did to those shifters in their hideout was more like a game of Candyland than real torture."

By this time the doorway to the bar was filled with the others, including Leila and Zachary.

Nichola's face changed with several emotions: anger and anguish, being but two of them, then he gave a sharp nod to him.

Devin looked at his mom who was looking at him with frightened eyes. "Mom would you come and get Anisa please?" He asked her gently, and Leila came out into the lobby and wrapped her arms around a pale and obviously frightened Anisa, who clutched at her with a sob as Leila led her into the bar.

Fred walked out of the bar and Devin looked at him expectantly. "I'll die before I let anything happen to her, Boss." Fred told him solemnly.

Devin nodded and looked back to Nichola as he started to say something. "Nick don't try to stop me. I am going to find out everything there is to know this time." Devin's voice was calm and controlled, which was more frightening than if he was ranting.

"I'd be honored to help you, Anisa's mate." Ssytis told him as he walked out of the bar to join him looking down on him from his seven-foot height.

Devin nodded once and proceeded to drag the man down the marbled hallway to the strongroom that housed the other captured hunter, accompanied by Ssytis. The hunter regained full consciousness just as they turned the corner at the end of the hall and the others could hear his wails of fear clear into the bar.

* * * * *

Looking back over my shoulder at Ssytis, who was sitting with his arms crossed, looking bored, on a folding chair against the door, in deadly frustration, I wiped the blood from my hands with a cloth that Aris had provided me. Still they would need scrubbing when this was all done and over; my skin was stained, and the gore remained beneath my fingernails.

It was strange, being hands deep in human blood. I wasn't feeling any particular need or desire to drink this guy dry. The only thing I was feeling was a deep-seated craving to draw and quarter this fucker; slowly, joint by joint. He wasn't food. He was a threat. He had tried to kill my Nessie. The only thing I was fighting at this moment was the overwhelming need to just end him, whether he talked or not.

We had been at it for an hour, but this asshole I was working on was much tougher than the kid was. Of course, when you looked at the small amount of damage I had inflicted we had really just started, and if he didn't start talking soon, it would definitely get much worse. I personally hoped he wouldn't talk too soon.

The man's screams were fading to be replaced by sobbing moans.

"Tell me what I want to know and this all stops." I tell him intentionally keeping my voice gentle; knowing that it was a lie.

The boy from earlier was bound to a chair in such a way that he was able to see everything that I was doing to his comrade. His face was drenched in sweat, his pupils dilated in fear due to the adrenalin rushing through his veins and his body was racked in fearful shivers. The emotions that he was pushing through the air was just as delicious and fulfilling as they had been earlier. I looked at him briefly and he shrank away from me in terror.

"You can stop this too if you know the answer." I told him quietly.

"Don't you fucking do it, Johnny! Don't you fucking do it!" The man who was strapped to the table missing his fingernails shrieked out in a sob at the boy who was beyond his eyesight.

"Enough! You have decided to not be part of this conversation!" I told him abruptly, driving a slender, but sharp and deadly, silver stake that Aris had found in their rooms through the palm of the man's hand and into the table below, causing him to squeal in agony, and Johnny to start against his bonds in his chair. "I am so pleased that you are experiencing the pain and damage that these motherfuckers can do firsthand. Never thought that would happen when you brought them into our house did you?" I bent low, telling him over his squealing screams as his blood dripped to the floor, causing my nostrils to flare at the aroma. "I wonder how it will feel when I nail your dick to this table?" I asked him, then focused on Johnny. "I suppose we could see how Johnny responds to having his dick nailed to his chair first."

Johnny started shrieking also. "Stop it you sick bastard! Stop it!"

"Stop what? I have seen the films you fuckers took." I looked between the two of them and they abruptly stopped screaming, to look at me in shocked horror. The only sounds were the pained gasps of the man on the table. Johnny himself looked like he had forgotten to breathe as tears ran down his face. "Did you guys get off on cutting parts off of those shifters? Talk about sick fuckers. I haven't even started compared to what you fucks have been doing. I must say, those films were certainly inspirational." They focused wholly on me now in dawning desperation. "I am sorry, were you holding out for a rescue? It's gone, fellas. It's all gone. Burnt to the ground. The only thing I want to know is who else is there in this villa that works with you? Who killed the girl and dumped her body in the cooler?"

Their gazes became hard and unyielding.

"Okay, we can just kill all of the humans; there are only a few left that we haven't fully cleared anyway. We can torture every single one of you. Either way, we still get you all." I told them keeping my tone reasonable, as I studied their continued resistance, cold and detached on the outside, though I could feel myself becoming more furious by the moment.

Surprisingly, I think this fury of mine was what was keeping my bloodlust relatively at bay.

But, still, these hunters were really pissing me off! The fucking morons are causing their own pain and since they hadn't denied, at all, that there is still someone in the villa helping them; they are doing their utmost to protect them. Yet, they know that we have them in captivity now.

They know that they will all die sooner or later. So why take down other humans who are innocent; who have nothing to do with this? Who are nowhere near supernatural?

And, surely, they must understand that there are several ways to die? What would I choose? Quick and painless, or, bloody and in pieces? Since I knew that me and my comrades were going to die regardless, I think I would like to choose to die well if I had a choice.

"What do we care about a bunch of blood whores? They are either fucking and feeding you or profiting off of you. They are traitors to the human race!" The man on the table gasped then moaned as his fanatical, hateful speech caused him to spasm against the stake that still held his hand securely to the table.

Ssytis spoke behind me. "Little vampire, might I have a try?"

I turned to him, and he stood up as I motioned to them, "Be my guest."

"Like we give a shit!" The man on the table ground out between clenched teeth, steeling himself for another round of torture.

I looked at Johnny as he gasped, his body finally remembering to breathe. "You fucking vamps. You are all a like!" Johnny's voice a soft, hateful, panting.

Ssytis smiled widely at them both as I took his seat against the door. "You are mistaken, hunter!" He said stripping off his clothes.

Oh, my God! If he starts raping them with that double prick of his I am out of here! I am not sticking around to watch that shit!

"I am not a vampire." Ssytis told them and started to transform.

* * * * *

He was the most terrifying thing that I had ever seen in my entire life! Including that psycho that had killed Billy.

Unlike the wolf shifters, who when they transformed, simply 'swallowed' their human form in a symphony of growing hair, sinew, and shifting bone to become another creature quickly and seamlessly; Ssytis's transformation was an explosion of flesh!

It was as if a gigantic snake burst through his human body, leaving chunks of himself splattered on the floor as his form grew to at least nine feet tall, his arms lengthened, and his legs fused and lengthened into a ten-foot tail that flowed along the floor to support that nine-foot height; part of which was as wide as my waist.

He was red, scaley, the large hands at the end of his long, muscular arms were equipped with black, lethal looking claws, and his eyes which had always been a yellowish color, but still had retained the shape of a human in his human form, were huge, yellow, and bulgingly reptilian. His rounded head had twelve-inch fangs protruding like daggers from his mouth, just like a viper. His hair was gone because his human scalp was now on the floor along with whatever had remained of his human body.

I found myself on my feet gazing up at him as the hunters who had been in as much of a shocked silence as myself started screaming their bloody heads off.

"What the absolute fuck!" I whispered and he looked down on me giving me an unblinking, creepy look out of those baleful eyes; and I swear one side of his mouth lifted in a smile.

* * * * *

I laid in the small rolling bed curled up with my hands over my ears trying to shut out the now continuous horrific screams that were echoing throughout the villa.

The bed that Aris had provided, was set up next to my mother and Iris, who were recovering well. Both were conscious and my dad and Aleksei had perched themselves to hold them closely in relief.

Still, no one else in this bar where we had all been put to 'keep us safe' from the hunter threat, even seemed bothered by the continuous screaming! Even Zachary, Devin's brother, seemed wholly unfazed by what was happening. He just sat next to Fred and those wolf shifters from the ranch at the bar and drank! He's human too! You would think that this would bother him!

I just couldn't take it anymore. All of that screaming that was going on, every echo that flowed through the marble hallways of the villa, was driving me crazy and the fact that Devin was causing all of it was making my heart seize.

I leapt out of the rolling bed and ran out of the bar area.

"Anisa!" Zachary yelled sharply and Fred's corresponding, "Miss Anisa!", as I ran down the hallway toward the screams.

Then I could hear he and Fred giving chase, their cowboy boots beating out a rapid sound on the marble floors of the villa.

I might be small, but I am fast and had gotten a good head start; there was no way they were going to catch me before I got to my mate to make him stop this!

* * * * *

I heard a pounding on the door. That was okay. Ssytis and his stunt had secured us the information we needed. After the initial screaming had started Johnny cracked and started babbling at the top of his lungs, while the man on the table never stopped screaming.

We had a name for Aris of a barback who worked in the bar, a location of an apartment in town where several of them lived along with their names, and a location and names in the town where Ssytis had been staying. Even with my vampiric abilities I could barely write fast enough to record all of the information.

I opened the door, and due to the continuing din behind me, only realized at the last moment who it was.

"Devin Sutton! You stop this right now!" Anisa yelled at me launching herself into my arms. I held her tightly to me and glared over her head at Zachary and Fred who were running down the hall obviously in pursuit of her, and when my mother rounded the corner, I knew that Nick wasn't far behind. Zachary and Fred slid to an astounded stop about ten feet away looking above my shoulder to one side of the doorway.

I felt Anisa stiffen in my arms and then give out a stunned gasp as she stared up.

Following her gaze, I looked up and to my right to see that the Naga had poked his head through the door over my shoulder and was looking down at her calmly in my arms. His two-foot forked tongue flicked out of his mouth, tasting the air.

"Oh, my God, Ssytis! You are a mess!" She exclaimed with absolutely no fear.

She wasn't wrong. He was covered in blood and gore; of course, it was his own, but still he looked pretty nasty.

He gave her an unreadable look, lifting his snake lips over his fangs and teeth.

God, I hope that's a smile.

170

Finally Secure

I stood in the shower of my suite for several minutes letting the hot water flow over my skin, just relishing the heat and steady sound of the water. I finally grabbed a bar of soap to run it over my body to try and wash away all of the blood and frankly terrible and conflicting emotions of the past several days; at least those emotions of pleasure that I had gotten from torturing those humans.

I wanted to feel bad, I wanted to feel shame, I wanted to feel horror over what I had done. God, help me, if I could bring myself to do so. They tried to kill my Nessie and I didn't feel sorry for them. They got what they deserved; and as far as I was concerned it could never be enough.

It had been easy enough to get a confession out of the barback, on the murder of Trudy, the bartender; especially after he saw Ssytis's terrifying true form. I was ashamed that I had never known her name until after her death.

Aris and Vuk's Beta, Blackie, who had arrived on the scene while Ssytis and I had been enjoying our torture fest, and a few members of the wolf shifters and vampire security team had taken the hunters, loaded them into some vehicles, and left the villa. I had overheard Aris telling Nick that he would make sure that they all were never seen again, either dead or alive. Frankly, I didn't care enough to know the details as long as that was truly the case. As long as the shifters were involved, I felt certain that it would be.

I don't know how I feel about trusting Vuk's wolf shifters to make sure that the job got done properly more so than my own kind here at the villa. But, it is what it is.

Unbeknownst to Aris, Nick had watched him leave the villa with a hard gleam in his eye. It was evident to me at least, even if to no one else at the moment, that Nick had made up his mind for who to place blame for the security fiasco at the villa. If the only thing that Aris lost was his posh job of running the villa, I would be very much surprised. I knew that Nick wasn't one to forgive such a fuckup such as the one that we had dealt with over the past two days.

The only good thing that had come of it was the enormous amount of information that we had been able to gather on the hunter organization and their European affiliations. That information helped to secure Vuk's cooperation to not only present, but strongly advocate for, a vampire-shifter alliance. Which was fortunate, because Vukasin Vasileiou, the Alpha of the Skoteinó Fengári Pack, was a powerful force among the shifters of Europe.

With him as an advocate not only should the alliance pass, but it should thrive. He had also kind of adopted Mitch and had offered to send his own daughter to the ranch to be our doctor. She had just graduated from Medical School last year and he wanted to see her safely ensconced in America; where though we have hunters, they aren't considered to be nearly as hatefully rabid as the ones that are running around Europe.

Just like with human terrorists, things seem to be safer and their activities less prevalent across the pond. Seem being the optimum word.

Having such an alliance would be a good thing for my wolf shifters and a good thing for Vuk too.

According to Beta Blackie's report, he had sent pack members to the locations that Johnny had revealed and would grab up any of the other hunters, they had orders to handle them with extreme prejudice, and if the hunters returned to their burnt-out headquarters, the shifters would know about it and eliminate the problem.

Unfortunately, it seemed to both me and Zach, who viewed all of the activities with an intelligent and critical eye, like he always does, that the wolf shifters in the region were a hell of a lot more organized, secure, and prepared for a war than the vampires here were.

I am not sure what lesson to take away from that. Maybe age has something to do with it? At over three hundred, maybe Aris had developed a laissez-fare attitude about life and what could happen, which you know would be fine if he wasn't in charge of security for others.

Still it could be like Ssytis told me, while he was switching back into his human form, which thankfully was not as nasty to witness as switching into his true form was: *Sometimes the easiness of this modern life led you to forget your priorities where security was concerned.* He says that these modern times lull you into an attitude of safety; and you forget to make sure that you take the proper steps to survive.

Of course, I personally think it's because Aris is just a natural fuckup. Harsh? Maybe. But him listening to his dick over everything else almost led to the death of my mate; so, I am thinking not so much.

Anisa stepped into the shower with me, though her bruising was evident, they looked to be yellowing and she looked to be healing rapidly. I glanced surreptitiously at her still perfect, small, curvy body out of the corner of my eye and through the flow of the water on my face. She had her long, golden-brown hair pulled into a high ponytail to prevent her hair from getting wet; obviously she wasn't here to get clean herself, she was here for me.

I felt her small hands run along my back as I leaned on the wall of the shower in front of me. She took the soap and ran it over my back to massage my tired muscles and while I appreciated her efforts, if she knew how badly that I wanted to be fangs and balls-deep in her right now she would be nowhere near this shower.

She reached around me to stroke my hard cock and I barely held back a moan. I turned around to face her, knowing that my eyes were red, and my fangs were out. She didn't even flinch.

Fearless. My Nessie is fearless.

I reverently cupped her beautiful face and looked deeply into her gorgeous blue eyes and brought my lips down gently onto hers; careful not to pierce her perfect pink lips with my fangs. She never stopped stroking my cock with her soft, small, and when she touched me like that, perfect, hands. When she gently cupped my balls I couldn't help but groan. Okay, if she wanted to give me a hand-job…who was I to tell her 'no'?

* * * * *

I feel so tired, but I just can't sleep.

Devin didn't seem to have that problem.

I laid next to him with my head propped up on my hand watching him while he slept. I wasn't sure when the last time it was that Devin had slept, though according to his mother, he needed to sleep more because he was a young, developing, vampire.

Even though young vampires seemed like full vampires in many ways, they needed to sleep in the beginning because their bodies were still in transition, and it actually took months and sometimes years before that transition came to a conclusion. Rest as well as having plenty to eat helped them with their bloodlust; helped them to maintain their control. His mother had told me that even she still slept every day and when she did, she sometimes, slept extremely hard, almost as if she entered a phase of stasis.

I could believe it looking down on Devin's face. He hadn't moved at all since he had exhaustedly climbed into our bed after his shower a couple of hours ago; almost like he was comatose.

He seemed so young while sleeping. I gently smoothed one of his long chocolate bangs away from his eyes. Well, I guess he was, young. I knew he was only twenty-seven, but there were often times that he seemed so much older. I think that is because of everything that he had experienced since his transition began and I could sense that he really tried to keep himself under control; especially where I was concerned.

Then there were times when he acted like such a teenager! Especially when he was goofing around with his brother, Fred, and those wolves. He and his friends had even adopted Castor Blood as one of their peer-group. I smiled thinking about how close he was with them all.

I tried really hard not to be jealous of him and his friends. I had never known another male vampire to seek out other male companionship like

Devin did. My Dad didn't have any close friends other than Mr. Tsoukalous and Aleksei; still it was almost always just he and my mom; and I knew it was the same way with Devin's mother and Mr. Tsoukalous.

Maybe it was generational? Maybe it was just all Devin? Maybe it would change once we had been together longer? This was still so new between us and there had been so many bad, crazy things happen since it had started.

Still, he didn't seem to be in any hurry to make love to me. Sometimes I think that he really wants to, but he is holding back for some reason.

I want him to make love to me. For a lot of reasons. I want him to mark me as his. I want him to want me; like I want him.

I want him to need me.

I want him to love me.

I worry that he doesn't, and this connection is just something that he can't resist anymore; and so he finds himself just stuck with me.

Maybe, I am just being silly because of everything that we have been through? Maybe, I am just overthinking it all.

I hope that is most likely it. I want to believe that it is.

"Your worrying is keeping me awake, Nessie." He suddenly said softly.

I gasped, "Can you hear what I am thinking?"

"No. But I can feel you worrying." Devin said opening his eyes lazily to look up at me calmly. "You don't have to worry about anything, my Nessie, everything is going to be okay." He smiled softly and reached up to stroke a finger along my cheek thoughtfully and his pecan-colored eyes were warm.

There were times that he was so sweet.

* * * * *

The guys looked up from their breakfast to see Devin and Anisa walk into the dining room hand-in-hand. He was wearing a tight grass-green t-shirt that emphasized the cut muscles of his chest and abdomen, with his normal boot cut jeans and cowboy boots and she was dressed in a soft peach-colored long sleeve blouse and matching knee-length flowing skirt and brown flats.

The peach color emphasized her light tan skin, sparkling blue eyes and the slight blush on her cheeks as she looked around the dining room sliding a glance to where her mother, father, Leila, Nichola, Vuk and Louve, and

Iris and Aleksei sat as Devin easily pulled her over to his table.

Fred grinned widely and rushed to bring an additional chair to the table to sit next to Devin's chair, bobbing his head at Anisa who smiled shyly at him, as Devin settled her into the chair.

"Good morning, Ma'am!" Fred beamed at her, his hazel eyes shining, as he sat on her other side.

"Ma'am." The wolf shifters nodded to her with smiles.

"Good morning, Anisa." Zachary said looking up from his tablet on Devin's other side with a soft smile, then taking a sip of his coffee.

"Miss Anisa." Castor told her with a pleased grin.

"Good morning, Anisa and Anisa's Mate." Ssytis said with a smirky smile. Devin gave him a slight eyeroll in return.

"Good morning, everyone! You are looking much cleaner this morning, Ssytis." Anisa said to him cheerfully smiling widely.

Ssytis returned her grin.

* * * * *

"Don't they look well together!" Esmeralda gushed quietly nudging Leila's shoulder with her own.

"I must admit they do." Leila smiled in return.

"How will she handle all of those rugged, handsome men?" Iris asked quietly with a humorous little lilting sigh in her voice, her eyes gleaming naughtily.

"Auntie!" Leila exclaimed. "You are being bad." Though her voice held a threatening giggle.

Louve gave out a coughing little giggle, her eyes sparkling.

The men just glanced at each other as if in long-suffering patience and continued to eat.

* * * * *

"Did they ever find the porcine blood?" Devin said to Castor.

"Yes." Castor held up his glass.

"Did they test it to make sure that it didn't have any poison in it?" Devin asked looking around for a waiter, then turned back to Castor when he didn't answer.

Castor had a concerned look on his face.

"I am sure it's fine." Devin told him quickly.

"I hope so since I have been drinking it all morning!" Castor exclaimed worriedly.

Zachary burst out laughing and Anisa chuckled, covering her mouth with her fingertips in humor at Castor's slightly fearful look.

Nelson suddenly walked over to the table.

"Wow! Buddy!" Devin exclaimed standing and holding out his hand. "What are you doing here?"

"I got in a couple of hours ago. Lord Tsoukalous requested that I come to help out with some staffing issues." Nelson said with a smile grasping Devin's hand. He and Devin had become fast friends over the proceeding months in Peru, and he had helped both Devin and Fred contain, and move when needed, their traveling poker game. After all he was an excellent majordomo, and always knew what was going on in his hotel. "I wanted to come over and offer my congratulations, personally, to you and Miss Anisa."

"Oh, thank you, Nelson. That is truly kind." Anisa told him tearing up slightly.

"I thought we would have a special evening of dancing after dinner tonight if you would like." Nelson told them. "I am expecting several guests through out the day to be arriving and a small event would seem to be appropriate."

"I don't know Nelson. This place isn't like Peru. I am not sure that they have a full-time band. I have only seen them play once the whole time we have been here." Devin told him. "I wouldn't want to bring in any strangers after all of the problems that we have had."

"Master Devin, I assure you that the villa has a full-time musical staff onboard. Just like all of the other residences. Let's see if we can get them to play nightly like they are supposed to." Nelson told him with a slight smile and a gleam in his eye. He grasp him lightly and affectionately by the shoulder and bent to kiss Anisa's fingertips gently, giving Devin a reassuring smile as he made his way over to the older vampires.

Devin sat back down next to Anisa. He was so happy and frankly relieved that Nelson was taking security of the villa in hand. It was like a weight was lifted from his shoulders and he could actually relax with his little mate, instead of constantly being on the lookout for things that might kill her.

He glanced speculatively at Anisa as she laughed at something that Fred was saying to her.

"You mean that you are a teacher?" Mitch suddenly chimed into their conversation.

"Well, I just got my secondary education certificate last June when I finished my internship." Anisa told him. "But I was considering going back to school for my master's degree and becoming a school counselor instead."

"What's a secondary education certificate?" Ric asked.

"Well, in my case that means that I can teach through high school level. I specialize in English. But when I started out I was considering being a math teacher." Anisa told Ric and Mitch's eyes gleamed.

"Uh-oh." Zachary said with a smirk.

"Uh-oh?" Anisa asked him in bewilderment.

"Yes, honey." Devin said leaning back and smiling softly, putting his arm along the back of her chair, and looked over at Mitch whose gaze was fixed intently on Anisa. "I think that you are about to get a job offer from the Alpha of The Diamond Wolf Ranch."

"Who is that?" She asked Devin curiously.

"Me." Mitch told her with an ingratiating smile.

"You are?" Anisa looked at him confused.

"Yes, ma'am. And Miss Anisa, our little ones sure could do with a good teacher on the ranch."

"But don't they go to school now?" She asked him slightly concerned.

"Of course they do, ma'am. But it is a local human school and as you know they ain't human. It's like they don't fit in with the other kids, you know, because they are keeping a big secret. It makes it hard for them to have friends. Also, we always have to worry about their safety outside of the ranch." Mitch told her looking sad. "It would be so much better and safer for them to be able to go to school on the ranch. You know with a real teacher helping them learn. Somebody who understands what they are. Somebody who they don't have to pretend with."

"Oh." Anisa told him. "I can see how that would be ideal."

"See how he slid right in there, right in for the kill." Zachary murmured to Castor and Ssytis.

Mitch ignored him. "You don't have to decide right now, ma'am. We will all be going home after the conclave next month. 'Course you will be living there too; seeing how you are the Boss's mate and all. You can take a look at the situation when we get home."

"I will absolutely consider it, Mitch." Anisa told him sincerely. "Maybe Devin could build a schoolhouse for the children?" She looked at Devin sweetly.

"I am not quite sure how I got roped into this." Devin told her, then smiled at her when she reached over to hold his hand.

* * * * *

"Would you like to go for a walk on the beach?" Devin asked Anisa, then looked up to find his mother, aunt, Esmeralda, and the Luna standing around the table.

"No. We are taking her." Esmeralda told him.

"Taking her? Where?" Devin demanded.

"To the spa for a relaxing time with us ladies." Iris smiled compellingly.

"But…" Devin started only to be cut off by his mother.

"Nelson says that we will be having a celebration tonight. It takes time for we ladies to prepare." She smiled at Devin who gave her a disgruntled look. Leila looked at the other men at the table dressed in their jeans. "You gentlemen will be expected to dress for dinner this evening." She said with a smile. "Mr. Ssytis, I am not sure if you have a suit, but these gentlemen can take you to the tailor if you need one made." Leila told him with a smile.

"Thank you, Lady Tsoukalous." Ssytis told her graciously, surprising the rest of the table.

"You gentlemen have a productive day." Leila smiled at them as Iris pulled Anisa from her seat.

"Mom!" Devin protested.

Leila reached over placing her fingers beneath his chin, bending to give him a small peck on the cheek, telling him softly, "I love you, Devin." He gave her an annoyed look out of clove-colored eyes, and she whispered in his ear this promise, "You will thank me later."

He watched the women hustle his little mate out of the dining room crossly, and Anisa turned back briefly to give him a small, sad, wave. He waved back briefly in irritation, a frown on his handsome face.

"God, I love women!" Ssytis burst out jovially with a chuckle.

"Me too!" Fred told him with a laugh, while the rest of the men looked at them in confusion.

"What do you mean? They just hijacked my mate!" Devin said.

"Anisa's mate, when she is returned to you this evening she will have been primped and pampered, her hair and skin will look and feel like silk, she will be dressed beautifully, and she will smell so good you will want to eat her..." Ssytis sighed as if in remembrance.

"Sounds to me like they are getting her ready for a sacrifice!" Ric said appalled.

"Only Anisa's mate can answer that." Ssytis told him with a sly grin.

"You should get her a piece of jewelry, Boss!" Fred said. "Women love jewelry."

"That is true." Zachary murmured sipping his coffee engrossed in his tablet.

"What would you know about it?" Devin demanded.

Zachary looked at his brother to tell him calmly. "Quite a lot actually. I love women, more importantly, they love me." Zachary smiled largely at Ssytis, who returned his smile.

"I have this problem also, my friend!" Ssytis told him.

The rest of the table groaned loudly.

* * * * *

"Come Devin, we are going into Katerini. Vuk's Beta has called, and he has secured the employee that poisoned the women during dinner." Nick commanded approaching the table.

"You are not worried about security here at the hotel?" Devin asked in concern.

180

"No. The pack is spread throughout town and have supplemented the day security here at the villa." Vuk told him with confidence.

"I might as well go with you then." Devin told him, as if he actually had a choice. "It looks like I need to go to the jewelry store though."

"Oh, good! Women love jewelry." Nick told him with a smile.

"Diamonds are usually a good gift." Vuk told him advisedly.

"Anisa likes something called rose gold." Rom told him clasping him around the shoulders affectionately as Devin stood up and they all headed into Katerini leaving the others behind.

The Realities Of Being A Mated Vampire

I was trying to tie my tie and not doing a particularly decent job of it, and on top of that, I seemed to be surrounded by idiots.

My brother, Castor and the wolf shifters were lounging in my room waiting for me to finish getting ready and they were all disgruntled over the fact that they had not received personal invites to go into Katerini with the others. If I would have known that they would be such babies about it I would have just taken Nessie tomorrow to the jewelry store and let her pick anything she wanted in the store; then they could have come along!

"You know what the issue is, don't you?" Zach, who was lounging in one of the oversized chairs in the sitting area of my suite, was telling me as I struggled with my tie. "They were just softening you up to lead you to slaughter!"

"What are you talking about?" I replied with a roll of my eyes looking at his reflection in the mirror. I just couldn't help it, he was being so dramatic!

"Yes. They are all mated. They are happy to see you leg-shackled also. Misery loves company. So, they are happy to see you join their exclusive little club!" He stated emphatically.

"Oh, my God!" I muttered, starting over with the tie in frustration. For some reason I found myself inordinately nervous about this evening. It was like I was getting ready to attend my own wedding and these guys weren't helping my nerves!

I understood that tonight was important for Nessie and me; for the vampire community it was the first real function that we would be attending together as acknowledged soulmates. Thinking about it like that, I guess it was kind of like a wedding! That thought didn't make me feel any better.

"That's probably true in a way." Castor said reasonably. "There are so few mated pairs."

"Even amongst shifters." Mitch interjected.

"Yes, even amongst wolf shifters." Castor agreed. "Let's face it. You being mated is kind of special in our communities. Especially since you are such a young vampire. I have been around for three hundred years, around all kinds of females, human and vampire, and nothing even close like it has ever happened to me." Castor nodded in a sage way. "And I have never seen it happen from start to finish to anyone other than you. When you are together, you and Anisa resonate.

I can actually feel it in the air. I felt it this morning at breakfast. It's the same feeling I get around Rom and Esmeralda, and Uncle Nikolaos and your mother when they are in the presence of each other. So, the others are probably really happy to have another mated male around."

"That's probably true. I feel something similar when Vuk and his Luna are together. It's like an energy connection. If you are paying attention, you just feel their connection strum throughout your body." Ric said with a nod of his dark head.

Mitch nodded in agreement.

"From your perspective you should consider this a good thing. You have other males to talk to if you have questions about what is going on with you." Castor told me sincerely.

I threw my hands up in defeat. I couldn't get this tie right!

"Here let me." Zach stood up and came over to tie my tie quickly and easily in a perfect half-Windsor.

"Hey, that looks pretty good, brother." I said admiring the tie which was almost the same blue as my Nessie's eyes, in the mirror.

I glanced at the guy's reflections behind me. We all made a pretty handsome group of young men in our finery. I smiled at them all as I put on my silver two-toned suit coat, smoothing it over my black suit pants and looking down at my shiny black dress shoes making sure that they weren't scuffed.

I held my arms out to them.

"Well?" I asked nervously.

Castor and the wolves nodded eagerly in approval.

"Well, you won't embarrass her at any rate." Zachary said with a smirk next to me.

I punched him in the arm and the others grinned.

These guys were my friends and family, and I was glad that they were here with me.

"Where the hell is Fred?" I asked looking around realizing that my companion was nowhere to be seen.

"Oh, he has the best job tonight." Ric said with a huge smile.

I looked at him in confusion.

"Yeah, he's on 'lady duty'." Zach said with a funny twist of his lips and a light chuckle. "It's something that Uncle Man told him. He says that now that Fred has a lady to look after he needs to make sure that she is taken care of before you. So, you are basically on your own now, Dude. Anisa is officially more important than you, where Fred is concerned anyway. He is taking his new job very seriously." Zach laughed.

"Strangely, Brother, that actually makes a lot of sense to me." I told him smiling in return.

* * * * *

"Oh, my, God!" I said breathlessly. "I can not breathe!" I said as my mother held my hands tightly and Iris pulled on the strings of this torture device that they had me laced into. "Why do I have to wear this?" I panted.

"Because Devin is going to love to remove it from you!" Iris said with authority.

"I really don't think he cares!" I said with a gasp to Iris. "I can't even believe that I am able to wear this at all." I told them breathlessly as they pulled me. "I could barely move yesterday morning!"

"That is because you are healing like a vampire." Louve the Luna told me.

"Yes. That is because you are in close proximity to your mate. You are picking up some of Devin's vampiric healing abilities. It is one of the good things about being mated, especially for a human." Devin's mother explained patiently as Iris finally tied the strings.

They had tortured me all day. I had been steamed, waxed, buffed, painted, washed, dried, and curled and my tolerance level was almost zero at this point. Now they were trying to take away my breath with this damn corset!

"Honey," Devin's mom said to me. "It's a special night, which deserves special clothes and special activities. He probably doesn't care right now, but I guarantee you he will appreciate it and remember it fondly forever." She smiled at me as she brought me over to sit at a table in her room to start applying makeup to my face.

"And Anisa, this is so much fun! If we were at a larger resort, we really wouldn't get to do this together. We would have hair and makeup people to help with all of this. This is so much better because you have all of your family around you." Mom said to me encouragingly, and I could see a slight sheen in her eyes like she was tearing up.

"I remember when we were in Florida, Es." Devin's mom said with a happy sigh applying my foundation. "I was so nervous that night, though I didn't really know what was going on."

"Oh, I remember, Nikolaos took one look at you and didn't want to go into dinner!" My mother laughed devilishly. I had never heard her laugh like that before. "Speaking of which, Ani, Devin will take one look at you and decide for an early evening also. Don't let him get away with it! He can wait to open up his gift. Waiting is half the fun!"

"I can barely breathe, let alone eat, mother!" I exclaimed.

"Anisa. Think about it this way. If you open all of your gifts on Christmas Eve, it makes Christmas Morning anticlimactic. The excitement is built by the wait." Devin's mom gave me a sweet, knowing smile.

"If you think so, Lady Tsoukalous." I murmured.

"Call me Leila, sweetie. You are my son's mate after all." Now she was starting to tear up also.

My mother stood on the other side and held open a rainbow case of eyeshadows for Leila to look at. Iris stood behind me with a beautiful dress so that Leila could see it as she viewed them.

"I think this one." She pointed at one of the colors to my mother. "It is a couple of shades darker than the dress and will bring out the blue in her eyes."

"I agree." My mother told her, and I saw Iris nod behind me in agreement.

"And with this." Louve held out a tube of lipstick.

"Oh, yes. That's lovely." Leila said to her, her eyes lighting up in excitement and my mom and Iris nodded enthusiastically.

Of course, no one asked me my preference. I was just the Barbie doll along for the ride.

* * * * *

"Fred!" I exclaimed walking out of the suite with the other ladies.

Fred was looking very handsome, his normally wild straw-like hair was slicked back, and he was dressed in a very smart dark gray suit.

"You look nice! What are you doing here?" I asked noticing for the first time that Mansuetus was also with him in the hall, and he was also looking very handsome in a dark blue suit.

"We are here to escort you ladies to the dining room, ma'am." Fred said with a soft smile as Mansuetus held out his arms for Leila and Iris, and Fred held out his for me and my mother. "Let me be the first to say, that you look very beautiful, ma'am." Fred smiled reassuringly as I found myself suddenly incredibly nervous.

Nessie Is A Monster's Name

My heart lurched in my chest. I had never seen anything so heavenly beautiful in my entire life.

Nessie was coming down the hallway on Fred's arm dressed in a long champagne-colored silk gown, gathered beneath her soft breasts, a la grec, with a fashioned flowing silk sash that cascaded over one of her lightly tanned shoulders and down her back, leaving the other shoulder and both of her arms bare. Her golden-brown hair was gathered on top of her fine head, with several long ropes of curls dangling over that bare shoulder seductively.

God knows how I envied those curls that brushed her peachy silken skin! It was exactly where my fingers itched to be.

Castor and the wolves, who had been waiting impatiently with me, were stunned into silence.

"Wow!" I heard Zachary say next to me in awe.

Such an understatement.

I was aware as Rom took hold of Esmeralda's hand and led her away to their table, smiling at first at his daughter and then in my direction. But I could not take my stunned eyes from my Nessie; and as a widely smiling Fred led her forward to me, her gorgeous, striking blue eyes never left mine.

"You are exquisite, my Nessie." I told her softly reaching to take her hands in mine; and I meant every word. I had never seen a woman more lovely in my entire life.

As the others left to head to our table, she blushed in response, raising a hand to my lapel smoothing an imaginary crease, and said, "You look very handsome tonight too, Devin." She smiled shyly at me, but I had never heard her use such a seductive tone before.

I leaned down to look at her striking eyes with hunger. "I can order something up to the room." I struggled to keep myself under control, but it was extremely hard, along with other things.

She gave me a beguiling smile. "I think we should stay for a while." Her hand ran over the hard, velvet covered, jewelry case in my inside breast pocket. "What's this?" She asked tapping it with her fingers, and curiosity lit up her cerulean eyes.

I smiled widely. Under this seductively beautiful exterior there was my sweet, curious, little thing. "It's a gift for you." I told her and she smiled up at me.

"You got me a gift!" Her melodious voice was suddenly excited. "Oh, but Devin! I didn't have time to get you anything today." Her blue eyes dimmed a little.

"Baby, you are my gift." I murmured giving her a soft, brief kiss on her luscious peachy-pink lips. Reaching into my pocket, I pulled out the long black velvet box and opened it so that she could see it.

She looked down on the rose gold diamond tennis bracelet in awe. "Oh, Devin, it's gorgeous."

"Not nearly as gorgeous as you deserve, my Nessie." I told her sincerely.

Each stone was a perfect half caret and sparkled brightly in the light of the dining room. It had cost me more than my truck, but looking at how she tenderly looked at me, I knew that it was worth every penny.

I had also started a little trend, since the other's decided that they should buy jewelry also. I think our purchases made the store owner's year.

"Here let me put it on." I told her removing the bracelet and looking around for a place to put her box, suddenly Fred was there to take it from me, slipping the empty box into his pocket with a smile then disappearing.

If he thought being on hand for 'lady-duty' meant that he was moving into our suite he had another think coming.

I fastened it around her left wrist, and it looked beautiful against her lightly tanned skin. I smiled as I gave her small hand a brief kiss and then led her to our table with all eyes in the dining room upon us. With her by my side, I felt like the luckiest man in the world.

* * * * *

When we were finishing dinner, I noticed several strangers in the dining room.

"Who are all of these people?" I whispered to Devin as he sat next to me drinking his blood at the table. I had noticed that he and Castor both ate food and drank blood openly around me. My parents had never done so, at least not that I had ever been aware of.

"Most of them are members of the Skoteinó Fengári pack. That man there is the Beta," Devin nodded toward a rugged man with pitch black hair, even blacker than Ric's. "That man next to him," he nodded at a ruddy looking man with reddish blonde hair, "is the Gamma."

"What's a Gamma?" I asked quietly, curious. I knew what an Alpha and Beta were but had never heard of a Gamma.

"He's the third in command of the pack. The Diamond Wolf Pack's Gamma is a guy called Lenyx. He's back home overseeing the construction projects and keeping an eye on the ranch."

"But some of these new people are vampires." I stated in a whisper looking around curiously.

"Several people arrived this evening from Ukraine. Everyone is afraid that some sort of war is going to break out there. I don't personally know about that, I don't really pay any attention to geopolitics. But the concern is enough for many of the vampires of Ukraine to go on an extended holiday. I heard that several of them have plans to leave for the hotel in London or the one in Egypt and this is just a stay over thing. Though Nelson is expecting several guests to be moving in and out over the next several weeks." Devin told me, then continued.

"Nick is insistent that conflict is about to break out. Vuk and the shifters agree with him. Originally we were coming here to hang out for a bit with mom and Nick and we were going to head to the shifter conclave in Kiev. But then the location changed to Skopje because the small council and the shifter council are convinced that something is going to happen. Either way, even if they are wrong, Skopje is better for us because it is closer to the villa. So, with everyone kind of nervous about whatever is going on, we will probably get to meet a lot of new and interesting people before we have to go to Skopje." Devin smiled at me reassuringly.

"Do I have to go to Skopje with you?" I asked nervously, I had been around vampires for most of my life, since my birth parents had been murdered, and knew how to behave with them. But except for Mitch and Ric, who acted just like everyone else, I was still a little nervous around shifters. "Can't I just stay here while you go and do what you need to do?"

"Nessie." He said gently, coaxingly. "It will be fun. Besides, after everything that has went down recently, I am not sure when I will be comfortable with you staying anywhere when I am not there." He smiled at me, holding my hand tightly.

I tried to smile at him in return calmly; though I kept finding myself increasingly nervous as the night went on.

"Would you like to dance?" He asked me suddenly, standing to pull me up without waiting for an answer.

He led me to the dance floor pulling me close to him with a strong leading hand on the small of my back.

Don't be nervous my Nessie.

I heard his voice in my mind and looked up into his smiling reddish eyes.

I am going to take exceptionally good care of you. I promise.

* * * * *

I am trying really hard to be reassuring towards my little mate. I know she is growing more nervous as the night is wearing on and though I am not picking up any specifics, I can guess why. She barely ate anything tonight at dinner and I thought about ordering her a glass of wine, but I had made plans for later this evening and really didn't want her to be too drunk.

It has been really difficult holding back my eagerness for this night to be over; though I don't think that she has noticed with all of her nervousness

190

flowing through her. My cock trembled slightly in anticipation of finally making her mine; and if not for the length of this jacket it might be quite embarrassing.

Sitting next to her as she enchanted our whole table was something to see. I had already known that she was smart and funny, but I never realized how sweetly elegant that she was. How disarmingly charming and graceful she could be. As I had sat next to her and especially now as I twirled her around the dance floor in my arms her scent of chocolate, popcorn, and figs weaved her spell of desire around me until I was intoxicated by her by the time the song ended, and everyone was leaving the dance floor.

Please tell me that you are ready my Nessie. I ache for you.

She nodded at me shyly as I took her hand and led her out of the dining room.

As soon as we hit the lobby I grinned down at her and scooped her into my arms, which caused her to squeal in laughter and using my vampire speed ran us up the stairs.

She bent down from my arms and opened up our door and I entered our room, kicking the door closed behind us.

She laughed hard as I sat her down gently on the floor inside the doorway of the suite, "Oh, my gosh! I have never moved so fast in my entire life!"

I smiled at her looking at her back in hunger as she walked into the suite to gasp out in surprise and then I reached behind me to lock the door securely.

* * * * *

From the surprised, overwhelmed look on Anisa's face, Devin was glad that she had wanted to stay for dinner.

Because Nelson had outdone himself.

There were red rose petals sprinkled over the floor of the suite and over the bedspread of their bed. There were crystal vases of long-stemmed red roses throughout the suite and a dozen more roses in a crystal vase on the tray next to a chilling bottle of champagne; knowing Nelson it was probably the absolute best he could find in the wine cellar. Which means it should be something incredibly special.

He leaned his shoulder against the wall as she turned around the room

191

watching her turn in a circle to look around the suite in wonder.

She finally turned to him with tears in her eyes, "Oh, Devin, it's beautiful." Her voice was a breathy whisper.

He pushed away from the wall to lightly pull her against his body. Reaching to stroke his thumb against her cheek he said, "I told you, my Nessie. This is what you deserve." He bent down and took her lips with his own to kiss her tenderly, suddenly pulling her tightly against him to deepen the kiss only pulling back when he felt her tremble slightly against him. He smiled down into her eyes briefly, then told her, "Let me pour you a glass of champagne. Oh, I am supposed to tell you that your mom left something in the bathroom for you."

"Devin," She said in a tremoring voice as he started to head for the champagne. "Would you unzip me?"

He met her eyes suddenly with a flash of hunger and she lowered hers demurely and presented her back to him. He slowly moved aside the sash and then grasp the zipper firmly and lowered it leisurely down her back. He gently kissed her bare shoulder, breathing deeply of her scent as he moved his face through the silken curls resting on her shoulder.

Suddenly, he stepped away from her, saying softly, "Let me get you that drink."

Blushing deeply, she practically ran into the bathroom.

* * * * *

Ani,

I wanted to tell you how much I love you and how proud of the young woman that you have become. May you have a wonderful life with your soulmate! It is something that your father and I always wished for you.

You should know somethings about soulmates. Sometimes it may be hard. This is the closest that you will be with another living being and Ani, sometimes it may be awfully hard. Sometimes you may need time and distance from each other. And sometimes you may get bored with one another, especially when you have been together centuries.

Sometimes you may hurt each other. It may happen over insignificant things, important things, and even ridiculous things. There will be many hard discussions

between you over the centuries; remember even though you are soulmates you are
still two different people. Always be honest with each other, and importantly with
yourself. When you are wrong, say it. Be slow to condemn and quick to forgive.
Learn from mistakes and move on and be gentle with each other.

Because, Ani, Devin will be the only person that you will ever truly crave: his
scent, the way he feels, his soul.

Each day together may not be perfect, but I can tell you from experience that you
will find having a soulmate to be the most wonderful thing to ever happen to you.

Remember, Ani, you will always be my little girl no matter the passage of time
and I will always love you.

Mom

I felt the tears flow over my cheeks to land on the deep cleavage of my breasts, bound up in this torturous corset.

I looked up and Devin was standing in the doorway, with a concerned look on his face. His coat was gone, his dress shirt was open, and I could see how tan his smooth skin looked against the whiteness of the linen shirt. I looked down and his feet were bare, and suddenly I found myself smiling widely.

I ran to him wrapped my arms around his neck and with little resistance from his now shocked countenance pulled him down to kiss him deeply. He hesitated for all of three seconds before pulling me to him with a groan and then lifting me up wrapping my legs around his waist to carry me back into the bedroom.

"What in the world do they have you trussed up in, Nessie?" He asked. "No wonder you are crying! You must be in terrible pain!"

"I am fine, honey." I laughed as he sat on the bed placing me on my feet in front of him to turn me around between his knees to face away from him and start undoing my stays. Right now he was my god! "Your mom says that I am healed because I have borrowed some of your healing abilities." I looked behind me as he was speedily working on the stays. "I think you are supposed to be taking them off slow and sexy like." I giggled as he gave me a look.

"You are beautiful in this get up, but you are also beautiful in anything. If you were in sackcloth, I wouldn't want you any less than I do right now." He frowned in frustration at the stays. "Okay, slow and sexy is going to have to wait for another day. Who in the world did up this mess?"

"Your Aunt Iris." I gasped as he gave it another tug from behind.

"She's probably laughing her ass off right now." He grumbled and I looked behind me to see one of his thumb nails grow.

"Don't you dare cut them, Devin! I think that you have loosened them enough. Here." I ordered and turned around to face him so he could undo the metal loops and studs of the front closure.

"This is better." He said undoing the fasteners from the top down with his strong fingers. He did slow down when he realized that he was exposing my breasts with every loop and stud. "Oh, this is much, much better." He growled softly and buried his face in my deepening, exposed cleavage, breathing me in as he kissed my skin gently.

I wrapped my arms around his head with a smile kissing the top of his silky head.

* * * * *

He ran his hands down her smooth silk encased legs, then back up to unhook her garters from her stockings, never removing his lips and nose from the skin of her breasts. He slid the silk stockings down her legs and as she lifted each leg to help him, off of her tiny feet. She kept her arms around him holding his head close to her, giving little sounds of encouragement.

Sliding her panties down her legs, he returned to work on the metal loop and studs of the front closure on the corset. Adjusting his arms and removing them from the sleeves as she pushed his shirt from his muscular shoulders.

Soon the corset ended up with the other articles of their clothing, laying upon the rose petals strewn about the floor and she stood naked before him. He ran his hands over her, looking for any leftover bruising. Ensuring that she was unharmed he finally fastened his lips over one of her pink-tipped breasts with a groan, running his large hands over her rounded plump ass.

"Oh, that feels good." She whispered to him as he suckled her, holding his head tightly against her.

Soon she was running her hands over the solid muscles of his back moaning softly and he softly stroked the fingers of one of his strong, long fingered hands higher and higher up the silky skin of her inner thighs; eagerly wanting to touch a small piece of heaven.

Suddenly, he gripped her outer thighs and stood up with her to turn and lay her back onto the middle of the rose petal scattered bed.

He looked down letting his gaze rove over her lightly creamy-tanned body and met her cerulean blue eyes warmly with a gentle smile, standing at the end of the bed, his hands undid the waistband of his pants and let them drop to the floor. They were quickly followed by his black silk boxers.

Her eyes widened at how long, hard and intimidating his cock looked.

"Don't be scared, my Nessie. I told you I will take very good care of you." He told her sweetly as he put a knee on the bed to crawl up and over her.

He softly stroked up and down her body, becoming firmer on each pass of his hand causing her to gasp in desire and he took her lips in his, kissing her deeply, stroking his tongue against hers, sucking on her tongue and lips and exploring her mouth lazily with his.

Finally she felt his large fingers slowly stroking between her legs, gathering her wetness on his fingertips to spread and rub over her clit, causing her to raise her hips up to seek his hand.

I am going to make sure that you feel so good, my sweet Nessie.

"Oh, Devin!" She gasped out against his lips hearing his voice in her head and her legs fell open like the unfolding of a flower to his exploration of her body.

He ran his fingers gently up, over and around her clit as she felt a deep need take hold of her belly, and her hips moved in the rhythm that he was playing on her body as she moaned out her pleasure.

As she felt the first wave of her orgasm overtake her, she felt his finger fully enter her causing a little pain which was soon forgotten as her body clenched tightly around him and she gave out a small cry.

He slowly steadily stroked her pussy, as his thumb glided gently over her throbbing clit. Her hips moved in time to his strokes.

Again, my sweetheart, again.

She felt him enter a second finger, stretching her, and applying pressure to her clit. She exploded around his fingers with a soft sob, drenching his hand in her juices.

He removed his hand from her, and she could feel him stroking her juices over himself and then he was stroking the head of his cock against her pussy, running the head over her clit causing pleasurable ripples and spasms throughout her body.

He thrust slightly with his hips, groaning faintly and she felt the head of his cock enter her body, causing her to gasp and her body to stiffen at the intrusion.

There will only be a small pain this first time, my lover.

His voice in her head was reassuring, seductive, soft, and totally in control.

She wrapped her arms around his waist, sliding her hands along his hips, to grasp his ass suddenly thrusting herself up his length, piercing her maidenhead with a small cry of pain.

"Jesus, baby!" He gasped, as he scented her blood, his nostrils flaring and suddenly looked down into her eyes; his eyes red and fangs extended.

"Don't hold back, Devin!" She demanded of him totally without fear.

He gripped her hips tightly to thrust deeply, fully seating himself in her pussy with a harsh groan and his control shattered.

She wrapped her legs around his thighs and held him to her as he thrust shallowly into her.

He fought against his instincts, trying to give her time to adjust to his length as he ground against her clit with his pelvis causing her to cry out with need as she brushed her lips against his shoulder, running them along his neck.

Every gasp, every cry from her sweet, sexy lips was driving him to the edge.

"That's it, Nessie, take me." He whispered encouragingly into her small, shell-shaped ear as he lengthened his thrusts, steadily grinding against her clit as she gripped his ass guiding his strokes, pumping herself against him.

She could feel herself tighten around his length, and suddenly she saw stars, as she cried out, coming around him, pulsating up and down his stroking cock.

He stroked against her several times pulling the longest orgasm from her body to finally thrust himself deeply into her with a sharp cry, and she felt him pulsate within her as he came hard, his body shuddering against her as he buried his face in her hair along her neck.

I will always be yours, Nessie, just as you will always be mine. I love you, Nessie.

His voice flowed strong in her mind, and a tear flowed from the corner of one eye in relief as she held him tightly to her, kissing softly over the line of his jaw, her heart overflowing with her love for him.

* * * * *

Anisa woke up to a darkened room, only illuminated by the light coming from the opened bathroom door and Devin lying next to her gently washing her between her legs with a very warm washcloth.

He squinted slightly at the blood on the cloth, before tossing it across the suite and through the bathroom door to land on the tile.

His eyes were warm as they met hers. "Are you okay?"

"I'm fabulous!" She giggled at him in happiness.

"Yes, you are." He smiled at her. "Let me rephrase the question. Are you sore?"

"Maybe a little. But I am sure that you can make it go away." She smiled wrapping her small hand behind his head to pull him down to her lips.

He pulled her close against him as he plundered her sweet soft mouth with his.

"Have I created a monster, Nessie?" He asked her with a groan against her lips as he felt her hand encircle his half-hard cock and stroke it firmly.

"You once told me that Nessie is a monster's name." She laughed against his lips.

He was enchanted with her happiness which caused a joy to spring forth in his heart as he pulled his insatiable monster beneath him once more.

Bowling Anyone?

Castor looked at Devin and Anisa's empty chairs at the breakfast table the next morning with a look of curiosity at Zachary.

"I wouldn't expect them to come up for air for at least a day or two." Zachary told him calmly taking a bite of toast.

"I tried to check on them this morning." Fred said meekly.

The others looked at him like he had rocks in his head.

"He threatened to shoot me through the door." Fred told them.

"I would expect so." Mitch said then looked at Ric sharply with a growl. "I would expect people to leave me alone with my fated mate for at least a few days."

Ric looked at him offended that he would even think that he would do such a stupid thing. "Of course, Alpha."

Mitch nodded at him.

Ssytis walked into the dining room with a tall, elegant, beautiful blond vampire, with snapping black eyes. He escorted her to a table where a pretty, young, flame-haired human woman sat. She looked to be slightly older than Anisa. He bent low over the vampire's hand turning it at the last moment to place a lingering kiss along her wrist. The vampire woman sighed deeply. Ssytis stood to give the young woman a small nod and made his way over to the table sitting in his designated chair in between Castor and Mitch.

"Did you have an enjoyable time last night, Ssytis?" Zachary asked quietly, giving him a knowing perceptive look, as Ssytis motioned over a waiter.

"Very." He said with a slight smile then noticed Castor who was still looking over at the table where the beautiful blonde vampire sat with the red-head.

"Who is that?" Castor whispered to him.

"The Countess Catherine. She and I are old friends." Ssytis told him with a satisfied smile.

"No. I know the Countess. Who's the girl with her? A companion?" Castor had shaken himself out of his reverie to look at the Naga.

"The Countess says that she is her granddaughter. I believe that her name is Katja Frost. Until recently, they had been residing in Kiev. Nice girl. The Countess is inordinately proud of her; she has a good head for business she says." Ssytis told the table sipping the coffee that the waiter poured for him.

"She's pretty." Zachary stated generally. "That's good, maybe we will have somebody to dance with in the evenings, since Devin is going to hog Anisa to himself at least for a few days. It is going to be awfully boring around here until we go to the conclave in a couple of weeks with just you guys." Zachary told them typing on his tablet. "We got to figure out something to do! Going to the gym and walking the beach is not going to cut it."

Castor nodded his head still looking over at the table, a puzzled look on his face.

* * * * *

I looked up from my tablet to see my mother, Iris, Es, and Countess Catherine and her granddaughter standing next to our table.

I stood up, basically because if I didn't I knew my mom would gripe at me about how atrocious my manners were. It seemed like manners were everything in the vampire community.

Everyone behaved well.

Well, until they didn't.

Let's face it, these creatures had fangs, claws, moved super-fast, and had a sometimes insatiable thirst for blood; as well as other attributes depending on the individual.

They could be extraordinarily dangerous.

But if they needed structure, like extreme, and sometimes very old fashioned, displays of manners to keep their shit together; who was I to balk their system or the way their community operated?

Especially since it could actually be mine one day.

Might as well try to learn it and fit in, at least until I figured out what I wanted to do with my life.

Since my mother became a full vampire, at least when she was without Nick, she always seemed to be surrounded by other women. In all my years of her raising me, she never had more than a few select female friends, one or two close friends at the most. Now, she ran with a posse most days.

When I got a moment I had plans to ask her why.

"Good morning, mother." I said smoothly.

She gave me a proud smile and introduced the Countess and her granddaughter to the table.

The granddaughter shyly nodded her head to me and the guys as I introduced them. She seemed a little out of her depth like she hadn't been around a lot of people, other than her grandma for a long time. I kind of felt bad for her. As a human surrounded by vampires and other supernatural creatures all of the time, I knew it was a lot to take in.

One on one, like with me and my brother, or with me and my mom, or even me and Nick? That was okay. But totally surrounded by a bunch of others who were not only strangers but supernatural to boot, and on top of that being the odd man out? That could be a little overwhelming. Especially for a kid. I pegged her at about twenty-one now that I was looking at her closely.

She's younger than I originally thought she was when I saw her from across the dining room.

"Zachary, the ladies and I are going to have a spa day." Mom was telling me with a smile.

Not sure how to answer her, since I wasn't sure if 'spa day' was code for hanging out and feeding from humans, I smiled in return and said, "That's nice."

"Can Katja hang out with you gentlemen today?" She asked sweetly with a purr to her voice.

Great, my mother seemed to be plotting something.

I looked over at Katja, who was as red as her fiery hair in embarrassment.

"Sure." I said happily as if I would love to hang out with strange girls all day.

It was best to deal with my mother in an affirmative manner when in mixed company to avoid later scolding.

My mother gave me a kiss on the cheek smiling sweetly saying softly to me, "You are the best of sons."

"I know." I replied steadily.

"Just don't tell your brother I said so." She said saucily with an impish grin that was a twin of my brother's, her teal-colored eyes sparkling with mirth. I was quite aware of where he got that attribute of his character.

I pulled out a chair for Katja and she sat down in resignation and the vampires filed out of the dining room.

Once they were out of earshot, she said, "Listen, you guys don't have to babysit me."

"You are an American!" Castor exclaimed in surprise. He had been giving her his intense vampire stare since the ladies had approached the table.

"Yes." She said with long-suffering patience. Obviously, this was something she had heard a lot. That would make sense with her living in a foreign country like Ukraine.

"Nonsense." I said replying to her statement. "We are going to go into town today and go bowling anyway, you might as well come a long."

"Bowling!" Fred and the wolf shifters exclaimed excitedly.

"Yes. I found it on my tablet when I was Googling what to do in Katerini. Why not? There is not a lot to do here in the villa. Might as well get out and see the town since it is more secure now."

"I heard about your recent problems here." Katja told me. "We were having some problems in Kiev ourselves with a hunter group."

"Yes, I know, if Uncle Nikolaos had allowed me and my team to stay for a while longer, we could have taken care of that problem for you." Castor told her, looking at her with his continued intense look. "I don't believe I have ever been 'bowling'." Castor said turning to me.

"That is not surprising to me." I told him.

He seemed to be one of the oldest, most dangerous, most inexperienced creatures I have ever met.

All business and no fun.

I actually felt bad for the guy.

"How about you Ssytis? Want to go bowling?" I invited the Naga.

My brother was really grateful to him for saving Anisa, and seemed to like him a lot, despite his scariness. I might as well get to know him better myself.

"No. You youngsters have fun. It is a bright, shiny, and sunny day out. I think I am going to change into my true form and nap on the beach." He told us with a large smile.

Fred and the wolf shifters made little faces as their eyes bulged slightly at the information.

I personally didn't want to think about the details of that or the mess that it would leave behind. I had heard enough from Devin and seen all I wanted to see of that.

"That sounds nice." I said encouragingly as he stood and left the dining room.

Fred opened his mouth to speak, and I held up a finger at him. "Don't say it." I told him glancing sideways at the girl.

"Do you think that I have time to change into a pair of jeans?" Katja asked and I looked at her light green blouse and skirt.

For some reason, vampire women and even most of the wolf shifters, all wore skirts when at the resort. I failed to see the reason why, other than to show their beautiful legs off.

I have to admit, I have been seeing some very pretty female limbs lately. Her grandmother had probably insisted that she dress 'appropriately'.

"Absolutely, I have got to get a car set up with Nelson in any case." I told her with a smile, and she got up and headed out of the dining room.

I noticed that Castor was still watching her intently.

If he was going to be weird, he was staying here.

"Dude, you're being a creeper. Knock it off." I told him.

"What?" He asked in surprise.

"I don't know what your fascination is with that girl but keep your fangs in your mouth and your dick in your pants. She's just a plain old human; not a blood donor and you are being obvious. We will be out in public today, and I don't want any trouble." I told him bluntly.

Because he had truly little experience with humans, other than as a food source, sometimes you just had to be candid with Castor.

Saying as if appalled at his behavior, "I was obvious?" He placed a long-fingered hand on his chest in surprise.

"Yes!" Ric told him.

Mitch and Fred nodded in agreement.

"Okay. Sorry." He told us all sheepishly.

* * * * *

It was kind of strange walking into Efkarpidi Polychoros, the Bowling Centre and Billiard Parlor in Katerini with these five guys. It looked just like any megaplex that you would see in the states; bright neon lights, glossy lanes, lots of games.

As I had learned from Zachary, he was a human, Castor was a vampire, Fred was a companion, and Maverick and Mitchell were wolf shifters, which was kind of a shock as I had never met any shifters at all since I had been living with Grandmother over the past two years in Kiev.

And now this mixed group was going bowling.

It was very surreal, but at the same time kind of nice to be normal too.

It had been a long time since I had been around normal.

I knew that Mr. Ssytis was something weird last night when he escorted Grandmother to her room. I just figured that he was a really old vampire.

Come to find out that he was some sort of a snake man called a Naga!

Just the thought of my strait-laced Grandmother getting her groove on with a snake man was enough to freak me out.

I wonder if she knows?

Fred seems to be really different from all of my Grandmother's companions. They seem to be really dull compared to him. He is almost like an independent human.

I couldn't believe when they told me that he was Zachary's brother's companion! I know that my Grandmother's companion, Karl, would never like to be too far away from her unless ordered.

Karl would probably be here with me now if it wasn't that Lady Tsoukalous's son was escorting me.

Zachary seems like he is okay. He seems to be really relaxed and self confident around everything that I have referred to for the last two years as 'the weirdness factory'.

I found out that the celebration that was going on when we got here last night was because of his brother and his new mate, who just happens to be human.

That is really strange, and I had to admit to myself interesting.

I hope I get to meet her soon.

I didn't even know that vampires had mates, though I met two more this morning when I met Lady Tsoukalous and Lady Esmeralda. All of the vampire ladies that I met this morning behaved perfectly normal.

In fact, most of the vampires that I have met since moving to Kiev to live with my Grandmother have pretty much acted the same way.

Exceedingly polite, but wholly uninterested.

Which is good, because Grandmother always tells me to not allow myself to be alone with any of them, because mostly they are not to be trusted.

Grandmother says that I am a human after all, and even though I come from vampire stock, most vampires would be tempted to take a nip if they could get away with it.

Grandmother says that to some of them it would not matter that I am not a blood donor. So, I am to always be on my guard.

She also told me that I probably will be very safe at the resort.

The rules are strictly enforced at the resorts, blood drinking from humans is strictly consensual. Any violations of the rules and the vampire will lose resort privileges.

Which to them is a profoundly serious thing because there are very few resorts in the world, and vampires, generally don't mix in public places like they used to.

They generally keep to themselves and their own kind.

Which is why it has been uninteresting living at Grandmother's home, even though for me it is a foreign city.

Because she is a vampire, and really cognizant of making sure that I am safe, we don't really do a lot and when I go out by myself, even during the day, I always have one of her companions, usually Karl, trailing me.

So, though I would never tell her because she has been really worried and exclaiming like Chicken Little for the last week and a half that *The Russians are Coming! The Russians are Coming!*, I was really excited to leave Kiev for my very first stay at a vampire resort.

Beyond the odd vampire gathering, which I found very tedious, living at Grandmother's was very boring.

So, even though I am going bowling, which I haven't done since I was a kid, it was wonderful to be doing something different.

Something normal.

Something human.

Even if it was with a bunch of guys, the majority of which, were other than human.

Though out of all of the guys I am with, that Castor guy seems like he's a little weird.

I almost fainted when he walked right out into the sunshine today when we got into the limo.

I have seen vampires deal with sunshine before, but it usually includes long-sleeves, pants, overcoat (no matter the temperature) hat, gloves, sunglasses, and an umbrella.

Regardless of the protections, it is a big deal and braving the sun is only done when absolutely necessary.

Now, it seems like you could get a treatment and as long as you protect your eyes, the sunshine isn't much of a bother.

The vampires of the resort are really different compared to my Grandmother's friends; they seem more modern and they are very human-like; and so far seem really pleasant.

But then again, I have learned that most of them seem that way.

Until they are not.

I have noticed that Castor guy staring at me a couple of times this morning with a strange look when he thought I wasn't paying attention.

Though, he seems to have gotten over whatever his problem was since I got changed and met them all in the lobby to leave.

Still, I hope he doesn't make me have to bash him over the head with something because he is very handsome, and I really don't want to create a scene.

My Grandmother would not be pleased.

* * * * *

I try not to alert the others that I am watching her.

Especially Zachary who is watching me with the sharp eyes of a hawk.

But there were times that I could not help myself.

When she walked down the stairs in her tight black jeans I became fascinated with her long curvy legs, rounded ass, and neon pink tennis shoes which matched her neon pink crop top giving the illusion of still longer legs.

I had never seen a red head intentionally wear pink that shade before. Her fashion sense was original and seemed to work for her.

I couldn't stop myself from watching her intently as she slipped on a black canvas jacket that was not quite long enough to cover the luscious curves of her ass.

Though not a tall woman, unlike her Grandmother, she was still about four inches taller than Anisa and much smaller than I.

Still her legs were long in proportion to her body almost as long as my own. I wondered briefly what they would feel like wrapped around my waist.

I quickly schooled my gaze to one of nonchalance.

Though I found her absolutely fascinating.

Her eyes are so green.

Like the green of a jewel and flash with a beguiling intelligence and her long wild curls are like flame.

Her hands are slender and lovely, even unadorned by jewelry.

Her small nose is straight and slightly upturned at the end and cutely perfect.

Her lips are dark red and when she smiles they frame straight, white teeth.

Her skin is flawless and unfreckled, not like you would find in most red heads.

She is not classically beautiful.

Not at all.

Still I am entranced, and I find myself wondering what the rest of her looks like.

* * * * *

"These shoes belong to other people!" Castor was telling Zachary appalled.

Zachary was looking at him like he was losing his patience as the man behind the counter watched with interest.

"Dude! It's bowling. You rent the shoes!" Zachary told him.

"Are they vermin free?" Castor demanded of the man behind the counter in fluent Greek.

"Yes sir. We disinfect them after they are returned from each patron." The man told him steadily.

"Why don't you get him a new pair of socks?" Zachary said to the man as Castor scowled.

"Shoe size?" The man asked Castor.

"Forty-four." Castor replied sullenly then took the shoes and the socks from the man.

"And you miss?" The man asked Katja.

"Thirty-eight." She replied taking hers also.

"She needs a new pair of socks too." Castor told the man dangerously and the man handed her a pair of ladies' socks.

"I was okay, Castor." Katja told Castor in surprise.

"Used clothing always carries vermin. Trust me on this." He told her sincerely.

"Okay." She answered him giving him a small unreadable side look.

"Fine. Get us all new socks." Zachary told the man with a slight note of exasperation and the man smiled seeing a large, unexpected profit coming his way for sales of the day. "But you are going to have to help us Americans convert into Euro Sizing."

"No problem, sir." The man said with a large smile.

* * * * *

"I thought I told you I did not want to draw unnecessary attention!" Zachary told Castor as they took their things to their assigned lanes.

"Vermin! You do not know what it is like to have vermin crawling on your body because you are unfortunate enough to have to wear other people's clothing." Castor was starting to go on a tangent and drawing more attention.

Zachary could feel his skin start to crawl at Castor's insistent description.

"Fine. You. Are. Right. I don't." Zachary enunciated in a hushed voice. "Now come over here I am going to show you how to bowl. Which before you get any ideas of throwing a heavy bowling ball into those pins down there with your superior vampire strength, rolling it on the lane is required." He looked at Mitch and Ric. "That goes for you guys too."

"Don't worry about us. We know how to bowl." Mitch said with a grin.

"Good." Zachary said with relief.

* * * * *

"I do not know why it is continuing to go into the gutter!" Castor yelled in exasperation, his light green eyes had long ago turned red in frustration and the only reason why I hadn't called this outing to an end is because we pretty much were the only patrons in here.

"It is doing that because you are pushing it into the gutter!" Ric said throwing his ball and getting a 7-10 split. "Damn!"

"Castor," Katja said to him, and the vampire was suddenly directly, supernaturally, before her, all attention that she should call on him, looking down into her dark emerald eyes with his creepy intense stare. She blinked up at him in surprise at the speed of his response to her. "What hand do you write with?" She inquired sweetly and calmly as if speaking to a person who was on the edge of a rooftop and about to take an unfortunate leap.

He held his left hand out to her silently and she looked at me.

"Jesus! You are throwing with the wrong hand, buddy." I told him.

"I am throwing it just like you are." He told me with irritation.

"But, buddy, I am right-handed! Try doing it with the other hand."

And due to the fact that Castor was well-endowed with super-ultra-supernatural grace, that was the last bowling game that any of the rest of us won.

* * * * *

They were heading over to play some pool when Castor suddenly exclaimed, "Ah, billiards." Then he looked at Katja. "Women don't play billiards."

She nodded at him and gave him a dangerous look, to which he seemed oblivious, then said in general. "I am going to go and wash my hands. I will be right back."

"I will attend to you." Castor told her starting to follow her.

Zachary stepped in front of him. "No you won't. Fred." He nodded at Fred who followed Katja, sedately, smart enough to give her some space.

Castor glared at Zachary affronted.

Zachary returned his glare with steely blue eyes his arms crossed over his chest.

"Do you like that girl?" Zachary asked him quietly.

Castor was startled by the question. "She's nice."

"Yeah. Uh-uh. Then quit being a dick." Zachary told him.

"What?" Castor asked.

"You heard me. You are being not only a creeper, but you are being obnoxious. That girl was not born in the 1700s! She was born this century and she's an American too. She has rights, and the last thing a man should say to a woman of this century is that she can't do something. She can play pool if she wants to." Zachary told him harshly.

Castor looked disgruntled for a moment, then said, "Okay."

"Okay." Zachary started to walk away, then turned back to tell Castor, "And when we get back to the villa, get something to drink, because your eyes have been red for a while now and if you freak out in public, I am not taking you out with us anymore!"

"Okay." Castor said sullenly.

They waited a few minutes for Katja to get back with Fred and then headed toward the billiard rooms.

Castor stepped in next to her, "I apologize." He said to her quietly. "I am not used to modern women."

She looked at him. "It's okay." Then walked a few paces faster and turned slightly back, her green eyes flashing fire. "But don't let it happen again."

Castor was wholly entranced.

* * * * *

"This is bullshit!" Fred leaned over to say to Zachary as they watched Castor once again running the table to trounce Ric at pool. "He's cheating! He's using his vampire abilities!"

"That's rich coming from you! That's why no one will play poker with you anymore." Mitch murmured on Zachary's other side.

"Yeah! Well, my skill is developed over a century and thousands of hands of cards!" Fred defended himself.

"Well, he is a vampire. And he says that he learned to play billiards when he was a young man at Oxford when he was living with Uncle Man and Nick." Zachary said quietly to the two of them. "That doesn't mean that he is unbeatable." He looked to Katja with a small smile who was standing next to them waiting to play Castor.

She smiled at him conspiratorially.

Katja, was quite good, and had held her own against the four of them. Leaving only Castor left to play.

Zachary had been impressed with her pool skills and they had a plan.

* * * * *

"Where did you learn to play pool?" Zachary had asked her when they were playing together, and she had sunk her third ball in a row.

"I grew up in Stanford, Connecticut and played a lot of pool when I was growing up. I graduated early and went to Cambridge for school." She paused to look at the table trying to select a shot. "I didn't quite fit in. Probably because I was so young, and I was away from home for the first time. So in my spare time from studies, I played a lot of pool."

"Cambridge? You went to MIT?" Zachary said impressed.

She laughed bitterly. "Well for a couple of years. I didn't graduate. I am not a rocket scientist. I didn't get a scholarship or anything. My dad was a businessman in New York and Grandmother paid my tuition. I really went to MIT because it was close to home, but not still home if you get my drift." She smiled at him. "And I am pretty good at math."

"So why didn't you graduate?" He asked curiously.

"My parents died in a small plane accident in the Bahamas on a business trip the summer after my second year. I was actually supposed to have gone with them, but I didn't feel like it." Her voice was bitter for a moment. "As you can imagine, hanging out on a hot beach is not my thing." She held up one pale arm. He smiled gently at her in sympathy. "So, I stayed home." He stayed quiet as she tried to make her shot and missed. Sighing, she looked at him. "After their death, Grandmother came and 'collected' me. Seems like I am the last known member of her human bloodline. I had no idea that Grandmother was even a vampire before my parents died, because I had never met her. My father just always referred to her as his Ukrainian Grandmother."

She stepped back as Zachary was picking his shot. "I have been staying with Grandmother ever since. Mostly now, I help oversee her business interests and invest her money. I have found I am rather good at that also." She gave Zachary another smile.

"I tried to take a couple of classes at the University of Kiev when I initially moved in with her. School was fine but being around humans with this secret is difficult. It's hard to have friends over to the house." Katja smiled bitterly. "Then of course my Grandmother can be all up in my business. You should see her when I want to go on a date with somebody. She's like all Sherlock Holmes on them." She laughed, making a little dramatic terrified face.

"I know, I got a mom." Zachary laughed with her. "And I agree. It is a hard secret to keep."

* * * * *

Castor, even though he was beating everyone at pool, was not happy with Zachary and Katja speaking and laughing together. He realized that they may have a lot in common, both of them were humans after all.

But he found that he did not like her attention being on anyone other than himself.

He tried to shake this from his mind. He had no claim on this particular female; not that he wanted one.

She was human and he just wasn't used to dealing with human females in a social setting that's all, his small amount of time with Anisa aside.

She was just a different human, like Anisa was. They were both off limits for food.

Still, Castor had never felt about Anisa like he was feeling about Katja and since she was not food, he didn't like this feeling.

He didn't like it at all.

* * * * *

"Just because you are female, doesn't mean that I will go easy on you." Castor was telling Katja arrogantly chalking up his pool stick.

"I don't expect you to." She returned softly doing the same to her stick while the other men looked on; Zachary was grinning widely at the exchange.

"I tell you this, because after your defeat, you may feel the need to cry. Do not be ashamed of it. Females frequently cry." His voice held a note of sympathy.

She looked at him suddenly out of fiery emerald-green eyes. "You know I had almost felt sorry for you." She murmured dangerously and he gave her a confused look. She swept her hand towards the table, "It's your table."

He looked at her arrogantly setting the cue ball in the middle of and slightly left in the table's kitchen and bent over to take aim to take his break shot.

She leaned forward at the very last moment to whisper in his ear breathlessly, "Don't miss!"

Castor abruptly hit the cue ball with surprised force, missing all the other balls that had been racked up and sending it sailing off of the table.

Ric, Zachary, and Fred ducked and scattered, and Mitch snatched it from the air with one of his large hands just before it would have crashed into the wall.

"Nice catch, Jeter!" Zachary told him with a grin, which he returned.

"My turn!" Katja sang out and taking the cue ball from Mitch proceeded to run the table.

* * * * *

Castor, who glared at all of them throughout the limo drive back to the villa, had been furiously silent about his defeat to Katja. As the limo doors were opened by the doorman, he climbed from the vehicle to stomp through the entrance just as Devin and Anisa walked down the stairs hand-in-hand.

"Hi Castor!" Anisa said brightly.

Ignoring her he yelled out as he stomped up the stairs, "Nelson, send a donor to my room!"

"Of course, Master Castor." Nelson replied looking at the others curiously who were walking in and grinning widely.

"What's up with him?" Devin asked Zachary and they all started to laugh.

"He's in a snit because he got his ass handed to him by a girl." Zachary leaned close to his brother saying softly as the others laughed loudly. "And one that he likes."

"Really?" Devin looked at Zachary in surprise and Zachary nodded with a smile.

"Hi! I'm Anisa, are you human?" Anisa was asking Katja brightly.

"I'm Katja. Yes, I'm human." Katja gave Anisa a small bashful smile.

"Oh, that's wonderful!" Anisa smiled widely and hooked her arm with Katja's and led her into the bar area. "Did you and the boys have a fun time? What did you do? Where did you go?"

Zachary and Devin watched them head into the bar with Fred and the wolf shifters following closely.

"She's very friendly." Devin said with a smile about his little mate.

"Yeah, she is. I'm a little surprised to see you already. So?" Zachary asked with an interested look and a raised eyebrow to his brother.

"Bro, I am not giving you any details." Devin told him with a secret smile. "But this break is really for me. She's exhausting me, man."

"Are you happy?" Zachary asked grinning and putting his arm around his brother's shoulders.

"Yeah." Devin gave him a large smile and a half hug in return. "Really

213

happy."

Then they followed everyone into the bar.

Making New Friends

"**I** like her." Nessie whispered to me as I assisted her into a chair at a table in the bar a couple of days later.

"I know you do." I said with a smile.

"It's nice having another human girl around."

"I am sure it is." I agreed with her.

"When all of this wolf shifter business is over with we should invite her for a visit to the ranch." Nessie told me.

"Can we put it off for a while? I would rather be alone with you." I whispered in an intentionally naughty voice into her ear, giving her a small kiss on the neck to which she giggled seductively in return.

"Guys! Get a room!" My brother said coming into the bar with the guys and Katja carrying the poker chips and cards.

I gave Nessie a suggestive look, motioning out the doorway with my head to which she replied, "You stay right there, Devin Sutton. I want to learn how to play poker!"

"Yes, ma'am." I replied with a grin.

She and I have had so much fun over the past few days just being together and especially waking up in each other's arms every morning.

She has brought joy, love, and laughter into a life that I had previously thought held only boredom and booze for me.

She has showed me a better future and I was embracing it wholeheartedly.

So after teaching her to bowl and play pool over the last couple of days, which by the way she was terrible at, but it hadn't made any difference because she still had so much fun doing it, I was now supposed to teach her how to play poker.

* * * * *

"What are they doing in there?" Nichola asked Leila as he heard the loud laughter coming from the bar as they left the dining room. He poked his head into the bar, and said with irritation, "Are they gambling in my villa?!"

He headed into the bar with Leila rolling her eyes behind his back and following on his heels.

"Are you teaching these young women to gamble?" Nichola demanded to the men around the table, who looked up at him.

"No, sir, we are not." Zachary told him firmly. "We are teaching them how to play poker. These chips are not backed by money. Everyone started out with the same number of chips, the person that has the most chips at the end of the evening wins the game."

"That sounds suspiciously like gambling." Nichola said.

"It isn't even close to gambling. It is strictly playing a card game. No money, no gambling." Devin told him with irritation. "Haven't you ever just played a game for the thrill of winning?" He asked giving Nichola a look.

Nichola stopped to stare at him a moment.

Leila pulled on his arm, "Nichola, stop harassing these young people." She had managed to get him halfway back to the door and then Zachary's voice rang out.

"We originally tried to get them to wager articles of their clothing, but you'll be glad to know that they refused to do so." The whole table burst out in laughter then ducked their heads, as Nichola's back stiffened in offense.

"They're being scandalous!" He told Leila in a harsh whisper.

"Yes, and you are being kind of a prig. Come back to the suite and I will teach you how to play strip poker." She told him with a seductive smile.

"Just the two of us?" He asked with a leer, his amber eyes lighting up at the suggestion.

"Of course." Leila giggled in a whisper.

He scooped her up into his arms with a sharp laugh and carried her away. Devin and Zachary just rolled their eyes.

＊ ＊ ＊ ＊ ＊

"Your mom is different than I thought she would be. She and Lord Tsoukalous seem to be really nice." Katja said to Zachary and Devin as she concentrated on her cards.

"Yeah, he's a pain sometimes, but she's crazy about him." Devin said his arm around the back of Anisa's chair as he looked at the five cards in her hands.

"This one?" She fingered a card looking up at him.

"No, this one." He pointed out another card to her.

"I'll take two." She told Fred, pulling two of the cards from her hand and sliding them over to him. Fred dealt her two cards from the deck in his hands and as she placed them in her hand, she got a large smile on her face.

Katja and Zachary groaned as well as the wolf shifters.

"I fold." Katja said throwing in her cards and the wolf shifters followed suit.

"Ah! What?" Anisa said.

"Sweetie, you have a tell." Devin told her not bothering to look at her cards.

"I do?" She asked.

"When you smile like that everyone knows that you have a great hand."

"But I win the pot, right?" She asked innocently.

"Yeah, baby, you win the pot." Devin said as she held her hand out to him to inspect the cards and Fred pushed a stack of chips at her which she gathered up with glee.

"Nessie, these cards are terrible." Devin told her taking the cards from her to study them, and the others stopped complaining to each other to pay attention to their conversation. "What were you smiling about?"

"I won the pot, right?" She asked him looking sideways out of the corner of her eyes and he saw a particularly impish glint in her blue eyes as she made little stacks of chips in front of her.

The others looked at each other in surprise.

217

"Oh, Nessie! You are so bad!" Devin told her taking her face in his hands to kiss her deeply.

God, he loved her so much.

* * * * *

Castor finally showed back up at breakfast the next day.

"Haven't seen you around for a couple of days, buddy. Everything okay?" Devin asked as Anisa sipped her coffee smiling briefly at Castor.

"I just needed some down time." Castor told him briefly, surreptitiously looking around the dining room.

"She's not down yet." Zachary told Castor not looking up from his tablet. "I hope that you aren't going to make an ass of yourself today." He finally looked up to pierce Castor with his hard blue-eyed gaze.

"I won't." Castor told him emotionlessly.

"Good. Because she's a nice person and you have no reason to be weird around her. It just makes everybody uncomfortable." Zachary told him.

"I understand, and I won't." Castor said seriously.

And Castor was being sincere.

He had pierced more veins and plowed more female bodies in the past two days than he normally did in three months and felt fully satiated and totally in control. He had determined that his reaction to Katja had to have been because he was feeling a lack of...a lack of something; whether flesh or blood he wasn't sure, but he had made sure to fully fulfill both needs.

He knew Zachary was right, his behavior had been bizarre, appalling and even worse, obvious, and he was determined to start again with the red-haired human girl; strictly to prove that he could.

Because after all, she was just a human, she wasn't particularly beautiful, she wasn't even from a particularly powerful vampire family, despite her Grandmother's ancient title; she was nothing special.

As soon as she walked in with her Grandmother and then made her way over to Anisa to sit next to her to start chatting animatedly, all of his good intentions flew right out the window.

I Can't Believe I Waited To Do This

Devin lay in bed with Anisa, his head propped up on one hand, a bright seductive light shining in his eyes. He listened to her giggle as he walked his index and middle fingers back and forth along her stomach.

"Decisions, decisions. So, where should I go?" He asked playfully in a sexy voice as if his hand was a separate entity. "These are wonderfully lush hills." His fingers walked up her middle to gently rub his index finger under the curve of one of her breasts. She let out a softly charmed giggle, and he walked his fingers further south. "But this. This is the source of all my world's sweetness and goodness."

Anisa let out a soft groan of encouragement.

"Of course it has always been my tendency to go for it all." He told her seductively taking a sweet pink nipple into his mouth and simultaneously plundering her with his fingers, causing her to stop giggling all together and to gasp out a soft moan.

Suddenly, he lifted her on top of him to straddle his legs, as he knelt on the bed, and he thrust into the slickness of her pussy. They had discovered this position a day or so ago, and she loved it as much as he did. She was wide open to him and able to take every centimeter of him, all the way to his root as he thrust deeply rubbing the head of his cock on her cervix. Which the first time he had done that had driven her into a screaming orgasm;

219

surprising them both afterwards.

He wrapped his arms around her small body holding her hips tightly as she arched back, and he suckled and tongued her nipples. He knew one day soon, he would nip her and so did she. But, until she begged for him to do it, he contented himself with simply grazing his fangs over the soft silken skin of her breasts.

"Oh, God!" He exclaimed in a husky whisper, thrusting deeply as he felt her begin to tighten and throb around him. "I can't believe I waited to do this with you."

She suddenly cried out as she clenched tightly around him, gripping his broad shoulders desperately. "Bite me, Devin. Bite me."

He pierced the top of her breast as gently as he could, only using his top set of razor-sharp fangs and swirled the ambrosia of her blood over his tongue, groaning deeply in ecstasy as he sipped her nectar, holding her tightly against him as he thrust himself into her with abandon. She cried out quickly again, her tightness clutching around him, and he came with a muffled roar his mouth against her breast; coming harder than he had ever come before, pushing himself firmly against her cervix, filling her womb with his essence.

As he tenderly held her small soft body against him, he gently closed the small wounds that he had made with his saliva, and he knew in his soul that he was complete.

* * * * *

I was propped up against the pillows of our bed, watching her lazily with contented eyes as she laid on her stomach next to me, lying across the bed, her lovely, smooth, rounded ass gently curved, as both of her small feet curled and waved in the air in happiness. She was talking to me in her sweet little voice tracing the ridges of the muscles of my abdomen, and I was paying only half a mind to what she was telling me because I was imagining taking her from behind as she knelt on the bed.

I could see it now. Her mouth would be open in ecstasy, small cries coming from her throat, as I thrust myself into her.

I started to stroke my fingers gently over that rounded ass in preparation of making my thoughts a reality when something she was saying caught my attention.

"What did you just say?"

She huffed at me in irritation. "Weren't you paying attention to what I was telling you? I said that I think that Castor is soul-mated to Katja."

"No." I told her and she nodded her head at me positively. "No way, Nessie! Yeah, he's been acting a little weird around her. But let's face it. He is a little weird around humans. It took Zach kicking his ass to get him to warm up to him. He just probably needs to eat or get laid or something."

"Nope, that's not it." Anisa told me with absolute authority. "According to Fred, he has drank from and slept with every female blood donor in the villa. That's what he was doing when he had disappeared for a couple of days."

"Now, Nessie, how would Fred know?" I asked her reasonably; making a mental note to talk to Fred about gossiping about other people's sex lives with Nessie. That's the last thing that those two needed to be talking about! There was always some rumor going around about people's sleeping habits at the resorts and my Nessie and my companion didn't need to be paying attention to that type of activity; and Fred should know better than to encourage Nessie's curiosity in such goings on.

"Cassie told him. Cassie has made friends with all of the blood donors. Cassie confirmed it to me. Did you know that Castor has a tattoo of a big green dragon on the side of his chest?" She asked me as if she was fascinated by such an item.

"Yes." I answered her not liking the fact that she was talking to Fred, Cassie, or anybody else about tattoos on other men's bodies.

"Why didn't you tell me?" She asked looking at me in disappointment with her beautiful blue eyes; like I should be talking to her about other guy's bodies.

"Because I don't want you to be thinking about other men and their tattoos." I told her sourly in a discouraging manner.

"Whyever not? I wouldn't want you to get a tattoo. Your body is perfect and having a tattoo would just prevent me from seeing how beautiful it is." She ran her fingers and eyes over the ridges of my abdomen again as if she was fascinated by them and I smiled widely at her words while she wasn't watching my face.

I stopped smiling, schooling my expression into one of disinterested interest in what she was saying to me, as soon as she lifted her head to look me in the face again.

"So, you see, I think that Castor acts weird around Katja because he is feeling the soulmate bond." She insisted.

"I suppose anything is possible." I told her steadily, and then with vampiric speed leaped out of bed to stand behind her pulling her into a kneeling position. "I think that I am wanting to feel my own soulmate bond right at this moment."

"Devin, you know that's not how it works!" She complained halfheartedly, then groaned sharply as I thrust deeply into her.

God, she felt wonderful!

"I know, my Nessie. This is definitely a bonus though isn't it, baby?" I asked pulling away from her slightly, then gripping her tight against me once more to thrust fully inside of her as she cried out a quick release; trembling around me.

I thrust in and out of her pulsating channel several times, eventually drawing forth two more orgasms from her body, loving to hear the sound of my name on her lips, before I found my own release with a shouted groan.

No matter how long I live, I will never tire of this; I will never tire of her.

Gathering her to me, I laid back on the bed with her, smoothing her silken golden-brown tresses from her flushed, lovely face so that I could look deeply into her beautiful blue eyes which shined with so much love. I was so thankful for having her in my life.

Joy overwhelmed me as it always does when she smiled gently up at me.

Kissing her deeply, I whispered against her pink lips, "I will forever love you, my Nessie."

Epilogue One

I knelt in front of her to gently kiss her rounded belly, getting either an elbow or a knee to my lips for my efforts making me smile.

It had come as a huge surprise when we realized that Nessie's flu-like symptoms months ago, were due to her being pregnant.

According to Gramps, I must have been just human enough to father a child with my still human mate! Aleksei himself had fathered children when he was human, right after he became a vampire, and as a fully mated vampire.

Who would have known that Gramps was the authority on vampire breeding practices? It would have been nice to know about these things when we were first mated; we might have changed the way we handled our sex life.

But, kissing my child and having it press against my face through their mommy's tummy, I am really glad we didn't; I couldn't fathom missing out on this wondrous miracle.

"It always moves when you are touching my stomach." Nessie told me with a giggle, running her fingers through my hair. I gazed up at her unable to hide my love as I knelt before her; she was my everything.

"It? I can tell you what the sex is, Nessie." I reminded her with a wicked gleam in my eye.

"Devin, I told you I don't want to know. Don't you dare tell me! I want to be surprised!" She said to me emphatically.

It had been an argument between us when she was far enough along for Dene to give her an ultrasound. She didn't want to know, of course, I just had to know and as soon as I could I cornered him alone and made him tell me.

Now all I wanted to do was to tell her and everyone else. I wanted to stand on the top of the ranch house and yell it to the horizon.

The only other person who knew the sex of our baby was my mother, who was staying with us just down the hall so that she would be here for Nessie when her time came, and she was sworn to secrecy!

Mom hadn't even told Nick. Which was okay, because he also was a big believer in the surprise department and didn't even want to know the sex of his own child, my new sibling, which according to Dene was due any day.

But of course, I knew.

The sex of the babies were my mother and I's little secret.

Nick had told my mother that he absolutely could not care less what it is as long as it and my mother are healthy, he would continue to be the happiest man on earth.

Boy, was he in for a wild ride!

Of course, there was no way he was the happiest man on earth, either, because that title belonged to me.

Epilogue Two

Nichola walked quietly back and forth in their suite at the ranch while Leila slept soundly, gently rocking his tightly swaddled daughter in his arms, intently watched by Princess from the foot of the bed next to the bassinet.

Princess had decided that the baby was part of her domain and kept a sharp eye on all who interacted with her. But for her size, she watched over her small charge with an intensity that would put any Tibetan Temple Dog to shame.

Even though far along in her own pregnancy, Leila had insisted that she come to assist Anisa who was due to have their first grandchild, now in a few weeks. She had stridently argued, when he had resisted, that both of them needed Dene, and everything would be easier in the same house.

His solution was that Devin and Anisa come and stay with them and have the baby at the Toronto residence. Devin was insistent that he wanted his child to be born in Texas.

American vampires! These youngsters still didn't understand that vampires were creatures of the world; not just one area or country. He himself had long ago stopped thinking of himself as just a Greek.

Nichola hadn't been keen on the idea but knew he would lose the argument before it really even started. He was helpless to deny her anything if Leila really wanted it; and she really wanted to be here with Devin and Anisa for the birth of her first grandchild.

Besides, as it turns out he was needed to help his sons through a plethora of issues, not only the running of the ranch, but also with the shifters.

He looked down on the beautiful face of his daughter in his arms, smiling gently. Feeling a love that threatened to burst his old heart. She gazed up at him with amber eyes the twin to his own and gave out a small yawn.

She had her mother's silky auburn hair, sweet smile, small dimples, and even though only a few weeks old, she was stubborn beyond belief.

She was a perfect mixture of the two of them and he was always in awe over what they had created together.

He crooned softly to her in his perfectly pitched voice; no words, just sounds and slowly her eyes closed in sleep. He slowly walked her back to place her in the bassinet, and Princess put her head over the edge to smell her gently, her tail softly wagging, to make sure that everything was in order with her charge.

As he slid into the bed next to Leila he realized that she was awake and watching him tenderly.

I love you. Her voice in his head was delicate and full of emotion as she reached to touch his face gently, her teal eyes brimmed with happy tears.

He took her hand in his and kissed her palm reverently thinking to her, *Meeting you was fate. You becoming my better half was a choice. But falling in love with you was beyond my control. Thank you for being a wonderful life partner; thank you for being my soul-mate. Thank you for giving me something I thought I would never have: a real family and a child. I will forever thank the Gods that you came into my life and decided to stay.*

Through life's ups and downs I give you my word that I will love you in the moments we're together and in the few times we are apart.

As Nichola lovingly kissed Leila's lips, he knew his life was complete.

Vampiris Bloodline – Foreign Language Glossary and Series Information

a gápi mou - my love

awki – prince (quechuan)

i allagí mou – my changeling

allaxiéra – changeling

ángixe me – touch me

agapitós - beloved

áse me na se agapíso – let me love you

áse me na se agapó gia pánta – let me love you forever

Château les Ténèbres – Dark Castle

Despótis – Lord or Master

Déspoina – lady or mistress

Dóxa to theó! – Thank God!

efcharistó – thank you

efcharistó, glykó mou, Se agapó – thank you, my sweet, I love you

éla gia ména – come for me

éla na to párei – come on pick it up

epitrépste mou na sas dóso efcharístisi – allow me to give you pleasure

fíla me – kiss me

glukó mou – my sweet

Glykó – sweet one

i psychí mou – my soul

i theá tis omorfiás mou – my goddess of beauty

Kyría – Lady, madam, mistress

Kýrios – mister, main, lord, master, sir

Le violeur vampire déchirant – The Ripping Vampire Rapist

lígo vampír – little vampire

maman – mama

mikró – little one

Mírame. Mirame ahora. – Look at me. Look at me now.

moró – baby

moy golub' – my dove

Naí – yes

No más oraciones, mi belleza oscura. Eres mía. – No more prayers, my dark beauty. You are mine.

Ñusta – Princess (Quechua)

nóstimo – delicious

Ochi agápi mou – no my love

Oh Dios, por favor, sálvame de este demonio – Oh God please save me from this demon.

o ómorfos ángelos mou – my beautiful angel

ómorfi adelfí psychí mou – my beautiful soulmate

O Theé mou – Oh my God

Panemorfi – beautiful

Parakaló agápi mou, Lypámai – Please my love, I am sorry.

páre me sto glykó sou sóma – take me into your sweet body

pio agapiméni mou – my most beloved one

pouliche fougueuse – spirited filly

Prépei na eímai mésa sou me ton éna í ton állo trópo – I need to be inside of you one way or the other.

Se agapó – I love you

se parakaló agápi mou – please my love

Se parakaló voíthisé me – please help me

Skoteinó Fengári – Dark Moon (Greek werewolf pack name)
Sulpayki – thank you (Quechua, pronounced: sool-pay-ki)
Sumag – beautiful (Quechua)
sýnchrones gynaíkes – modern women
thélo na eímai mésa sou – I want to be inside of you
tsingániki póli – gypsy town
Ypóschomai – I promise

Members of the Vampire Elder Small Council and their nationalities:

Nikolaos Tsoukalous: Greek
Johann Beutel: German
Charles Peake: British
Romulus (Esmeralda's mate (Es)): Spaniard/Italian
Prince Khaldun: Egyptian/African
Aleksei Ostrovsky: Russian/Eastern Europe

Major Locations throughout the series:

Château les Ténèbres – Dark Castle, Nichola's vampire resort in Ponce Inlet, FL

Temuco de Wila Tatitu – Temple of the Blood God, (Language: Quechua; the surviving language of the Incan Empire). Nichola's vampire resort in the mountains east of the Temple of the Sun that is near Machu Pichu, Cusco Region Peru.

Víla Xenia – Summer House of Hospitality, Nichola's vampire resort in Katerini, Greece. Katerini, Greece is where Nichola was born, grew up and lived as a human.

Diamond Wolf Ranch – Kerrville, TX, owned by Devin and Zachary Sutton.

Efkarpidi Polychoros – the Bowling Centre and Billiard Parlor in Katerini, Greece.

About the Author

V.P. Nightshade lives in Texas with her old grumpy husband, two hormonal (and nocturnal) sons, an extremely sweet Alien Dog, and a small, but feisty Cairn Terrier that talks.

V.P. loves horror stories and steamy romance novels and frequently mixes flavors of both in her writing. Hey, who doesn't love a reformed bad guy?

The Vampiris Bloodline is her first published series.

The First Time In Forever is her third published novel.

V. P. can be contacted at:

Facebook: https://www.facebook.com/VPNightshade.Author

Follow V. P. on Goodreads at: https://www.goodreads.com/author/show/21223301.V_P_Nightshade

Follow V. P. on Amazon at:
https://www.amazon.com/V-P-Nightshade/e/B0987X4LY1/

Also by V.P. Nightshade

The Vampiris Bloodline - A Paranormal Vampire Romance Series

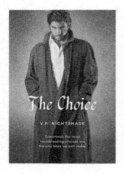

The Choice: A Paranormal Vampire Romance (Vampiris Bloodline - A Paranormal Vampire Romance Series Book 1)

Leila Sutton thought she was a normal wife and young mother.

All she ever wanted was to give her children a safe, stable, loving home.

Then the Change started and He entered her life.

He spoke to her heart and soul like no man had before and took her to heights of passion that she hadn't known existed.

For him she broke all her rules.

But, would she have to sacrifice her soul to protect her children?

Readers of paranormal romance will love this contemporary story about the struggle over who we love, what we choose, and the things that are chose for us.

Now, Always, Forever: A Dark Paranormal Vampire Romance (Vampiris Bloodline - A Paranormal Vampire Romance Series Book 2)

The inevitable always catches up with you. Leila knew that she would have to leave the human world to embrace her vampire nature eventually, she just never expected to do it for the same reason: her children. But now, she was out of choices.

For a vampire as old as Nichola, time meant very little, except when it came to being away from his soulmate. Then the years were torturous. Elated at having her in the vampire world again, he soon finds that an old rival is now interested in both her body and heart.

As the actions of a madman who craves the blood, flesh, and bodies of young girls intrude on their reunion, they are forced to fight for the only world that matters, theirs. Will they survive the fight for their family and love? Will they be able to protect both the secrets of the vampire community and the lives of humans?

This is the second book in a series! It is a True Sequel! If you have not read Book 1, The Choice, you will not understand the character motivations or enjoy this book. Please read The Choice first!

Printed in Great Britain
by Amazon

23008021R00137